BENEATH THE BLOOD MOON

BENEATH THE BLOOD MOON

DARREN WILLS

Matador
9 Priory Business Park,
Wistow Road, Kibworth Beauchamp,
Leicestershire. LE8 0RX
Tel: 0116 279 2299
Email: books@troubador.co.uk
Web: www.troubador.co.uk/matador
Twitter: @matadorbooks

ISBN 978 183859 262 2

British Library Cataloguing in Publication Data.
A catalogue record for this book is available from the British Library.

Printed and bound in the UK by TJ International, Padstow, Cornwall
Typeset in 11pt Adobe Garamond Pro by Troubador Publishing Ltd, Leicester, UK

Matador is an imprint of Troubador Publishing Ltd

malevolence – the quality of causing or wanting to cause harm or evil.

Dedicated to Ivar William Clarke (b. 15.05.2019).

Thanks to Mark Anson for his original idea.

AFTER THE WATERSHED

I had killed her, and I was glad I had killed her.

"I have to remind you that you have been arrested on suspicion of murdering your wife, Laura Walker. I will warn you again at this point that you should not say anything in your defence that you won't choose to rely on in court, since anything new you give in evidence will cause an adverse inference to be drawn."

"I'm innocent."

I lowered my head in desperation, but immediately realised that they might see this as some sign of guilt. I raised it again. I suddenly had the same attitude to these two that I had towards incompetent managers at work and, at the same time ironically began to feel like a misunderstood teenager in one of my classes. "You're just not getting it."

"Not getting what?"

"It's not how it looks. I'm no murderer. I'm a teacher, for god's sake."

"And that makes you innocent?" Sarcastic smiling filled half of the room.

"Teachers do carry out serious crimes sometimes. Teachers can sometimes be quite murderous." This was the junior of the two detectives, bespectacled and playing bad cop to his colleague's worse cop.

"Boston, two years ago." Taylor, leading the interview, now interjecting, had a knowing look on his face that was simultaneously irritating and intriguing.

"What?" Like so many times recently, I was in a world of confusion.

"Worked in a high school in the States. Maths teacher in Massachusetts. Pretty normal guy like you supposedly. Killed his entire family with a shotgun." There was no emotion in the policeman's voice, like he was reading out a shopping list. *"Bacon, bread, and a bit of mass murder."*

"Well not this teacher," I protested, albeit lamely. My wrists were aching from the harsh rubbing of the restraints, but I put that stuff to one side.

The senior Detective shook his head doubtfully. "No, Dominic. A job doesn't stop you pulling a trigger and taking a life. Counts for nothing. On the contrary, could be that the pressure of the job might have been the thing that sent you over the edge. There's a bottom line here. The circumstances more than suggest that you shot your wife."

"But I didn't."

He was undeterred. "You're looking at a life sentence. You do know that?"

I was undeterred too. "That's not what happened."

The senior detective, a superintendent according to his introduction, continued. "OK, if you say so. In your case, Dominic, we have a gun, gunshots, a dead body and a phone call made by you announcing the fact. Besides that, we have strangulation marks on the poor woman's neck." He paused, looking down at his sheet for something else to remind me of. He looked up. "You need to start co-operating with us now, if only to help yourself in the certain event of a court appearance."

By co-operate, he clearly meant confess. "Granted – all those things. I'm still innocent."

The officer gave a sigh of frustration. "Will you start then by telling me about your relationship with Laura. What's been going on?"

I couldn't help myself. I knew it wasn't a good idea, but it was such a difficult question to answer in a clear succinct way. Instead, out came a loud uncontrolled laugh that I found difficult to stop, and which caused the two officers to turn and look at each other with mutual concern. "I'm sorry, but the answer to that question is so crazy. I did try to explain some things in the car." I looked at both of their hard faces, full of their refusal to understand, before I spoke again. "The truth is, you need to know about Laura."

"Tell us about her." Taylor was naturally doing most of the questioning. Detective Superintendent Taylor, to give him his full title, had arrested me at the house, handling me aggressively, almost pulling off my arms to secure me despite my clear willingness to be arrested. I had him down as a rugby-playing Tory kind of a man, probably had a BMW, a Saab or some other car with plenty of poke, yet he was someone who was going to have to find a more imaginative side to his personality and do some serious listening if he was to own the truth. Was that going to happen? These people were notorious for not listening.

"She was beautiful." I sat up straight in my seat. Worst case scenario for me – I was easy pickings for a police statistic, a solved crime to help a policeman in his quest for promotion. Worst case scenario for them – I might make the water muddy and create too many shades of grey. Or would they cling to a falsehood for the conviction? Of course they would.

"Did you love her?"

"I loved her." I made a point of fully facing them. How would either of these two have coped? How would either have felt on this side of this table? Whatever could or couldn't have been, Taylor looked really comfortable in his state of relaxed supremacy I couldn't help thinking how things might have turned out differently if I had been a bit like him at certain times. Wisdom builds well on soft gullible errors, it seemed. I was betting that neither Taylor nor his junior had ever had a gullible moment in their lives.

Taylor leaned forward. "Of course you loved her. That's why you killed her. You couldn't have her, so nobody else could. Was that how it was?"

"Not at all."

"Come on now. Had she betrayed you, Dominic? She was leaving, wasn't she? Is that the way it went?"

"That's not what happened. I think you need to start listening to me. This isn't going to be one of those easy convictions."

"Are you serious? I've never seen anything more straight forward and obvious."

"No, you're wrong. You're going to have to do some actual investigating to get to the bottom of this one." He would have to play his police tricks for a long time if he was hoping to prevail; I was light years beyond them. Another time distant from now, that kind of approach would have worked, but I had been through too much.

Taylor continued. "Was anybody else at your house today?"

"Nobody. Apart from Leoni."

"Leoni who?

"Again, I tried to tell you about her on the way here. I never knew her surname. She was staying at the house."

"Staying at your house and you didn't know her name? How's that work?"

"It's easy. I never saw anything with her full name on, however hard to believe that is. You do need to find her though. She can unlock everything."

"How long has she lived at yours?"

"A few weeks. I don't know that much about her, but my neighbours will confirm what I'm saying."

"Tell us more."

She has brown curly hair, is about five feet two, and around thirty-five years old, I think, perhaps a bit younger. She was a big part of it all. You need to locate her."

"How was she important in all this?"

I tried to tell them, but about three or four sentences in, Taylor interrupted me. His eyes were glass, showing no sign of a response. "When was she at the house today?"

"I don't know. I mean, I didn't know the time. She left when the shooting started."

"So you're admitting the shooting?

"Of course I'm admitting it. But I'm not guilty."

I knew this truth of mine sounded outrageous, and their furrowed brows communicated how they thought so too. The Detective Sergeant, who had been introduced to me as Hawksworth, wasn't saying much, but was making detailed notes of everything I said. It was clear to me that both he and his superior needed to drop the disbelief and abandon the visible concern about my mental health. They needed to listen more and consider things outside the box marked 'how things appear'. I was doomed otherwise.

Taylor continued. "Did anybody else visit the house this afternoon, or this morning, even? No friends of yours? Laura's family?"

"She has no family. Not now. They're all distant or dead. Dead now." I allowed a decent interval of seconds to elapse. "They're worth considering though, in view of what happened.

5

In fact, you need to look into what happened to George and Lillian. You need to talk to Leoni's brother about that."

Taylor again leaned forward. "I'll tell you what. You tell us all about all three of them, Dominic, and we'll decide whether they're worth considering or not."

Before replying, I was distracted by my reflection in the glass opposite. I didn't look good – tense and disheveled. I was clutching this Styrofoam cup as if it was all that sustained my existence. It was different, drinking with hands secured – like a religious ritual. I knew what was happening. I was in the frame for murder and they were probably going to hang me out to dry.

"Are you going to reply to the question, or leave us hanging?"

"Laura's family? Yes, I want to tell you all about them. Totally relevant."

"How were they?"

"Well, they weren't her natural parents. Laura never knew her natural mother. Didn't even know who she was. She was adopted."

Taylor was clearly irritated. "I think we need to know about Laura's death, not her childhood, not even what happened to her parents. That doesn't really help us to understand why she died, does it?"

"That's just it," I said, knowing my voice was becoming higher in pitch and betraying my inability to control myself. I had been keeping myself so calm up to that point. "That's the crux of it all. I was not responsible for the killing of my wife."

"And Leoni's brother. What's his name?"

"I don't know. I believe he killed George and Lillian though. He has a drug problem, I think."

The two officers looked at each other, before Taylor spoke. "OK. For the purposes of the recorder, we are postponing this interview. We are just off to check on a detail or two." They left the room.

An appropriately miserable time for my appropriately melancholy situation. On this miserable autumn evening, where the rain was battering the pavements and roads outside, here I was banged up in Sheffield Police Headquarters, this mish mash of concrete and glass in the heart of the city. Here I was, handcuffed like a criminal in the center of the town that had been home to my first infant squeals, had formed the background for my early steps as a toddler and had been the setting of ninety-per cent of my life experiences. Here I was, going through shit.

I had always been more than reluctant to leave Sheffield. This was the town I had returned to after university, where I had spent my largely hap py childhood, where I had enjoyed school, the shops and the parks, where my mother and father were buried, where the shops, parks and concert halls that had shaped my youth and informed my adulthood were located. My football team, Sheffield Wednesday, lived here too. I had always thought this was the right place. Sheffield had meant life, history and everything.

At this moment, it meant nothing. Thirty-eight-years-old, in this unimagined situation, I was a man whose nearest moment to notoriety had been ruthless and vigorous apple stealing from neighbourhood gardens, some treacherous knock-a-door-running and the unscrupulous copying of music from the internet. In short, I was hardly a serial killer or one of the Great Train Robbers. but here I was, in the frame for murder. I had no solicitor. They had offered it, but I had shaken my head. If they didn't believe my truth, I was fucked, and no amount of clever words or legal assertions would help me.

As I sat wondering how events could unfold the way they had, the door of the interview room opened. The two detectives re-entered.

The questioning continued. "OK, so tell me, Mr. Walker," said Hawksworth, opening the batting for this innings. "What happened? How come there's a dead body and a gun with your fingerprints on it?"

"I don't deny that, but there are lot of details you need to know first."

"Give us the details."

"I don't know where to start."

Hawksworth carried on. "You said that Laura's childhood was important? What happened then that figures in this?"

Taylor gave his colleague a reprimanding look then turned to me. "Ok. Let's start with that. Why is ancient history relevant to you killing your wife? We're all ears."

"First of all, I never killed her. I would never do that. And it is relevant. Totally. George and Lillian adopted her, brought her up...Oh God, the poor bastards. Look what happened. They doted on her. George worshipped the ground she walked on. We all loved her."

"I can appreciate that but we need to get to the truth. Would you like to tell me how you gained possession of the gun that was used to kill Laura?"

"Forget the gun," I said. "The gun's not the thing."

"But Laura's dead."

"Yes. She probably is."

Taylor allowed a half smile to appear on his face. "Not much probably about it. She's on a slab in our mortuary."

They were going to have to listen to everything I had to say, but I could feel myself overheating. I was in no rush, but everything that was relevant had to come out in the right order if I was to avoid being charged.

"What is the thing if the gun's not?" asked Hawksworth.

"You're not going to believe me, are you? I didn't hallucinate this. I'm not a dreamer or a psycho, whatever you may think. I

8

didn't create this nightmare." I looked into Taylor's eyes in the most challenging way I could muster. "Have you checked out Sunny Vale Nursing Home yet?"

"Why would we?"

"I told you in the car. Weren't you listening to me then, either?

"We thought you were hallucinating, or at best, rambling."

"Why would I ramble? I was under arrest. I was trying to explain myself."

"It sounded too ridiculous to even consider. You were in quite a state when we picked you up."

"For God's sake, somebody has to believe me. Somebody has to listen to what I'm saying." I looked into the cold judgmental eyes of the senior detective. I couldn't see any signs of belief there.

At that point, in this sterile soulless room, I felt a warm breeze from the past. "Everything was just so great for Laura and me. We even had a holiday planned."

"What happened, Dominic? And how did you get that bruise? Did Laura do that?"

"I think I need to tell you everything."

BIRTHWRONG –
AROUND 35 YEARS AGO

"This is horrible. When's it gonna end?"

"Soon? Very soon."

Life was like this. Grey frowning clouds, floating with intent, bringing a depression northward above the rooftops of the drearily dismal row of tired terraced houses. This was to be another of those miserable and forgettable October afternoons. Grey was the colour, but it could and probably would darken further. The gloom was going to become blacker and wetter.

Below all this, at the top of the long winding street that was Thorpe Rise, were three teenagers with skateboards. Concentrating fiercely, they lined up their boards for their next death-defying journey down the twisting tarmac, a route that was deceptively menacing with its two blind turns, with the main road waiting at the end of their descent. At the very end, they would turn at the right time. Too soon and that would make someone the butt of a derogatory comment. Too late, and the evening news headline might feature a tragic teenager and a speeding car.

Three houses down from the top of the road, in a dingy upstairs room, a drama was unfolding. "I can't take anymore. I want it to stop." Judy Lawrence was in some difficulty, but it would be over soon. In her mid-twenties, but looking much older, Judy had this afternoon lost her customary eager-to-please smile, and her current situation now complemented the shabby environment in which she lived, where a couple of Neil Diamond framed photos on the downstairs wall would do little to distract any visitor from the squalor, neglect and general untidiness that dominated the house.

Smiling Judy, the neighbours called her to her face. Behind her back, they weren't quite so complimentary.

This afternoon she wasn't smiling. Her mouth was rigid and downturned with her suffering, and her utterances were high in pitch and volume. As the skateboarders roared past her house with all that teenage confidence, Judy was screaming out her woes for them to hear. In the sordid damp little box she called her bedroom, with its portable TV set resting on the cheap chipboard chest of drawers that stood between a grubby pair of blue and white floral curtains behind it, she writhed and grimaced on her grubby grey bedsheet. She formed a stark contrast of red face and unhealthily pale body, where all that sex, drugs and alcohol had come at a price.

Beads of sweat had gathered in every crevice, whilst her dyed black hair now formed an unpleasant moist spread around her head.

Looming above her, Lillian Stewart, with her blonde hair tied back neatly, was dressed practically for the occasion, sporting a white apron over a red jumper and Levi's as she spectated and supported simultaneously, as if she had been studying midwifery for the past fifteen years, not just the past month.

Judy moved her head from side to side. "Help me. Somebody please help me." The pains had gone on for about seven hours now and Judy was now clearly experiencing something towards the extreme end of that spectrum.

In complete contrast, Lillian was totally focused and seemed in control as she tried to mop the younger woman's brow. It was clear that she had both purpose and knowledge. She'd read all the books, had talked to a couple of experienced people, one being a retired midwife. "Come on. You're doing fine. Keep pushing…Soon be over."

"But it hurts so much. It's killing me."

"It's not, Judy. Really, it's not. You're doing so well. We're nearly there. Just push when you sense it's right." Reassuring words and a supportive mopping of the brow were meaningless and ineffective. There was no man to hold the younger woman's hand, so she had nobody to scream at other than herself, the air around her, and this makeshift midwife.

"Never again. Not for anything. Not for all the money in the world."

"Never again. Just this time."

The baby made its desperate exit. As the cord was cut, an immediate smile was closely followed by Lillian's loud voice towards the open door, the sound roaring down Judy's staircase. "George! George!" She wrapped the baby in a white cotton sheet. With the infant in her arms, she disappeared from the room. "It's a girl!"

In the downstairs room, sitting on an old wooden chair, George was a traditional man who had hit on a modern idea. George Alfred Stewart, similar in age to Lillian, ascended the stairs excitedly, entering the bedroom with an uncertain, uncomfortable look on his face and a collection of purposeful thoughts in his head. He was a fish out of water here. As far as he was concerned, this was one appalling shithole. Yet, being here today was a necessary evil and he was determined to get away from this place as soon as was possible.

Lilian, re-entering the bedroom ahead of her husband, was now holding the infant in her arms and cradling it like a new mother should. George put his arm around both of them, as if he was making a statement about protection. With Judy all bleary and semi-conscious, the older woman had a blissful smile on her face. All the mother could and would do was watch.

In her bleary-eyed state, staring at the ceiling, Judy was at best semi-conscious. Eventually, however, she managed to speak. "It's best if you go now." She attempted to make her voice stronger and tried to inject more firmness as she said, "I'll be all right."

"OK then," Lillian said. She looked at her husband uncomfortably then back at the sweat-lined brow of the mother not-to-be. "The painkillers are here." She indicated a packet in front of the portable TV. "If the pain continues, take two every hour."

George expanded suddenly, becoming a couple of inches taller. He positioned himself purposefully, facing Judy at the foot of the bed and staring down at her like a headmaster viewing a disobedient pupil "If you see a doctor at all, should you need to see one, remember your promise. Forget everything, especially us. Lay it on as thick as you need to. Claim amnesia. You've been paid enough."

Lillian interjected, turning her head away from the infant. "We will send you the rest in a month's time, so say nothing to anyone."

Judy made a dismissive gesture with her right arm in the direction of the door. "Yes. Just go. Please go."

George and Lilian left the inadequate attempt at a maternity ward with that precious cargo in Lilian's arms and they descended the stairs with the stealth of thieves.

In the top drawer of the chipboard chest of drawers was an envelope full of much-welcomed currency. George and Lilian had been more than reasonable in this department. As the front door closed loudly and Judy's offspring went out into the world early.

Judy clutched her stomach. "Oh my God." Her eyes were wide with pain. "No… No… Lillian! Lillian!"

She reached for the phone on her bedside table.

SUNSHINE DAYS

"What time is it?" I was bleary-eyed and barely conscious.

"Seven-o'clock."

"I'm getting up." That would be some achievement in my state of grogginess.

She was already dressed and putting on make-up as I rose myself from my slumber.

"I pulled open the curtains. What a lovely day."

"I know, babe. It's going to be hot today."

I panned the houses and gardens in our cul-de-sac, enjoying their sparkling uniformity and the colourful neatness of the gardens. "There are worse places to wake up to."

"Of course there are."

"Do you know what? I think I'm going to plant some different flowers for next year. Create more colour, more variety. What do you think?"

When I turned around there was only me in the bedroom. She'd gone.

The phone rang.

Three minutes later, I was still very much alive and on the phone looking out of the window of our spare room, my favourite part of the house, noticing how my car could do with a wash. This was the upstairs room that housed my extensive CD collection, where a willing carpenter had erected an elaborate set of wall-to-wall shelves, and where I hid all my secret purchases. Well, I reckoned being addicted to music was small potatoes compared to drugs and alcohol, although my wife would disagree, hence the secrecy.

"Anyway, that sounds ok. That's a long agenda though. I didn't want to go home tonight anyway…Don't worry about it. In fact, you can return the favour by washing my car. I'm just noticing that it's needing some soap and water…Of course I'm joking."

Next to a large glass vase in front of me was our wedding photograph. I picked it up to look more closely at it. What a day that had been. I never failed to enjoy that photograph, remembering how cool I had felt, how sexy Laura had looked and how fab the wedding had been. In the photograph, Filey Beach stretched out behind us like the pleasant passing of time.

As I came downstairs, I hesitated at the sound of a kettle being put down with slightly more force than usual. Laura must have heard the phone call. I took a breath as I swung round into the kitchen dining area with an attempt at joie de vive through a big warm smile and a cry of, "Morning, babe. Lovely day."

The steam from the kettle was rising towards the ceiling. Laura had her back to me.

I walked over to her and kissed her on the side of the neck. "Morning," I said. She had on that dark blue suit that she had bought in Meadowhall Shopping Centre a couple of weeks ago, looking very professional.

Without turning to face me, she asked, "Who was that on the phone?" There was an attempt at normality in the way she said it, as if she wasn't really all that bothered. Beneath that, however, I knew there was an underlying anxiety.

"Oh, just Tom from work, about the meeting tonight. Nothing much."

"It didn't sound like you were talking to Tom."

"It was Tom. Do you want me to pass the phone to you next time, so you can say hello?"

"Don't be clever. You've no right to be clever."

"But it's in the past. What you're troubled by is a distant memory."

"To you, maybe."

"And to you." I knew I always said the wrong thing, that the right words never came out, and today was no exception.

"Not for a long time," she said. "If it had been the other way around, if I had done what you did, how would you be feeling this morning?"

"Pretty terrible."

"Well now you know how I feel.

"It's a closed book. No need for you to worry. Not ever." I had gently turned her face to mine so she could look into my eyes and see that I was telling the truth. "That was just some stupidity that ended. A mad moment. Should never have happened. It will never happen again."

She pushed my hand away. There was pain in her face still. "I don't want to know. What I mean is…well, I don't know what I mean." She took a seat at the kitchen table.

I knew what she meant. "Just remember, we have a lovely home, a really good set-up, enough money to have a good life together."

"I want more than a cosy cul-de-sac and money, Dom. A nice house doesn't do it for me. I want a man I can rely on at all times."

"I know, and it's not just the material things for me, either. We're good together."

She looked up. "I guess I know how things are now. I want to forgive you, but I can never forget. Don't ever expect me to forget."

"I won't. Neither will I."

"I'm trying to get over it. It's just that you have no right expecting me to. It comes back, like a deep ache, if you know what I mean."

"I do."

"I want to trust you."

"I understand. Of course I do. I want you to trust me."

"It takes time."

Something else came into my mind as I finished making myself a cup of tea. "Did you wake up in the night again?" I asked, taking a seat opposite her.

"Of course. Just like the other nights. It's becoming regular as clockwork."

"The same thing?"

"Yes. Another black vision. If this carries on, I'm going to have to see someone about it."

Selfishly, I felt the blessing of a good night's sleep at having been unaffected by my wife's nocturnal disturbances. "I knew nothing about it. Perhaps you should have woken me up. Your problem is my problem, babe." I sat opposite her.

"No. I let you sleep off the Jack Daniels. Perhaps I should drink some of that tonight. It might help. Although maybe not as much as you had."

I smiled, if only to reassure her, whilst at the same time as thinking how sexy she looked in that outfit, clinging seductively to her size ten figure. She always looked so classy and elegant. "Well, I'm getting better. I only had two drinks last night. It's not like the old days."

Laura looked into my eyes mockingly. "Two drinks? They were half-pint glasses. I had a sip and could barely taste the coke."

"Now you're exaggerating."

"Am I? Well perhaps a little. It's just not good for you. Why don't you just have a drink at weekends, like me?"

"I will do. From now on."

"How many times have I heard that?"

"Well this time I mean it." Reassuringly, I took hold of her hand. "Babe, we're good."

"Well, I hope so. I think so."

"Anyway, tell me about your nightmare. Was it about you again?"

"God, yes. Totally. It was awful. I was going down this long black tunnel."

"What tunnel?"

"Well I think it was a tunnel. Actually, it might have been a corridor. Anyway, there was a tall shadowy figure at the end. It zoomed in like in a film."

"Perhaps you should write it down while you remember it. That's the trouble with dreams. They get forgotten really easily."

"Hard to forget this one. Very disturbing and dark. The shadow was like in a horror film, you know the type. Where an identity is hidden until the last moment. Anyway, it was suddenly revealed, and guess what? Yet again, just like in the other dreams, the demon was me."

"I don't get it. Why is it always you? In mine it's usually somebody from the past or an ex. If I'm lucky, it's Mum or Dad, like they're keeping in touch or something."

Laura leaned her head sympathetically. "Bless you. In mine, I'm the bad guy, the one who's going to do bad things."

"Well, you can be a bit bitchy at times."

"Are you kidding?"

"I did say a bit. Usually sweet, but sometimes a pain."

"Bitchy? Pain? Me?" Dramatically, she gave me an exaggerated expression of denial. Well, I'm being superbitchy in these nightmares. Last night I had a twisted evil expression on my face. It was contorted. Like I was so angry and wanting to hurt someone. When have I ever looked like that? I'm holding a knife blade up vertically in front of my face. Like this." She demonstrated with a kitchen knife. "Where do I get an idea like that? Can you imagine me being like that?"

"No, babe. Not ever. Perhaps it's just some phase you're going through. The dreams, I mean."

"Well obviously, Sherlock. I just don't want any more. These are not nice. I want dreams about holidays and excitement, not these nightmares. They're very scary." She touched my hand. "They frighten me, Dom."

"Why do you have them?"

"No idea, unless it's punishment for marrying you."

"Rubbish. I just don't get it. Having horrible dreams is pretty common I know, but for you to be the villain of your nightmare – well, I've never heard of that. I'm always the hero in mine."

"That's you all over. Sir Galahad."

I laughed. "You aren't going to go nuts on me, I hope? Do I need to hide these knives?"

Shaking her head, she said "No, and you can carry on sleeping with both eyes closed." She stood up. "While I remember, I picked up some brochures for us to look through." Laura went through to the other room and came back carrying some travel brochures, a beaming grin on her face. Holidays always had this effect on her. Clearly, she was motivated now by the blissful memories of Italy at Easter, and only two nights ago we had discussed spending a week away at October, half-term. "We could have looked through them last night. I've got to go to work soon."

"I forgot. Turkey looks good, babe. There again, we could always revisit Sorrento."

"Sorrento was fab, but there are too many places we haven't seen."

"Turkey, then?"

I shook my head, thinking of the recent news reports on television and things I had read in newspapers in the last few weeks. "We're not going there, the way things are right now. It's bang next to Syria and Iraq – too risky."

"Well, we could do Greece again then. We loved it last time."

I wasn't bothered about Greece, if the truth was to be known. The flight was a longer one than to Spain or Portugal, and I never enjoyed being up in the air. "Why don't we do a sporty holiday this autumn, for a change?"

She looked horrified. "You what? That sounds like a right drag."

"But you love sports when you bother to play them," I said. "We could do golf, riding, tennis, anything. Help you keep your sylph-like figure."

"Thanks, but not on holiday, Dom. We do enough here. What I fancy is two weeks on a beach. Just two weeks with sand and a swimming pool."

"So, a sporty holiday is out then? Somebody at work did recommend one in Spain to me."

"Listen, honey, and listen good." Her eyes widened, and her hands gripped mine as she leaned towards me. "In our two weeks of holiday I don't want to do anything more energetic than sex."

I looked straight back at her, knowing I had an uncontrollably massive smile on my face. She could always get me like this so easily, win any argument, regardless of the situation or time of day. "That sounds great."

"Anyway, on that bombshell, I have to dash now." She sprang up, her straight black hair hanging down as she grabbed her handbag from the kitchen worktop. "Got a meeting in half an hour. The oily surrealist from Leeds."

"Oh yes. Toby Ackworth. Well, I hope it all works out."

"I do hope so too, babe. Oh, I haven't told you, have I! I'll get a working holiday in America if today works out."

"How come?"

"Well if we come to an agreement today, I'm going to go to the States to link up with some galleries and shops in California and Nevada. Maybe do some real business. They're crazy about surrealism over there. Desperate for European originals." She placed a hand on my shoulder. "Anyway, whatever happens, I'll see you tonight."

"I've got squash with Jamie, and you're going out, aren't you?

"Oh yes. Obviously I meant later. Don't forget about my lift."

"Don't worry. I know the deal. I drive you home – just like you drive me crazy."

"Good. As long as you know your place." The door swung closed behind her.

It seemed like a world away. It had been a love-at-first-sight moment for me when I had called into the art gallery and shop she was working at, the Northern branch of a company based in London, to ask the price of a picture that was in the window. It was outrageous, the price of that picture, but equally outrageous was my attempt to have a conversation with this beautiful woman who even my mother would have said was out of my league.

"I know this is probably not welcome but I feel I have to say it. I would love to take you out for a drink or a meal."

"Which one? A drink or a meal?"

"Whichever one you would say yes to."

"I don't know. Depends what mood I'm in."

"Well, what mood are you in?"

"You won't get the picture any cheaper."

"Well, perhaps you can help me get past that disappointment."

At the time, I was sure she was humoring me, but we connected. There were no embarrassing or tense gaps in the flow of conversation that night and I recall that she did a lot of smiling. And what a smile. Within a few dates at the cinema and a trip to the seaside we both knew we were clicking big time. The long-term potential soon became apparent to both of us.

Hence, early dates soon become a full-on courtship, with an incredible physical dimension, and which eventually was summed up by a diamond ring and serious plans for the future. The planning reached a highpoint with the exchange of vows and home, initially an end terrace close to the entrance gates of Meersbrook Park, was a happy place. Waking up every day next to a sexy passionate wife was my ultimate dream.

Of course, that had all changed with the bump in the road last year. Three and a half years of marriage to a brilliant woman had not been enough for me, apparently.

"I have something to tell you." The Gallery had sent Laura to Holland to visit several Dutch galleries. After nervously picking her up from the airport and an uncomfortable drive home, I had seated myself away from her in the living room. There were horrible pauses throughout the ensuing conversation that were torturous.

Her expression had changed. "You've had an affair."

"I've been really stupid."

"Who?"

"It doesn't matter who?"

"Fucking who, Dom?"

"Just somebody I met in town."

"Why, Dom?"

"I don't know. I really don't get why I did it. I guess I was feeling a bit lonely, with you gone."

"Quit the self-pity. It doesn't suit you."

"I know babe. I'm just trying to explain it."

"Explain it? I've only been gone for three weeks. Couldn't you keep it in your trousers for twenty-three days?"

"Well I had a bit to drink. I ended up chatting to someone."

"Well, there would be drink involved wouldn't there. Why didn't you just chat? Why didn't you have the decency to avoid breaking my heart? You have any idea what this is like?"

"Babe, I don't know, and I'm sorry. And I know it's a cliché, but she meant nothing to me."

"Well she meant enough to you for you to fuck me over. God was I a fool for believing in you. I trusted you so much." Tears were rolling down her cheeks, which had become pale with mortification. Horrified by the disappointment she had felt, she became angry. "You know you've fucked everything up now, don't you?"

"I know. The last thing I would ever want is to upset you, but I had to tell you. I can't live a lie. I've messed things up big time and now I have to face the consequences.

"Was it just the once? I don't know why I'm saying just."

"Of course it was once. I've spent the rest of the time struggling. I've been trying to live with myself and dreading this. I do not want to lose you. I terribly don't want to have you not in my life." At this point, tears were rolling down both faces.

"So you've had a drink and slept with some slag. You've destroyed our marriage in the process, and guess what? I'm going right now to pack a case."

Sitting here alone on this weekday morning so many months on from that personal catastrophe, I didn't want to give it more than a split-second of thought. Even now it seemed so absurd and shameful. Thank God I had persuaded her to stay with me and after some tough months and too many upsetting conversations, we had eventually both managed to move on from it all. Well, at least to some extent. I guess both of us wanted the bliss we had enjoyed before. Those early months after my confession had been tough, with arguments, suspicions and insecurity, and too many awkward conversations that deservedly tore me apart. I guessed it needed to be difficult and awkward.

Thankfully she had been able to forgive me. At least, I hoped she had. We both felt we were getting back to where we were, and it was just the occasional punctuation of difficult conversations and reminders like this morning where I always strived to give this sweet woman the reassurance she needed.

These days, thankfully, I could focus on more positive matters. I switched on the computer and scanned the listings to see how my bids were doing. Two of the CD boxed sets I was after, both Tamla Motown collections to beef up my soul collection, had received higher offers, so I countered generously. Well, there was more than one way to get a buzz.

GOOD SPORT

I wasn't sure that I was in the mood for this. It was a warm summer evening with just a few suggestive silvery clouds floating above, but as always in this place, I had some difficulty finding a space for the car. My best mate was already here wearing his Wednesday shirt. One day he would buy a set of whites to match mine, he assured me, but obviously that day had not yet dawned.

"On time for a change," I yelled through the open window. I found an inconspicuous space at the end, next to the all-weather pitch.

As I approached him, he got out of his car, opened his boot, and with a broad smirk on his face, passed me three small square parcels. "Only three this week. You're slowing down."

What ensued was a strenuous hour and a half, with a soundtrack of sighing, swearing and grunting, and it was clear within minutes that we were no longer the young men we had once been. Ten minutes on the squash court, and we were red-faced and breathing profusely, looking very much past our sell-by dates as we toiled to keep up with a ball that seemed to have a mind and will of its own. After a lengthy rally, for one particular point, I reached to strike the ball and mis-hit it totally, sending it in to the bottom corner of the court. "What the hell was that?" In truth, we both remembered a time when the squash ball wasn't so independent and unpredictable.

"That's three points in a row. How much per point did we say?"

I gave him the finger and gestured him onwards with my sweeping arm. Jamie, a man I had lost contact with for two years. We hadn't had words or anything, but it had become a case of our paths not crossing very much, chiefly due to our different domestic situations. He had made a profession of chasing women on dating sites. He had been married on that day in Filey when he had taken on the role of Best Man and chief tormentor, but that relationship had crumbled a few months after that and we had just lost touch. We had luckily got back on track about six months ago, through a chance meeting followed by these squash nights and the occasional night out. We both liked a drink. As far as domestic situations were concerned, we would probably always be chalk and cheese, but so what?

I wiped the sweat from my face and breathed hard to get back some composure. "I'm not beaten yet."

It was a good job I knew how to be gracious in defeat.

Some strenuous minutes later, we were standing at the club bar waiting to be served. Jamie was savoring his victory. "I didn't think I would win that one. Your serves lost it for you. You need to be more precise in how you hit the ball."

"There's nothing wrong with my serve."

"All I can say is that it's a good job you're aggressive on the returns. Your racket skills aren't bad, but when it comes to you serving, no chance. In fact, I bet I could teach you how to do better. I could even show you how to beat me one day."

"Don't bother. It's only a game."

"I feel your pain, Mr. Walker."

I always gave as good as I got. "At least I have Laura to commiserate with me when I get home. How's your love life looking this week?"

"For the record, my love life is as good as it can be. Just for the record, with my hectic sex diary, you're lucky I'm here. I should really be somewhere else, having a more exciting time."

"Well, get you. Mister Big Time. The king of the dating sites, or what."

"Well of course. Skirt-chaser par excellence." He made an exaggerated show of checking his watch. "Anyway, should you be here? Sitting around here wasting time with me, with that minx you married? How is it that you're here wasting your time doing sport while you have that precious lady in your life. You know, the one who makes you go all puppy dog."

I grinned defensively. I was always happy to provide entertainment for the man who went by the name of Trojan on the sites, a name he probably chose because he thought it made him sound tough, although he claimed it was because he was sneaky with the women, like the Trojan Horse in Greek mythology.

"It's tricky, but I'll find some way to fit everything in." My feigned frown gave way to a smile. "I suppose we have to have to have a drink. Keep up this new tradition. Have to be a quick one, though. Promised Laura a lift home from town."

A young barmaid was suddenly across the bar from us, always a welcoming sight, since there weren't many things worse in my mind than waiting ages for a drink. Emptiness behind the bar and fullness in front of it were total pleasure-killers in my view. Whilst I ordered, Jamie was looking her up and down. It would definitely have been offensive if she had noticed him but he was crafty about it, shifting his eyeline to the optics behind her every time she looked up. He turned and gave me a knowing look. I could only shake my head in feigned disgust.

We found our usual table. He looked across the bar and declared, "She's well fit!"

"Yes, and it's a shame you aren't twenty years younger."

"I'd still pull her if I wanted, mate."

"Oh yes. And how would you do that?"

He pointed at his forehead, as if he was revealing some great philosophy. "I'd just give her my killer chat line. No problem."

"Fuck off. What killer chat line?"

He thought for a while. "I'd say to her, Hey lady, I'm seeing your future. I've got crystal balls and I see you in that old people's home one day. You know, you're sitting there not able to hold back the massive smile that takes over your face every time you think of that night you had with me."

"She'd interrupt you and tell you where to get off before you got halfway through that monologue. It's way too long for a chat-up line."

"Get out of here. How is it too long?"

"It's like a soliloquy from Shakespeare. 'Love's Labours Lost' probably. She'd have walked away before you even got to the end of it."

"Well, smart-arse, it worked a treat last week."

"Well, whoever it was must have been thick as a brick stupid, falling for that. I can't imagine I would have landed Laura, or any woman before Laura for that matter, with a line like that."

"Yeah, Laura." Jamie paused and looked at me. "I have to say something."

"About what?"

"Pretty strange, yesterday."

"How do you mean?"

Jamie was serious. "Have I offended your good lady in some way?"

29

"Not recently. Why?"

"Sure she's not feeling off with me for anything?" He looked serious and I was never comfortable when Jamie looked serious.

"What? She thinks you're funny. She always has. Knows you're a good mate."

"You're sure she doesn't see me as a bad influence?"

"Of course not. Because you aren't."

"She doesn't think I'm luring her husband into bad ways, then?"

"What are you on about?" Now I was really confused.

"I was just wondering if she might privately blame me for your indiscretion."

"No, not at all. She knows you were nothing to do with what happened. Christ, we weren't even in contact then. Why are you saying that?"

Jamie paused. I could see hesitation in his face, as if he was trying to come up with the right combination of words. "The thing is, I saw her yesterday. Did she tell you?"

"Did you? Where?"

"In town. On Fargate. She was walking past the Orchard Square entrance. It was weird because she looked straight at me, but didn't acknowledge me. She was wearing a black headscarf. Looked pretty chic. A bit Audrey Hepburn. Think Roman Holiday."

"Laura's always daydreaming. She won't have seen you." Laura did daydream sometimes, but was I just playing the loyal husband here, making a convenient excuse? Would she ignore Jamie? Very unlikely. If she had held anything of an attitude towards him for those rose-tinted, exciting times long gone by, she had never expressed it to me. I wasn't one hundred per cent sure, but I didn't want Jamie thinking that Laura had blanked him. "You sure it was Laura?"

"It was Laura. Umistakeable."

"But I don't think she owns a black headscarf. That's not her style at all."

"Well, she owned one yesterday. Anyway, if I hadn't put my arm out, she would have walked straight past me. She just looked at me and said she was in a hurry. I think she must have been on her way to work."

Laura being in a hurry was hardly a newsflash. She was always rushing around. "It's funny she didn't mention seeing you. She wasn't being funny with you though. I'm sure of that. She daydreams."

"Are you being honest with me? I can understand you sticking up for your wife."

"She's had a lot on her mind lately. It's that job. There's some right wheeler-dealing going with those pictures she buys and sells. It makes me glad I'm in teaching. There's less uncertainty with teenagers."

"Have you any idea how boring that makes you sound? Is your job that dull?"

"Never dull. Sometimes annoying, often frustrating, but never dull." I became defensive. "It's loads of things, sometimes utterly crazy, totally does my head in at times, but I wouldn't ever use the word dull to describe it." On the other hand, it had driven me to drink heavily on too many occasions, so it was no bed of roses.

"Are we having another? I fancy another Guinness before I dry up. After that, I'm meeting Angeline. That's in an hour."

"Who's Angeline?"

"Thirty years old, long blonde hair, and already thinks I'm lovely."

"Get you. Wait till she meets you."

"Yeah. It'll be heaven for her. About that drink?"

"Have to be quick," I replied. "Don't want to be late for my Laura."

"Well, don't let her see the parcels, or a sexy night will be out of the question. She'll put the block on. You won't even get to second base."

"As if!" I would definitely leave the parcels in the boot of my car.

Jamie shook his head. "Do they have a jukebox here?"

They had a jukebox. An hour and a half later, that same jukebox was playing the Arctic Monkeys and we were both singing along to 'Mardy Bum'. Jamie had a really loud and bellowing voice but hey, we were enjoying ourselves.

The music ended. For a rare couple of minutes, we sat there for a while not saying anything, and Jamie picked out a book that was on a shelf behind us. "You ever fancied writing a book, Dom?"

"Not really. What would I write a book about?"

"You could write about our adventures at uni. There's plenty of stuff to go at there."

"I don't think so. I don't mind remembering it, but I wouldn't have it in print."

"It would be funny. That lass with the stutter. You're d-d-d dumped."

"Embarrassing more like. Would be worse than your Best Man speech."

"Couldn't be worse than that. I excelled even myself that day.""

"Yeah. Why did you do that? That was horrendous."

"A bridegroom needs to squirm a little."

"A little? You traumatized me."

"Not really."

"Anyway, a book about those days would be agony to read and the embarrassment would never end. I wouldn't want anyone to read it, so what would be the point in writing it?"

"Well I definitely want to write a book." Jamie looked uncharacteristically serious again.

"Really? What about?"

"I thought I would write a book about the dating game, write down some of my adventures."

"Go for it. Why not? Some of the stuff you've told me, definitely why not? If you start, it might just trigger me off writing something. You could end up being my muse."

"Did I ever tell you about Tattooed John? He's worth a chapter."

"Who's Tattooed John?"

"A weirdo. He tattooed fifteen girl's names on different parts of his body. For every girl he met he got a tat, and eventually he had fifteen. After this, the story goes, he only went on dates with women who had one of his names. Bit of an obsession."

"He sounds like a right fruitcake."

"I don't know. A woman I met with had a date with him and said he talked about destiny and fate really emotionally and she ended up in bed with him. That's how she came across the tattoos. Apparently, he didn't hide anything, but it scared her."

"That's an interesting episode. Write it then, but try not to offend every woman in the known universe." This was all fascinating, but I stood up, having looked at my watch. "I've got to go. Same time next week."

Jamie smiled. "OK, but next time you are going to be even more of a beaten man. Give my love to Laura. Tell her I forgive her."

HERE COMES THE NIGHT

Did Henry Ford or Karl Benz ever envisage how the car might be such a blissful place for the relaxed driver? Could the inventors ever even imagine, great visionaries that they must have been, the possibilities they were creating for the kind of man who leaned back in his seat and wanted to appreciate the details of the environment around him. At the same time he could enjoy the delights of music, controlled from the middle of his dashboard. In any but the more extreme weather conditions, there was so much pleasure to be had cruising down country lanes with the lines of trees and the spreading sheets of green on both sides and ahead. The joy of the internal combustion engine. With the sunroof open, the freshness could engulf the car's occupants and create an envelope of true refreshment and exhilaration, a now traditional English pleasure. You could enjoy the idyllic scenery, the vibrant spread of greenery, embrace the wondrous and not so wondrous smells of nature, while upbeat sounds inside were equally stimulating. To top it all, you could even have your favourite woman next to you and savour the feeling that life could never be much better than this. Inescapable joy.

However, bliss was not quite the word I would have used this evening. The journey I experienced from Abbey Lane was lined with scornful streetlights and ahead of me were a series forbidding red traffic signals, alongside dreary frustrating queues of traffic, with, no doubt, like me, impatient men and women as occupants. The darkness just added a curtain of gloom. My mood was in a sharp and noisy descent and, at this rate, I would be psychotic by the time I hit the city centre.

I found my route into town characterised in an infuriating way by a number of temporary roadworks and every light seemed to be red. "Oh for crying out loud! Somebody's doing this on purpose." All I could see ahead of me was yet another soul-destroying stop light, and a lengthy series of brake lights that suggested this delay was going to be more than just a few seconds." My stress levels were going through the roof. I banged on the dashboard in frustration and looked around me for some kind of help, reassurance, or failing that, a bit of sympathy or undserstanding. "That's done it. Oh fuck! Fuck, fucking fuck!" When I lost it, I really lost it.

In the full knowledge that I was ten minutes late, ignoring the forbidding double yellows, I pulled up on the corner of Surrey Street, a thriving part of the City Centre, very close to a range restaurants and pubs, expecting tension and some kind of argument with Laura. The omens weren't good. On those occasions when Laura picked me up, she was never late, and prided herself on her reliability. "Always there when you need me, and always on time," she would say.

She emerged from a doorway. I watched with some trepidation as she conveyed herself up the road, with enough of an uncharacteristic lack of grace to suggest that she had been more than generously served at the bar. The smile on her face as she approached came as a massive relief. Perhaps there might be no friction tonight after all. Laura wasn't prone to mood swings, so we might just be OK.

"Hi, baby," she said as she opened up the door and dropped into the passenger seat. "I've had a fab time. Sorry I'm a bit late. How long have you been waiting?" She gave me a seriously wet kiss on my cheek as she settled into her seat belt.

"About ten minutes." Well, it didn't hurt to tell a white lie every now and then. "What was your meal like?"

"Ooh, delicious. I had calzone. Fucking perfect." Laura always swore more after alcohol, but it suited her. Most men like their woman to have a wild dirty side sometimes, and I was no exception.

"And how much wine?

"To be honest babe, I don't know. Put it this way, I think I'll sleep well."

As we drove onto Dewhurst Close, I was inwardly feeling pretty good; I knew the green light of likely intimacy was shining tonight like a divine blessing. Laura had had her hand on my leg for the whole of the journey, caressing my thigh, and I couldn't help feeling an excitement at knowing that Laura's nights out often came with benefits. Perhaps I should encourage her to go out more often. Perhaps not. I felt more inclined to have a drink when she was out socializing and, although I felt weak for thinking this, I did miss her usually.

As I unlocked the door, I knew what was going to happen. It had happened so many times before and I knew we were both feeling the same way. I was feeling amorous because I always fancied her beyond belief, whereas she always became frisky when she was intoxicated. Plus, she loved me.

True enough, the door was barely closed when our mouths came together and the energy of attraction took over. We were teenagers again. Our hands were frantically exploring each other. Laura was undoing the buttons of my shirt while I undid her skirt and allowed it to slide to the kitchen floor. Next, she removed my trousers and before they hit the floor she was on her knees looking after me in the way only a woman can while I closed my eyes and rested my elbows on the kitchen worktop to savor the moments. I whipped off her blouse and bra and the rest was a highly enjoyable episode, ending with us both upstairs and under the duvet.

Afterwards, I couldn't help saying, "That was lovely. Not really expected, but lovely."

"And how I love you, my beautiful man," she replied, holding my face in her hands and kissing me wetly and passionately, almost as if the sex was just foreplay for something more intense. We were always like this. A few weeks ago we had managed to have sex three times in forty minutes. I hadn't even known that was possible. I had almost emailed the Guinness Book of Records.

For about half an hour, we lay in bed talking. Laura had her head resting on my chest.

"I missed you today."

"I could tell."

"No, I did. Don't take the piss. I just feel so close to you right now. I think we're doing very well."

"That's the kind of man I like, utterly dependent. Fuel for my power trip."

"That's it. Scoff. Wait till the next time you feel emotional."

"Sorry, babe. I feel the same way about you. You know how much I'm yours, I'm just not as expressive as you are sometimes. You are a very expressive man. You are a man who can express. Like an express train can expressively move." She paused, then looked at me. "I'm just a bit tipsy tonight. Everything comes out stupid."

"You don't say?" I remembered the conversation earlier. "You didn't tell me you bumped into Jamie."

"When?"

"Yesterday. He said you were a bit abrupt with him."

37

"What?"

"A bit dismissive. In a hurry? Were you?"

Laura looked at me, bewildered. "I haven't seen Jamie since Liz and Joe's housewarming. What are you talking about?"

"Oh, I don't know. He just said that you were in a rush. You were near the town hall or something. He said you were wearing a black headscarf."

"That's weird. He's wrong. I was nowhere near there yesterday. Black headscarf?"

I lifted my arms. "Listen, don't shoot the messenger. I wasn't there."

"Well, that makes two of us."

"He just said you were in a rush and that you spoke to him. A bit dismissively, he said."

"Think about this, babe. Does that sound like me? Dismissively?"

"No, it's strange, unless you were blaming him in some way for some past stuff he had nothing to do with."

"I wouldn't do that. Why would I? He probably saw somebody who looked like me. It wasn't me, at any rate. He's been off work this week, hasn't he? I bet he'd been drinking."

"Perhaps," I said. "He certainly was enjoying the drink tonight."

"You know what Jamie's like. He is just totally obsessed with chasing women and can't get his head around much else." She paused. "Anyway, we need to address more pressing matters. What's next on our agenda?"

"I don't know," I replied. "To be honest I'm feeling tired now."

"I don't mean now, daft head. I mean next."

"Next?"

"Next."

The penny dropped. "I don't know."

"I really loved the last one."

"Outside again?" We had enjoyed an episode of intimacy on a walk last week. I turned to face her. Even in the darkness, I could see her eyes widening. "Is this what you want now? Broad daylight sin?"

Laura looked shocked. "I'm talking about another nice walk holding hands. Where is your brain at? Let me guess."

"Ecclesall Woods?" I asked, ignoring her.

She pulled a face. "Babe, just because we did that doesn't mean we need to repeat it." She paused. "That was a one-off. We just got caught up in a moment. It's hardly safe anyway."

"You're right. Especially in the daytime." I laughed.

"Too much stress for you."

"I don't know who was more shocked, that bloke, his dog or me." I wasn't very good with embarrassing situations and being caught in flagrante with your wife certainly qualified as that.

"That place was too hilly. Let's go somewhere more friendly to walkers. Somewhere with trees."

"Well, if it's trees we're after, what about Loxley Common? That's been fine for us before." I had grown up near that place. Unbeknown to my sweet demanding wife, as well as my outdoor adventures with her, most of my teenage sexual experience had been gained in that woodland.

"I think that's the best place anyway. We can do that. Back to just walking though this time." She patted my arm affectionately.

"Do you want to go tomorrow? It'll be busier in the early evening, with loads of people walking their dogs and children."

"What about later? Rugrats will spoil the mood." I wasn't sure if I was getting the wrong signals. I decided that playing innocent was probably my best bet.

"Could actually do earlier. I'm free last lesson in the morning so I could leave work for a bit and we could have a lovely lunchtime. There won't be many people around there then."

"Let's go for it, babe. We can have a wonderful walk and enjoy the countryside."

"My kind of woman."

In response, Laura gave me a reassuring kiss on the cheek and turned over to face away from me. "It's a date then. Tomorrow lunch-time."

MALEVOLENCE

I have some intentions. I have ideas and thoughts that I shouldn't have. Well, that's what most would say. There are directions that I go in and they are not nice, yet for me they are the right ways to go. I rarely hate my decisions. In fact, I like them because they stop my life being like everybody else's.

What do you do if you really want something? Do you let it go? Do you nurse your feelings like a sick child and carry that longing into eternity? I don't. Sometimes, it is easy to target a person who owes, and when somebody owes me, I am more than ready to do some taking.

There will be some suffering in the time ahead, but it won't be mine. For too long in my life I have been waiting, needing or preparing for changes, and here comes a big one.

I want better. There are things that have to alter and that will come soon. The world has something better in store for me.

Living my life has not been easy. So I don't think smooth. I've done too much fighting over the years, too much reaching out. I've not always won, but I've won most of the time. Too many have known me and too many have known me to their cost. I quite like to create a victim out of a fool. There are a lot of fools.

I once came into possession of a dog once, a poor pitiful creature whom nobody else wanted and it was obvious why. That was a few years ago now but it is still strong in my mind. I don't know why, since I don't do sentiment. This mutt had a desperate, needy ill-bred face with sticky out ears. and was so disturbingly hungry for something that nobody with a heart could do anything but give it some affection.

I gave him affection. I enjoyed stroking his fur, loved the walks we went on, and the creature seemed to like me too. He was some kind of cross-breed, possibly something like a Staffordshire Bull Terrier crossed with a whippet, which meant he had an interesting combination of strength and speed, but he still had that vulnerability of a creature needing love. I gave him love. Truly I did. For weeks I fed him, walked him and gave him shelter and I guess he felt like he had finally been welcomed by someone who would give him a home for the rest of his time on the planet.

Of course, it could not last. I know who I am. I could see ahead of me and would not be held back. I grew tired. Doggy had outstripped his welcome.

The creature seemed content enough at the end. It was a dark winter evening when the programmes on TV were at their worst, all repeats and patronizing bullshit. The poor mutt was laying in front of me, perhaps enjoying the TV, perhaps looking forward to 'walkies' the following day, maybe even dreaming of some in-season bitch in one of the local parks. Either way, he knew no suffering. It was all very humane, I suppose, for all those do-gooders out there who care so much about dumb creatures, so there is some reassurance to be had there. When I brought the blade down in that one quick arc of silver beauty, he did not have time to even see it, never mind think about it. I wonder what his last thought was? What was the last image in his mind?

Death came very quickly. The blood went everywhere, but that was to be expected. There were splashes of red on three of the four *walls of the room, with a massive pool of blood on the floor so I was left with a permanent reminder of how things had been. I got through so many paper towels, it was untrue. It took me ages to get the floor apparently spotless, but never really so. I could always see the redness. I still see the red blemishes. Sometimes it seems that the redness has spread through this little house, that it has spread into every room like a virus but that's impossible. My mind is a bit like that, though.*

It is hard being me. And, as I said, I do have these really bad intentions.

HAPPY FAMILY

On another 'glad to be away from work at last' evening, I was on my way home, singing loudly along with Queen's 'We are the Champions', wishing I was old enough to have seen Freddie Mercury on stage. Appreciating heritage was always fine and I did loads of it, but what must it have been like to have experienced somebody legendary like him as a reality? It must have been pretty awesome. I was tapping away dramatically at the steering wheel as I gave vent to my tone-deaf accompaniment. Perhaps up there, he was enjoying my version of his song. Yeah, right.

I had enjoyed myself all the way here, right back from the traffic lights at the bottom of Ecclesall Road and had not stopped singing since then. I credited this to how things were right now. Lunchtime with Laura had been lovely, and a nice break. As we had hoped, the woods had been deserted and we had had another lovely relaxed walking experience. No sex, but very sexy.

I looked at the dashboard clock to realise I had arrived just before six-o'clock, the first time in ages that had happened. I had left school early for the best of reasons. Normally, I stayed in school marking and preparing lessons until at least half past six and I tried to make sure that that would leave the rest of the evening for my real life with Laura. However, even now that wasn't always so, since at least one weekday night every fortnight, I had to mark assessments until midnight.

I parked in front of the garage door, knowing that Laura's Audi would be inside. I was going to make a point of leaving earlier than she was tomorrow, so I wouldn't need to park on the road today. As I retrieved my briefcase from the boot, only glancing at the tell-tale brown packages alongside it, waiting to be retrieved and hidden away at an opportune moment, I was smiling broadly. In my mind I was appreciating the fact that I was home with no work to do. On the minus side, however, I was now thinking about the evening in we were going to have, not an easy one.

I made my way straight into the living room. As I opened the door, Laura was looking through some papers that she had laid out on the dining table while she sat there, with a cup of coffee for support. She had a massive smile on her face as she acknowledged my presence in the room. Hurriedly, she started to put the papers into one neat pile, before putting them into a light-brown manila folder that was at the side of her on the settee. She held the folder tightly on her knee.

"Guess what, babe? Just had a call. We're buying all of Ackworth's paintings."

"Fantastic babe. A good day, then."

"Yes, and you know what that means. I'm going to New York."

"That's brilliant." I looked at her with an attempt at smiling, before the curve of my smile straightened more genuinely. "What am I saying? How will I cope?"

"You will cope very well. You'd better."

"When are you going?"

"Dates haven't been finalized yet. About ten days there."

"How many weekends?"

Laura picked up her phone obviously was checking her calendar app. "Only one. Miss me loads."

"Great marriage, this. I have to look after myself for a miserable ten days, while you go sunning yourself Stateside. And they say women have it tough!"

"Hey, perhaps you'll appreciate me more if I'm not around. This could be really good for us. Just don't fuck up this time."

I shook my head with a tight firmness. "No chance."

"And don't drink!" At this point her eyes had become intense and her demeanor betrayed a serious worry I knew she would have, one that needed putting to bed.

I sat down on the settee and I picked up the remote control, switching off the TV that had been silently shown some wildlife programme. "Things are already good for us. You don't have to go on."

"I know, but I will anyway."

"And I won't ever fuck up again so there are no worries on that score."

Laura stood up and stared down at me. "OK, don't get sulky. I know and you know. Everything ends if you fuck up again."

"I won't." I could feel a sharp edge of irritation in my voice, which should not have been there, since she had every right to repeat and every right to insist.

"Don't get grumpy."

I put down the remote and looked at my wife. "I'm sorry. I'm just tired." I stood and moved towards her, holding her hands. "I want you to do well in your job, sweetie. It's just... you know. I'll miss you."

"Well, that's good. Keeps you on your toes."

I grinned. "I take it we're having a takeaway tonight."

With the folder held close to her chest, she stood up and

moved to face me, looking down. "I can't be bothered cooking. Dad loves Indian food like you, so I've ordered some. Three Balti's and a Jalfrezi."

I made sure that I gave no sign of disappointment and forced a smile. "Well, I think I'll get a quick bath. Papa's coming and I don't want to make my usual bad impression."

"Don't even joke about that. You're getting there slowly. Just takes time."

"I don't mind that. I'm so good at being patient I should be in hospital."

"Is that the best you can do for a joke?"

"Makes my students laugh."

"I bet. Bottom set, by any chance."

"Ha fucking ha."

"Anyway, apart from that, just be very careful what you say. And make sure there are no references to our sex life, hidden or otherwise. No dirty asides, Shakespeare. Spare my blushes. At least till they're gone." Her eyes were again looking deep into mine, a clear sign that she meant it.

"Not even one joke?"

"Not even half of one. You need to win some brownie points, not black marks." She paused. "I enjoyed our walk today."

"Me too. Want to do it again tomorrow?"

"OK. I'll do it. Make it five at the five bar gate for a walk and talk. God, I'm so poetic at times." She laughed. "Maybe I should be an English teacher."

"I'd stay where you are."

Laura smiled. "Perhaps you're right. Anyway, it's bath-time for you. They'll be here at eight."

While we spoke, the right-hand window on the back wall of the living room was raised open for ventilation, allowing a gust of fresh summer air to enter the house and, looking at it all retrospectively, for our secrets to escape. At the time, we just could not imagine that anybody would hear us and were sure that nobody would want to hear us.

* * *

An hour later, the doorbell rang. For one of us it was the announcement of a welcome arrival whilst for another it was the signal for an evening of hard work after a day of hard work. Laura ran downstairs and opened the door with what would be a massive smile on her face. I continued to vigorously brush my teeth in the bathroom, standing there apathetically, with no inclination to rush. I gritted my teeth.

Subsequently, within the next hour, largely due to Laura's preparations, all four of us were sitting chewing some kind of fat after eating spicy culinary delights. The end result was a variety of chicken bones or ribs on every plate, with everything else having been mopped up by all four diners. Only one, Laura, had a substantial amount of rice remaining on her plate, but she was on that perpetual diet where it was always good to leave food. In truth, George and I probably both needed to diet more, but neither of us left anything. Isn't that always the way?

Lillian, a gentle woman in both appearance and personality, was doing a lot of the talking. "And anyway, I was in the Market and I bought a load of fish. I even bought swordfish and calamari, for a change."

"Calamari. I can't stand calamari." George, a formidable man both mentally and physically, looked at Laura and his wife as he spoke.

"It's quite tasty, fried." I said

"I expect it is," he said, looking at Laura, then turning to his wife.

"You could always have it with chips and mushy peas," Laura offered.

"Suppose I could," he said, smiling and looking at the pictures on our wall as if they were suddenly fascinating.

"Dom and I went on a lovely walk today. Didn't we, Dom."

I nodded.

"Lillian smiled. "That's nice. Where did you go?"

George was playing with something on his plate with his fork while Laura gave her mother the details.

Of course, they knew all the miserable details of our past year. Laura and Lillian were close, like sisters, and Laura, at her lowest ebb, had confided in her mother and had naturally been well-supported. Essentially, they knew that I had played away. Understandably, I had become the villain of the piece and it would be a while before we could all be comfortable in each other's company.

"Well you don't come to us all that often, so we wanted to make sure you'd be bigging us up after eating the food."

Awkwardly, I tried to make an enthusiastic supportive sound. Inside, I felt a really hopeless desperation, as though there was a demon hiding away inside me. I just wanted to make everything good for Laura. "That's right, babe. Let's get a reputation."

George gave me a quick meaningful look that made me more uncomfortable. He switched his attention back to Laura with a smile that might just have been forced. "Well, the food was nice. I hope it's as nice as this next week."

"Thanks, Dad. When do you two fly?" She had a nervous smile on her face.

Lillian spoke first. "We're off on Wednesday," Lillian said, showing the same unfelt positivity.

"Are you excited?"

"I am. I'm going to spend all week sitting in the sun while George works. If I can bear it, that is. It's so hot out there."

"I'd spend more time inside if it was me," I said.

"I might end up doing that. Thank God for air-conditioning."

Laura and she had talked of nothing else in their three telephone conversations over the past couple of weeks. As you might expect, Laura loved the fact that her dad painted portraits for a living. I was jealous of him. Everything I attempted with a brush looked unrecognizable and barely worthy of a seven-year-old. George, on the other hand, was a highly skilled artist and was paid substantial money for his efforts. For the past three years, his clients had mainly been wealthy Arabs and interest in the quality of his artwork was spreading by word of mouth, as it always had, with the wealthy out there queuing up to be his next subject. "I know I'm cheeky, but how much this time?" Laura asked.

George hesitated before speaking. This alone was a signal that it was a seriously lucrative deal. "Enough for our next ten holidays. As long as I paint it right, of course."

"Christ, Laura. I've changed my mind. You can buy me a set of paints and a brush for my birthday. I'm going to be an impressionist."

"You don't even know what impressionism means," Laura said. Lillian managed a faint half-laugh, probably out of politeness, whilst George maintained what might have been interpreted as a dignified silence. Hey-ho. Any jokes I made were bound to fall on stony ground these days and, thankfully, the clock was ticking, so they would be gone soon.

August jumped onto Laura's lap. "August! How are you, baby?" Laura began stroking the cat like he was a welcome escape from the tension of the evening and the cat's eyes closed pleasurably in response.

I decided at that point to take an initiative. "George, I need to talk to you about something. On the decking perhaps?"

Laura looked up at me, a concerned look on her face. I gestured with my hand that this was cool, and that I wasn't challenging him to a duel or a fist fight. In all truth, I would have lost either of those. I noticed Lillian giving the same look to her husband. He just looked blank-faced and picked up his drink, looking grim-faced, as if he would have welcomed a fight to clear the air.

I felt like a gunfighter without a gun. The two women were left looking at each other, with matching facial expressions. Don't worry, I signaled, this time with a wink, but with no confidence.

Facing the cloudy sky and beyond our fence, the park, I sat down and gestured for George to follow suit.

I cleared my throat then began. "I need to talk to you about stuff. I know you're pissed off at me and it needs to be sorted."

"Sorted?" The silence was allowed to continue for a while before he broke it. "You shat the bed big time. What do you expect me to say about that?"

"I know. She didn't deserve it. Don't think that I don't know that. The truth is, I was in a mess."

"That's no excuse."

"I know. We were having problems, largely my problems. I did something very stupid. I'll always regret it."

Stone-faced, he was still full of anger. "She should have left you. Judy would have left me if I'd pulled a stroke like that."

"Perhaps she should have. Perhaps I would have in her shoes. But she didn't."

"And I haven't a clue why she didn't. I urged her to get out."

"Well we're recovering. In fact, we're better than ever."

"What does that mean? You seemed happy last Spring."

"What it means is that you don't need to come here with the face on because I'm still with Laura. And treating me like a pariah just makes things unpleasant. You don't need to punish me, believe me." I kept a humble tone in my voice.

"You've got off lightly if you ask me."

"You're joking? I've suffered for it. Suffered big time."

"How is it big time? In what way? She never moved out."

"She didn't need to. I felt so bad. I hated the pain she felt. Laura knows that. She accepts my regret and knows that my promises are solid."

"Solid? Don't make me laugh."

"Come on, George. We're trying to get over it. We're trying to show you that we're getting over it. We want things to be normal."

"How can I trust you? How can I trust you not to go shagging somebody else the next time you're on a night out in town and Laura's not around. Like when she's in America soon. You've been a cheating bastard once, so why not whenever it suits?"

"It never suits."

He shook his head. "And to think we believed in you."

"You can still believe in me. I've been through hell at the thought of what I did and the fear of losing Laura has driven me crazy." As I said this, I studied his face, looking for acceptance. "All I ask is that you at least appear to put aside what happened."

"That's very easy to say."

"Yes. I know. I know you can't put it aside in your mind and how much it must hurt. I'm totally sorry about that. I'm not a mug, but I know I've been one. Laura is the best thing that could ever happen to me."

"The best by far."

"I know. It was just a mistake. A terrible, terrible thing I did. I…"

He raised his hand to stop me. "Well, time will tell. We believed in you, and you let us down. I needed a man to look after my daughter and give her a nice life."

"I know, and she's having a nice life now."

"OK." George paused, took a drink, a larger one than he usually took, whilst not taking his eyes off me for a split-second, and a few moments passed before he continued. "Let me sum things up for you. We're off halfway across the world next week. I can't forgive you very easily. To be honest, I wanted to batter you to the ground. But I'll give some ground, give it all a chance when we return. I want to feel better about you being with my daughter. I really do. Just you make sure you're a decent man for her and I might end up not despising you so much."

"Thanks. That's all I need. Just watch this space."

AN UNCERTAIN MIDNIGHT

As a child I had never needed to sleep with the light on. I was always comfortable in the blackness of night and generally, both as boy and man, slept soundly through whatever kind of night it was. My imagination did not reach into the darkness for something gruesome. My mind was sure that there was no bogeyman, no beast from the crypt, and, as I had grown older, I had come to realise that most crimes were committed in broad daylight anyway.

On this night, there was no wind, so very little was physically being disturbed, and everything around me had a calmness and serenity that was totally soothing to a man sitting alone with his thoughts and a newly-poured drink. I thought I was more hopeful, somewhere just above middle in the negative/positive spectrum, believing that overall, life at the moment presented opportunities and pleasures, if not quite perfect. Whatever was going to happen would happen, and I would make the most of it.

To consider the night's events and the harsh but not hopeless exchange with a man who had come to despise me, I had resisted the warmth of our home to sit in the cool darkness outside. In an attempt to be totally relaxed, I considered being exposed to the elements to be therapeutic. More practically, I had a white plastic bag of rubbish in my hand that was destined for the large black bin at the side of the house, but which I now placed down on the decking while I ensconced myself in the chair that George had sat in earlier, facing outwards at the restful flower beds and beyond. Tonight was only the sixth or seventh time I had sat outside so far this summer. I wanted to enjoy it.

Positively, the weather had been pleasant for most of the past month, but not enough to prevent us being ensnared by convenient diversions such as sex, Netflix and Facebook, alongside my not-so-clandestine love affair with music, when I would just sit upstairs in my culture room with the volume cranked up. However, it was always nice to sit outside. Whether it was a patio or a beer garden, it was funny how the warmth of these months suited both eating and drinking.

Laura, having gone up to have a bath, had left her handbag on the table and the glass of red wine was alongside it. This was typical Laura. She was unsettled after a difficult evening. Consequently, she wouldn't fancy her chances of getting to sleep any time soon, so she had sought solace in the bubbles and water. I had opted for one last JD and coke, albeit a treble. Eventually, I would retire to bed. Maybe then there would be some intimacy, dependent on Laura's ability to sleep after bathing, or else I would console myself with another chapter of my Stuart McBride novel to lead me to slumber. I had had plenty to drink, so either would be fine, with the latter probably being easier.

As I sat there with my hand cradling the glass, August came up and sat there staring. He was usually much friendlier towards Laura than me, probably because she had spent more time on him since we'd got him and had been the first to pick him up at the animal rescue centre. Do cats, like most humans, genuinely love anyway, or do they just want their needs satisfying?

"Here boy. Come to daddy."

August didn't move. August rarely moved when prompted. Being a cat, he had the right to consider the request for a while, when he could either assent or resist. I took a substantial swig from the tumbler. This was Friday night. I could cope with the hangover in the morning. Although no good at painting or do-it-yourself, I was still an expert when it came to becoming intoxicated.

Having clearly given the matter some thought, August gingerly moved forward and jumped up onto my lap. He settled quickly and within a minute or two, we were both purring.

I could have considered this. My beloved wife was happily bathing upstairs, happy that the evening seemed to have progressed ok with no conflict. Our cat, the only animal I had to think about at this moment in time, was in my lap, willingly receiving some affection that was possibly good for both of us while I was able to enjoy my favourite tipple, with the moon shining down approvingly from somewhere, although I couldn't see it from where I was sitting. All this was happening like a rebellion against under a calm black sky. How could I not be happy with my life at this moment?

I gazed up at the blackness and realized it hid the whole universe from view and was something magnificent but not necessarily benevolent.

Suddenly, something didn't seem right. I sensed a disturbance.

The universe might be ok from this chair, but something closer to home was irregular. My relaxed state had gone, and only August continued to purr.

I was suddenly conscious of not being alone out here.

At that moment, after some searching around the garden, I was beset by an instinct that prompted me to look at the far fence. It was a flimsy-looking wooden fence, formed from thin inter-woven strips, one that would surely one day fall victim to an enthusiastic storm. However, it was the kind of fence that would hide somebody on the other side.

Somebody was watching me.

I began to stare at different parts of the fence, trying to work out where whoever it was out there was hiding. Somebody was behind it. I knew this was not my imagination. I had a history of sensing things like this. Once I had sensed that somebody was downstairs in a house I had shared as a student. There were no tell-tale sounds or anything, but I had just had this intuition and the next morning we discovered that the lock on the back door was broken and the TV had been stolen.

I knew someone was there. I would let him know I knew. I slowly but purposefully left my seat and stood up on the decking. As I moved, I was listening for the sound of footsteps or a sudden burst of energy to get away. There was nothing.

As I stood there, staring outwards, I knew there was a hole in the fence, a hole that was probably a perfectly natural hole, made by the imperfect growth of a tree many years ago, but it was a hole that provided opportunity, which made me feel suspicious and vulnerable. It was about four feet up from the ground, a convenient height, too easy, for somebody wanting to look in at the occupants of the house and garden. However, as I stepped onto the lawn I wasn't merely seeing a hole. I was seeing something through the hole, something I should not be seeing. Unmistakably, unless the Jack Daniels was playing tricks on me in the darkness, looking into the garden, possibly, if not probably, monitoring me, there was an eye looking through that hole.

My heart was beating like some potential victim in a horror film. I was on my own here. The intruder could be armed, and I had no wish to become another statistic, another easy picking for a psycho with a blade or even a gun.

I considered alerting Laura and calling the police, but that would have made me feel like a wimp. It would probably be nothing. Whatever was going on, the JD inside me was stimulating bravery so I was ready for a fight if need be, although I would watch out for that knife. This was Sheffield, after all.

I was about ten feet from the hole when, even in this light, I could see that the eye had disappeared. Moving more quickly, I went right up to it, looked through it. I could see nothing, except the open space of the land beyond our garden that stretched right out to the playground and trees of the park. I heard nothing. Hurriedly, I examined other holes and gaps in the fence. These holes gave no sign of anybody or anything. There was an emptiness surrounding our garden, the kind of emptiness that we had seen as a selling point when we had bought the house.

I stood on tiptoe and looked over the fence. There was nobody. Had I imagined it? I had had plenty to drink tonight and hadn't slept too well the past couple of nights, so perhaps I had been imagining things. Perhaps I was going all Macbeth on myself and this was my ghost of Banquo, exposing my guilt over past sins. After all, who in the world would want to watch a man having a glass of JD on a veranda, especially round here, where nothing ever happened. Christ, this must have been one of the quietest places in the Solar System.

I stood there for a couple of minutes listening for any tell-tale sounds. Nothing. I had definitely imagined it.

I decided enough was enough. I turned and returned to the decking. Purposefully, I picked up the white rubbish bag I had placed down there and took it round the corner to where the bin was. I lifted the bin lid, dunked the white bin bag in there, then replaced the lid unceremoniously. Slightly unsettled by my unproven and therefore dubious intuition, I opted to go back into the house, picking up my glass as I went. Before I entered the house, I took one last look at the fence and put the disturbance of my good feeling down to alcohol, ever my fatal flaw.

MALEVOLENCE

I intended to look at them closely, listen to them intently, and now I know a bit more. I am always curious. I was especially curious this evening. I just need so much information. I want to know everything about this bitch and him. I am committed to this and I need to prepare properly. Life may have been a mixture of the difficult and the eventful, but here is an opportunity for something quite perfect. The time is right for something dramatic. Now I want to transform and take. I have done my share of being on the receiving end of suffering and recovering from suffering, which have made me stronger. That strength has enabled me to take advantage on so many occasions. Now it is time for some serious wrongdoing. There are no limits to this. I have seen some of what I need to see, added to what I already knew, and there has been food for thought.

The best way to avoid disappointment and frustration is to be active. It is always better to do things than to sit around waiting for whatever life wants to give you. You go looking for it and do what's needed like Malcolm X said. "By whatever means necessary."

I hate what I know about these two. She is so comfortable and complacent. Doesn't she just deserve something to happen? He too, like a showroom dummy, looks so easy because he's stupid. He probably doesn't realise how stupid he actually is. They are both waiting for me, but they aren't aware of it yet.

They will be aware of me soon.

I will be in their lives in time. In fact, I am already in their lives, but they do not know it. It will be easy for me make the moves. I just need to sort out some of the details. That's where the devil is, where I am. The ground needs to be made right for the storm that is coming. In whatever time needed, it is time to take a wrecking ball to all they think they have.

Like most things, all is dependent on timing. It's knowing when to stick and when to twist so that the world turns nicely and I end up with everything. Winner takes all, and losers don't always survive.

I have to keep on thinking, re-thinking, then re-thinking some more. This grand scheme of mine needs to happen in the right way.

It has been a long time coming. I never knew I had so much patience. But patience is crucial. What is going to happen will be classic but I need to keep a sense of caution. It could so easily fail. I must pay attention to all the relevant details and refrain from striking until I am totally ready.

AS IT SHOULD BE

We had both needed something. As we enjoyed the final moments of another delicious episode, our arms were wrapped around each other in a harmonious show of blissful mutuality. We could only congratulate each other in grunts, sighs and tight gripping in recognition of the beauty that we had just enjoyed but that was plenty. Disentangling ourselves clumsily, I enjoyed how Laura's face glistened from her exertions in our erotic moments as we fell into place, side by side, bodies half-covered by the duvet and impervious to anything that could detract from that.

Laura lay on her side, looking outwards, away from us. I knew she was thinking about something. "What exactly did you say to Dad tonight?"

"What I told you I said. I just told him how good we were. It needed sorting, babe, if only to shorten his long face. He was like a miserable horse."

"Don't be so hard on him. It's only because he cares about me."

"I know that."

"He knows how much you hurt me."

"I think I convinced him that I hurt myself more. I tried to anyway. I know how much he cares about you, babe. But then again, why wouldn't he?"

"Yes, he's a sweetie really. Always there. Mum's the same."

I gently pulled her round to face me, knowing that I was about to steer the conversation in a different direction. "Do you ever wonder what your real parents would make of you now you're older?"

She looked at me and paused before turning her head to face the ceiling. "Not really, no." There were a few silent seconds that were never going to mark the end of the conversation.

"Occasionally I think about her, and whoever he was, but wouldn't anyone? Just a sperm donor, apparently, and she was just a surrogate. Dad and Mum told me everything I needed to know about both of them, to be honest."

"They are still people, sweet. Aren't you more curious about them? I think I would be."

She shook her head firmly. "Of course not. For me, the bottom line is this. When she sold me, she gave up every right to be in my thoughts. So, she's not in them. Not ever."

"OK. Do you ever think she might have had a change of heart, though?"

"It makes no difference to me. Let's put it this way, I'm not going on 'Long Lost Family' any time soon."

"What if she was under pressure? What if she felt compelled to give you up?"

"Who sells a kid or gives it away? I wouldn't. Not ever."

"Oh, right. Is that a reference to our kid, by any chance?"

"Our kid?"

"Our kid. The one we're having in the not too distant future?"

"Let's not go into that again. That's long term and massive. We've some way to go before we'll be ready for that."

Now I became lost in my own thoughts. This was just like the previous occasions when she had made the same suggestions about waiting and the timing. For me, the only thing that mattered was how strong we were together and how we had so much to offer. I felt we had come a long way since those destructive days of last year. From Laura's point of view, however, we still had some way to go before she would be ready. Yet, if Laura said there was more waiting needed, then I would wait. "If you're sure?"

"Totally and utterly, babe. We don't need a baby. We just need to rebuild us." She gently clasped my hand and looked searchingly into my eyes. "You do understand, don't you?"

"I think so. But you're definitely the right woman for me to have a child with. I hope that one day we'll be of the same mind." I lay back. "That's it. That's my last mention of a little one for a while."

"Thanks. We just need some more time. You're on the way to being my whole world again, babe, getting there, so you never know. It's like I was telling Jenny on Facebook the other day."

"Who's Jenny?"

"This woman who I used to go to school with."

"You never mentioned her."

"She contacted me a while ago and I accepted her as a friend. To be honest, I didn't recognize her from her photos but people change sometimes, don't they? I think she's a bit lonely. She was really interested in my life, my work and you and we chatted loads about relationships, hobbies and food. Bit pitiful really. She wanted to know how she could make her relationship work as well as ours does. Wanted to know how we made each other happy day-to-day. Her bloke's a builder, self-employed, apparently, and I don't think life is very good for her."

"Well, it never hurts to touch base with your past. Did she know about your reunion party?"

"I told her about that, but she wasn't interested. Not the face-to-face type. Shyness, I think. She does seem like a lovely woman, though. She just wants us to be online friends."

"Hey, be careful. She might be a creep who turns up at the house unannounced." I reached switched off the lamp, plunging the room into darkness. "Anyway, it's sleep time."

MALEVOLENCE

In the darkness a dustbin can be almost encyclopedic. Any search in a container of rubbish will surprise in the amount that can be revealed about a person or two. It helps when the darkness inside is matched by the blackness outside, where there is a protective hum provided by the gentle swaying of trees in the breeze. Nothing else stirs. Nobody can see.

Almost nobody. While some find sleep, a condition I have had problems with most of my life for one reason or another, a determined figure, acting quickly and silently, can operate in the darkness. The plastic lid can be gently lifted and you can find the truth in so much detail.

This wasn't my first time exploring human residue. It was the sort of necessary evil that often gave an advantage. Theirs was no different. This had been my fourth attempt to stealthily delve into their filth.

I had learned from previous raids that the bitch liked Clarins make-up products, was on the pill and had eight thousand pounds in her bank account. He, pretty stupid if you ask me, read football and music magazines, and drank too much Jack Daniels than was good for him. Great. I didn't mind him dying from liver failure, whenever that might happen. In fact, his dying in the not too distant future was fine by me.

I placed valuable and informative items in my black rucksack. I was constantly alert, ready to run, or strike if discovered.

On this particular evening, just like the other times, nobody witnessed my activity. I slowly lowered the lid and made a swift exit. I was getting good at this.

AS IT IS

For Laura and me, everything had an edge. When we were together, there was such an intensity, such an understanding that everything we did carried its own excitement, whether it was shopping or watching a film. "We're just kind of magical, aren't we?" she had said to me one evening while we were curled up together watching a movie. Of course, there was always such a good feeling generated when we were side by side. We were such a good fit. The sex was tremendous and was as magical as it could be, while the emotional side always kept us feeling good in its way too. We just knew exactly how to optimize pleasure for each other, and we would both become lost in our conversations, cuddles and intimacy.

We had been walking. There was an early evening breeze in the air, but it was warm enough for neither of us to need a coat and for the beer garden to be an attractive proposition. We walked towards the road that adjoined the common, holding hands and only interested in each other, just as we had always been. We kissed each other as we walked, and I was thinking that we would have all the foreplay done before we reached the car.

"Hey, that car's there again." Up the road, about fifty yards from our two vehicles, was a metallic blue Ford Fiesta, just like the one I had owned ten years ago. "It was there the last time we were here. Abandoned?'

"I don't know. I don't think so. Who would abandon a car here?"

"Do you think somebody could have had a heart attack or something?"

"I doubt it. It will be some dog-walker. They probably used the other entrance and went towards the fields rather than the woods. If it's a woman, she will have preferred that. Safer."

Laura laughed. "You make me laugh. I bet there hasn't been a crime committed here in the past ten years."

"Except for the crime of you refusing to let me give it to you against that tree." I pointed behind me.

"Since when was being careful a crime? I want to come here again." She looked at me. "Oh, there's a bit of lippy on your neck. Stand there."

I stood there while she cleaned me up with a wipe from her handbag. I looked at my watch. Six-ten. By six-thirty, I would be back at Dewhurst Close and giving my wife the good news. We just had to get home first.

MALEVOLENCE

The TV is great, for most people. It gives so many of the sad bastards and bitches entertainment and a buzz. To me it gives nothing but a deep negative feeling and a need to do something to make my situation better. I hate television. I get sick of seeing smug smiles, false expressions from artificial people. They don't know what tough is. I have a serious loathing of the things that people get off on from on that screen full of shit. Besides, too much on there is emotional stupidity and nobody gets anywhere by being emotional. Emotions just get in the way of the good stuff.

Popular television is awful. In fact not much on any of the channels is better than utterly shit. Programmes show a world that's nothing to do with me and if I force myself to watch them, they make me want to declare war on all humanity there and then, which I guess I am partly doing anyway. People on shows have been too lucky, avoiding obstacles and discomfort that are necessary in life, and they end up offering pathetic ideas to equally pathetic people and making everybody think that victories are achievable where they are not. I hate people.

I don't dwell on it, but my life, particularly in the earlier years, has been a troubled kind of soap, one that could and should perhaps be shown late at night. People need to see the horrible stuff that can influence a life, rather than the shitty storylines in dramas and documentaries that just make me sorry that they and me supposedly share the same world.

A great storyline is present in my mind right now and it's about to unfold. I only regret that I'm not very good at writing things down.

And then there is the news – The News! Supposedly, it is interesting but it always features people who don't deserve life, arrogant idiots who need to have their existence ended, whether they be the smug survivors of disasters, selfish politicians and leaders of countries, or people in the strange world of the celebrity who have done nothing good but feel that they have done everything. I will be doing my bit. I am bringing some fab news to my favourite couple when the time is right. They might not survive the disaster I am bringing, and they may even achieve celebrity status like the victims of Jack the Ripper, only with more suffering.

It could be worse. The Jack and Jill of my murder rhyme could be in advertising. I become particularly violent when I think about advertising. I have wanted to kill after seeing the unreal squeaky-clean sugar-coated world presented to me by the commercial moments between and within programmes. Mars is more like where I live than the world that they try to show me. Nobody who puts on a smile while they sell the qualities of a cooking ingredient, a toothpaste or a fizzy drink should have to cope with life. They have presented a version of living that is a totally stupid and which needs a reaction. They needed to see my life growing up and then make their advertisements. After these two, I will go looking for people in the world of the false image.

All that most of television (and the world outside television for that matter) needs is someone to act as the ultimate avenger, a bold soul to wage war on the shit that pollutes all existence. To sort out or remove the shit people and make the world a more honest and real place.

This is me. At this point I take a step forward. I am happy to do my bit for world truth.

INTRUSION

9F were horrific. They were always a tough group to teach, with some lively minded boys who liked to encourage each other to disrupt through smiles and laughter and were in no hurry to accept what I was trying to achieve with them. We were at the end of the lesson. I had kept a few offenders behind afterwards because their names had been written in black marker on the board and I was letting them know that there was a price to be paid for crossing Mr. Walker, the kind and knowledgeable English teacher.

"Can I go now, sir? I hardly did anything." With plenty of emotional expression, this was a boy who clearly paid better attention in Drama lessons.

"This is a five-minute penalty. You mucked about. You delayed the learning of others in the class. That's not on."

"What about me, sir? I only spoke across class once. I'll be better next time." I imagined this lad in the dock in a few years' time, trying to reduce his sentence. Perhaps I was being harsh here. Not many of my ex-students became villains.

I fiddled with my watch. "OK. Silence now. Five minutes silence. You disturb the silence, the five minutes starts again."

One of the detainees sighed, all too audibly. Another one not yet ready for the world of employment, where we all sighed inwardly.

"OK, it starts now. Five minutes from now."

A dagger of a look was given across the classroom. This was Friday, fish and chips day. Being late wlould mean that all of the fish would be gone and a meat-ish pie would be the only option. None of the six boys in front of me wanted that. Silence now took over the room.

My classroom door suddenly opened and Hazel, the school secretary came in. Looking around the room, she quickly appreciated the punitive nature of the situation and came round to my desk to whisper to me. "Thomas Huxton's mum is in reception. Is this a bad time?"

"No. I'll be down in two minutes. Just making these characters sweat a bit."

Hazel smiled at me and left.

"Right boys, we need to make a deal," I said.

* * *

Gwen Huxton was here to see me about her son being bullied by a group of idiots in the year above. It had all been about something Thomas had said about a girl, apparently. I had managed to convince the boys who had threatened Thomas that this was a case of Chinese Whispers, that it was better to move on from any conflict situation, especially since three students had been permanently expelled for bullying the previous year so carrying on any ridiculous dispute might not be in their long term interest.

"Anyway, Mrs. Huxton, I think it's sorted. The school's anti-bullying policy is pretty strong. We don't accept it. When I spoke to them, the boys were receptive to what I was saying and they seemed to realize that what they did wasn't right. I don't think there'll be a repeat."

She seemed positive about this matter, at any rate. "Well, I want to thank you for sorting it out. Tom was very worried about it."

"You should tell him that if anything happens, he should see me straight away."

"I'll do that. Are you going to be Tom's tutor next year?"

"It's highly likely. I want to take the form through to Year Eleven."

"Well, I hope so too. I know that Tom will. He really likes you as his form tutor. So do I."

Was she flirting with me? The platitudes were great, and this woman was hot, but I wasn't allowed to enjoy the idea, even if it was a fantasyland that in all truth I would have ultimately turned down for obvious reasons. Outside the room, Hazel was once again seeking my attention and signaled to me from outside.

"Excuse me."

I stepped up to the door. Hazel had some news, as her highly serious demeanour conveyed. "Your wife has been on the phone. You need to ring her. You've been burgled."

* * *

I expected much worse. In my mind as I had driven home, I was seeing the jagged ugliness of broken windows, destroyed furniture and tell-tale spaces where key possessions were missing. In my head I was anticipating difficult conversations with soulless individuals representing the insurance company, as they failed to appreciate the emotional impact of such an unwelcome intrusion. A colleague of mine had been burgled a few months ago and the cretin who had broken in had shit in the bed, so I guess that had somewhat coloured my journey home from school, especially since on that occasion they had taken his fifty-five inch plasma screen television, whilst the two passports disappearing had suggested all kinds of horror in stolen identification and bogus credit card debts. I just hoped they hadn't taken my Starship Enterprise. That die-cast metal wonder had pride of place in my culture room.

With all the nervousness of a dental-phobic going for an extraction, I let myself into the house. I walked through the hallway, seeing nothing disturbing, but when I reached the kitchen, Laura was standing with a cup of coffee in her hand, watching a man in dodgy dungarees removing broken glass from the smashed kitchen window.

Straight away, some emotional intelligence kicked in and I went up to my wife and hugged her. Knowing Laura, this would be traumatic and I knew she would be needing plenty of reassurance. She accepted the hug, before gently ushering me away from the kitchen into the dining room.

"What's been taken?" I asked, trying to force a relaxed smile that I thought might help.

"I've been through everything. Nothing seems to be missing. Two police officers were here. We have a crime number, but they were baffled. Nothing's gone. One of them reckoned somebody broke in and had second thoughts."

I could see she had been crying so I had to say something to lighten the mood. "You mean they didn't even take my Enterprise?"

Laura gave a welcome laugh that I wanted to last for a lot longer. "No. It looks like we had a burglar with taste."

"Sounds like a nutty burglar to me. Was nothing taken then? Not even the telly? Have you checked your jewellery?"

"Nothing's gone babe. I've been through everything. Another suggestion the officers made was that the burglar was disturbed soon after breaking in. It could have been August. I left him in the house when I left this morning."

"August the guard cat. Now there's a revelation. I would have thought the smashing of glass would have scared him off, or even better, might have alerted one of the neighbours."

"The window wasn't smashed. The sergeant said it was done professionally. A cutter had been used to make a hole big enough for a human to get through. It's so fucking weird, Dom."

August sauntered in like he was the king round here. I watched bemused as she picked him up. "Hey big boy. You probably deserve a treat today."

"You don't know for sure that it was anything to do with him that we didn't get ransacked. A professional burglar wouldn't be scared off by a cat. Although why a professional burglar would pick our house beats me. What the fuck do we have that's worth stealing?"

"Well, it probably was this fellow that saved us. Trust me on this, babe. He deserves a double helping of dinner today. Don't you, baby?"

Surprisingly, I wasn't feeling as positive as Laura. "So, didn't the twat go upstairs at all?"

"The policemen said he probably got no further than the kitchen. There are no signs of anything more than a broken window. I wonder who it was."

"I told you somebody was at our back fence the other night. I bet, whoever it was, was sussing things out then."

"But why? To take none of our valuables?"

"What valuables? Yeah, that is odd. It's good, but what kind of burglar breaks in professionally and then doesn't take stuff. Oh well. We managed to hang onto some privacy, anyway. Nobody rifled your sexy knicker drawer. We're ok for tonight, sister."

"And he got nowhere near your Enterprise. He would have only felt sorry for you."

"In awe of Captain Kirk more like. Anyway, Mrs. Klingon, you can take yourself back to work now. I've got the rest of the day off, so I can take care of the glassman. I'm going to ring about getting a burglar alarm fitted as well. I don't want this to happen again. The journey here has aged me ten years. I'm now too old to be your husband."

MALEVOLENCE

An old cliché in life it isn't what you know, but who you know. I know someone who works in a shop selling electrical and building equipment, a quality staff member. I wouldn't say that I had him under my control, but let's just say I have a bit of leverage. He is somebody who knows stuff. He has expertise. There is nothing dysfunctional or worthy of criticism about people who know stuff, useful stuff. Everybody should know useful stuff.

I had a special task in mind and he pointed me in the right direction. The guy seemed to understand me totally and was very helpful. Who knows? I might shop here again.

To cut a long story short, I had left that shop with some important equipment and came home knowing how to use it.

Knowledge is power. Mission was accomplished. I achieved today what I wanted and some important details are now achieved.

Someone once told me that anything is obtainable. I believe that. It all depends on how far you are prepared to go to achieve. I think it is clear how far I am prepared to go.

I am sitting in my room. I count eighty-seven items in front of me spread out across the floor around the bed, items that would never be missed by any but the most obsessive individuals (and these two oafs are far from obsessive), items that give me a real understanding of what I need to understand. A page of a bank statement sits next to a letter which is alongside a photograph of women on a night out. I took some good photos of things that might be useful, like their living room and bedroom. Everything is coming together pretty well.

They're now easy meat. They think they're safe, fixing the window. They're becoming mine, but they don't know it. I will get what I want. It's about time.

WHITBY

"It's just a mass of green and brown. It looks like it stretches all the way to the horizon."

"I know, babe. Sinister beauty, if you ask me." This was the North Yorkshire moors, a part of Britain I had no positive feelings for. "I think there are terrible secrets here"

"What do you mean? It's only Yorkshire." One of Laura's favourite novels was Emily Bronte's 'Wuthering Heights' and I think that fact was having an influence here.

"I kid you not. Missing people are going to be buried underneath the heather around here somewhere, or not-yet-captured killers could be roaming around, sheltered by this wild beast of a landscape."

"You're going psycho on me, Dom. This area's pretty. So natural."

"Pretty? I bet there's an actual wild beast roaming around here, like a large panther or some man-eating dog or two – perhaps even a pack of them." The whole region for me was shrouded in natural expressionless gloom. I knew I wasn't being logical. Perhaps this feeling I had was historical, that there was terrible guilt from a lifetime I experienced long ago. Either way, I was always happy to pass the Moors and see it in the rear-view mirror.

On this Saturday morning, we had taken the two-hour drive to Whitby, something we had arranged to do several months ago. Whitby was just…special. Laura and I loved it – the harbour, beaches and the eccentric shopping opportunities, and it was probably our favourite place in the UK, with Cornwall being too far away to drive there regularly. She once had said, "Whitby's my Paris." I had laughed at the absurdity of that but I could understand her point. We would spend all day hand in hand there, walking along the narrow lanes and scrutinizing the shops and bars, enjoying the many things the place had to offer.

Laura and I particularly loved the idiosyncratic shops. This was a wide range of businesses selling an incredible array of Goth clothes and trinkets. We had bought various meaningful and meaningless things from these places, enough clothes and ornaments to fill a wardrobe and a cupboard over the past few years, although we had only done one of the Goth weekends they have twice annually there. This was when the town became enriched by people who looked like escapees from Bram Stoker's story, dressed in all kinds of finery. We liked the weirdness.

As always, the journey to Whitby was a positive part of what was always a positive experience. We stopped at the Highwayman Cafe, where, over a cooked breakfast for me and beans on toast for her, we talked about our plans for the weekend, when we like two kids making plans for Christmas. Laura dared me to feed the Highwayman's geese that were separated from the people outside by a flimsy wire fence. I rose to the dare and tried to give one of the birds a piece of bacon but wished I hadn't as it nearly took my arm off. She laughed loudly, attracting the attention of other visitors to the café, who looked on in disgust.

Being late-June, the weather was glorious, about twenty-six degrees. Parking the car was the hardest bit, and Laura told me off for being impatient, but I just couldn't wait to be out of the car and walking on terra firma.

We checked in at Barnhall House, a smart old hotel with a fab little bar, where we had a four-poster bed waiting for us and we always made good use of our sleeping arrangements. The arrival sex reflected our enthusiasm for the trip. I could have stayed in bed with her for the rest of the day chatting and musing over how great we were, but this was Whitby and that would have been a waste. Well, at least she thought so.

"This is lovely, babe," Within a half-hour, we were sitting comfortably outside the Marine Restaurant on the corner next to the river at a little table where we could observe the comings and goings of the wide range of people walking along the road. Laura, radiant in her sunglasses, had that contented no-work-today smile on her face that was always there when we came here. She was taking in the details of the fortune teller who was based opposite this restaurant, the same signs she had read on every visit here, but which she always found fascinating.

To this day, I don't know whether that was a factor in anything, but her calm expression suddenly changed to something more tense and not quite so comfortable. Contentment suddenly became concern and she became much more focused. "I have something to tell you soon, something big. I don't want to tell you today, because it's not appropriate."

"What do you mean?

"I'll tell you soon."

"What is it?"

"I can't tell you. Not today. Trust me on this, babe. I will tell you, but not today."

"You're not pregnant, are you?"

'Please don't quiz me or speculate, Dom." She paused. "I wish I hadn't said anything now."

"Why did you say something, then? You know what I'm like."

"Because it's something important to me, and I couldn't hold it in."

The look of concern on my face must have been dramatic. "It's nothing terrible or out of this world fantastic, just something. Now can we leave it at that?"

Laura had that look in her eyes that I had seen so many times before. If we hadn't been in Whitby, I might have pursued it further and risked an argument, but having a brilliant two days was crucial to me, and probably to her too, especially after the burglary that wasn't. Besides, knowing Laura, she would tell me what she had to tell me when she was good and ready.

Several hours and five pubs later, we opened the door of our room rather worse for wear. I had suggested we have a brandy and port three hours ago and from then on we had both drunk a succession of double gin and tonics. Apparently, Laura slept on the bathroom floor that night, although I couldn't remember anything about it after opening that door. I was on the floor when dawn broke, feeling like there had been a fight and alcohol had won, not for the first time.

It was late Sunday afternoon when we set off home. There was a characteristic reluctance about our walk to the car. It was always depressing leaving Whitby. Laura looked across at me, studying me, making me feel quite self-conscious. "Let's go to the countryside tomorrow. A walk somewhere. I fancy some excitement, babe."

MALEVOLENCE

He's soft, this clown. I was looking at the website of the school he works at and found him on one of the pages. It didn't take me long. There's a picture of him with some kids on some school trip to some ridiculous place or other. It reminds me of one of those pictures that companies use to give a good impression and hide the bastardisation and abuse that really goes on. It's a photo, but I can see into his eyes, see his inner thoughts and attitudes. He's soft. He's the kind of man who is easy to boss, easy to fool, only good when it comes to mastering little kids and putting them through it. Well I'm no little kid. I can make mincemeat out of this sap without even breaking sweat.

And as for her, well she's made for me. She was designed that way.

My plan is just about ready. I've gone over everything in my mind so many times now and I actually think the time is right for the thing to happen. What's the worst that can happen? I get rumbled and that's a year or two inside. That doesn't scare me one bit. I'll be the meanest one inside so what's the fucking big deal? I'm going for best case scenario. That means I'm going in search of the life I'm entitled to, the best life I've ever had. God knows it's worth doing something dramatic to get that.

They're not expecting me. I've heard their conversations, seen their smug faces and how up their own arses they are. They don't know that I'm even on their horizon, I'm hiding so deep in their shadows that neither has any sense at all of what is coming. This is going to go like clockwork. I've done some wonderful things in the past, but this will be my personal best and I'm going to find plenty of reward for my trouble.

At school, teachers used to belittle me, say that I would never amount to anything, that I had a bad attitude. Well fuck them, and the horses they rode in on. They were all shit anyway, just nobodies who thought they knew more. In reality, they knew fuck all, even the one I fucked and killed.

He's a teacher too. As full of shit as they all were. He's going to do some learning. I'm going to show him what belittle means.

Laura? Dominic? What kind of names are they? Even their names are a dead giveaway. This is the coming of change. Here I am to do some changing.

WHERE AND HOW?

This summer in Sheffield was a real one. There was too much heat and too much need to hide inside. Sunbeds abroad held no novelty for us this year.

One stifling week after Whitby and we were given a much-needed break from the assault of the sunshine as the temperature dropped for what was predicted by Carol on BBC Breakfast as 'a four-day lull'. At last we all had the summer weather we were used to, and in truth, we were relieved about that. Thankfully, we were nearing the end of the school year, when I was going to have six weeks without daily toil and early get-ups, with regular morning breakfasts in my local Wetherspoons.

This particular Monday was an overcast one, with the all too usual gathering of frowning grey clouds that loomed ominously, when the roasted lawn looked like it needed more by the way of rain or the blessing of an only partly invigorating hose pipe, but perhaps I would be able to pay more attention to this with more time on my hands.

Pulling into the staff car park to start my working week, I heard the familiar bleep of a text being received on my phone.

'Can't wait,' it said. "I won't be late." Laura was texting me unnecessarily, I thought. She didn't usually feel the need to reassure me of her presence. I still found myself smiling as I made my way into the school building. Good times.

All that day, I found it difficult to concentrate at work. Thankfully, there was no meeting taking place after school so I had been able to make a quick getaway. I was meeting Laura for a walk. The 'can't wait' text made me think she was wanting more of an outdoor physical experience than just two or three thousand footsteps, so like a lot of hot-blooded males, I became excited.. "Bring it on," I replied to her.

Punctual as ever, I turned up Long Lane. I arrived at Loxley Common and felt optimistic. Whatever happened here, it was going to be fun. We were nothing if not predictable.

Well, almost predictable. Where was she? I had arrived to see Laura's Audi parked in the place I expected it to be. So where was she?

I sat in my car for a few minutes, assuming that she might just have gone for a comfort break somewhere. I was still excited. She would emerge from either the left side of the road or the right, with that welcoming smile that made everything seem brilliant.

I checked my phone for texts from her. Nothing. I left my car again and walked towards hers. I peered inside. All I could see was a folded piece of paper on her passenger seat. It was face down, but was partly folded over and I could just make out the words *PLEASE and MEET* in capital letters.

After five minutes or so, I decided to ring her. There was no joy, just an impersonal soulless voice telling me she was unable to answer the phone right now. Perhaps she was where we had been before, waiting for me. Maybe she was going to surprise me in some way that I would like.

Venturing into the Common, as I went beyond the first line of trees, I tried her phone again, but got the same annoying emotionless voice. This was odd

This time I decided to leave a message. "Hi, babe. Listen, I don't know where you are right now, but will you ring me. It's a bit hard to hook up with the Invisible Woman." I didn't know what to do so all I could think was to go deeper into the wood, to places we had been in the past when visiting here, just in case she had gone ahead after all. I was scanning all directions. I did three-sixty after three-sixty in the hope that I would suddenly see her and the uncertainty would be ended.

At an old wooden bench where we had spent half an hour sitting and musing three weeks ago, I decided to sit down. I was trying the mobile every couple of minutes, each time with the same frustrating outcome. This wasn't the fun I had anticipated. After sending a text that urged her to get in touch now, without kisses at the end this time, I decided to head back to the car.

I walked past a field, considering the nonsensical notion that Laura was playing some kind of practical joke on me, which was totally not her at all. Another thought suddenly struck me. Perhaps she had taken a walk somewhere and would return to her car. I shouted out her name. No reply. I waited and listened intently. Still no reply.

When I reached the road, Laura's car was no longer there. There was a sinister gap where it had been. How could that be? How could she have driven away without even looking for me?

Beginning to feel uncomfortable now, I was dumbfounded at how she would drive away from here without any communication with me.

I stood there for ten minutes, but it soon became clear that she wasn't coming back. If it was some uncharacteristic joke, the joke was on me. No doubt, in that case, she would be well on her way to our house by now. Perhaps she had, for some other reason, decided to go home anyway, like if she had had a bad stomach ache or unexpectedly bad period pains. I decided to head there too. I was perspiring. There was something altogether ominous about this.

I began to consider best and worst-case scenarios. The best case was that Laura had gone somewhere, that she had been called away from here for some reason, before she could meet up with me. In this case she would join me later. That seemed highly unlikely, though. Laura wasn't the kind of woman to be called away at the last minute when we had an arrangement. That wasn't how we worked.

There was a worse case. The worst case was that something had happened, something that would stop her returning to the house. What if somebody had taken her – some pervert or psycho, while I was sitting in the woods feeling sorry for myself? Imagine if somebody had knocked her unconscious and dragged her away to somewhere more secluded. I dismissed that idea. This was Sheffield 6 and stuff like that didn't happen in this area. However, I needed to see Laura and know that she was ok.

I had decided to drive back to the house. Perhaps, for whatever reason, that was where she was now. I put my foot to the floor as I ascended one of those steep Sheffield hills. A sixty-pound fine and three measly points would be worth it if travelling a few miles quicker than the rules allowed prevented the unspeakable happening.

Driving off? What the fuck was that about? Why would she do that? It didn't make sense, because Laura had never pulled a stunt like that ever. She was meant to meet me there, had even sent that text confirming it, so what the hell was happening? Then there was the piece of paper on her passenger seat. What was that about?

Just as it began to rain, I arrived at the house. Laura's car wasn't outside and I felt that same dull feeling that I had felt at the Common. I checked the garage, but that was empty. I ran up to the door and tried the handle, but the door was locked. Fumbling, I managed to find the front door key and made my way inside. I shouted "Laura' several times, but the lack of response to my first call should have been enough. The house was empty too.

Had there been anything unusual about her that day? I tried to remember. If there was, why hadn't I noticed it? But then again, why would I? I was always so busy with work.

Well, I was certainly seeing reality now. I nursed a JD and Diet Pepsi in front of a silent television, all the time listening for a recognizable car engine or key in the lock. I turned the TV down a few times in the hope that her car was creeping in quietly. There was nothing.

I decided there was only one thing for me to do. Go back to Loxley Common. What if she had gone away and come back, and was now waiting for me. On another level, what if she was hurt and in that area somewhere, needing somebody to rescue her or save her in some way? That wouldn't explain the disappearance of her car, but perhaps the assailant had taken that away after attacking Laura. I had to be back there again. She would ring me if and when she was able. I was sure of that. Unless her phone charge had run out, wherever she was, as there was always that possibility. That might explain everything. It could also explain nothing. She did have a charger in her car. I was in the grip of a nightmare that could only be ended with Laura's smile.

I went. I pulled up in the same spot as before. Laura's Audi was still gone. I was desperate to see her and know that she was ok. My heart, still relentlessly beating, betrayed the horrible fear that was now taking hold.

Was this payback for last year? Was this a cold dish of revenge I was now being forced to consume? Was this an act of a woman leaving her husband? She had said, on numerous occasions, she would try to forgive but could never forget. Had it all become too much for her?

Was it something even worse than that? Surely not? This part of Sheffield wasn't known for bad stuff happening.

"Laura! Laura!" My eyes were everywhere.

Nothing.

I carried on running in one direction then another, trees ahead, around and behind me and I knew what was becoming an inescapable truth. Laura wasn't here.

At one point on the public footpath, I halted. This was where we had stopped for a while to have a picnic last year. That was over eighteen months ago and the memory was so vivid, with the pleasure all too easily re-lived.

So where was she?

"Laura!"

Why wasn't she here?

I began to think. Had she somehow never intended to be here tonight? Had she sent me a bogus message, knowing that it would have added to my excitement and anticipation? I was still pathetically and desperately considering the ridiculous idea that this was some kind of joke and if so, how far was she going to take it? If it was, her acting skills were incredible, since this morning and last night she had given the convincing impression of somebody wanting little more than a lovely walk with her husband. I knew she had done some play-acting in her university days but was she that good?

I continued to wander around the area, in and out of the endless trees, to the edge of the golf course, surveying that area, looking perpetually for some slight detail that Laura was here somewhere, watching me and amused by the mayhem she was creating in my head.

Still no sign.

As I walked back to the car, the only other possibility was that she had for whatever reason gone home, even if she had been delayed for some reason. In this case, perhaps she would be home already, and the worrying could end. However, I had to make sure she wasn't here first.

In what was to be a final sweep of the area, in which I snaked through the area of trees, there was no sign anywhere I looked. I came across nothing. I didn't expect to, since she had obviously driven her car away. She wasn't here. I had no option but to go home.

Up the road, I noticed a green wheelbarrow next to the hedgerow that looked like it had been dumped by some fly tipper. I hated fly tippers. I wasn't sure, however, why anyone would dump a wheelbarrow.

As I drove back home, I felt a darker mood coming on.

By the time I reached the supposed comfort of Dewhurst Close, most of me was seething, ready to do some serious sulking. I wasn't going to speak to her and would go straight upstairs and have a bath in protest at it all. She would know that she had gone too far. I would await a profuse apology. At the same time, I would have a sense of relief that she was back home, since I had been worried about her. I wouldn't let her know that though, well not straight away.

Frustratingly, the red Audi was still absent. Where had she gone? Slight possibilities remained. I supposed she might have gone to the supermarket, or maybe the dry cleaner's, as I knew she had a suit in there she wanted to pick up and she could have had an urgent request from work that coincided with a battery failure on her mobile phone. What was needed now was for Laura to communicate.

I hadn't texted her for over an hour, and I hadn't phoned her for more than that. I definitely needed to show less vulnerability.

I just let myself into the house like it was a normal evening. I went straight upstairs and began running the bath water, keen to be in there soaking myself when she eventually and inevitably got back home. I put my suit on the hanger and closed the bathroom door behind me, like I didn't want to be disturbed. That would show her.

The heat of the water was soothing. But after half an hour, Laura still wasn't home. I went downstairs and grabbed my phone.

Laura's mother answered. I was relieved that it was her and not George.

"Hi Lillian, it's Dom. Is Laura with you?"

"No Dom. We haven't seen her. Is she still at work?"

"Not sure. I expected her to be here by now."

"I'm sure she'll be home soon, love. She's probably got sidetracked."

"Yes, I suppose so. Sorry to bother you." Sidetracked by what? I hung up, totally frustrated. The only thing I could do now was switch on the television and distract myself from the nagging feeling of insecurity. Normally she would text me to tell me if she was going to be late, so why hadn't she done that tonight? What would cause such a reversal in attitude? I decided to text her yet again, this time somewhat more amicably.

Hi babe. Where are you? XX

At this point, my indignation had all but evaporated and worry had taken its place as the dominant emotion. I was sure she would ring or, at the very least, text me back as soon as she saw my message.

Groggily, I awaked uncomfortably and awkwardly. I had fallen asleep and had been that way for over an hour. I looked at my watch to see that it was now nine o'clock. Four hours had passed since Loxley Common. I shouted upstairs for Laura but there was no answer. I went up and looked around, in the vain hope that she was hiding, continuing the joke that wasn't. I checked my phone. She hadn't replied. There was still no Audi in sight. What exactly was going on? Was I the victim here, or was Laura?

Had I upset her? I went through the past few days and tried to find something that might have offended her in some way, something that I might have said that was clumsy and insensitive. I could recall nothing of significance.

Had she met someone else? Now there was a rub and a half. I hadn't entertained the idea prior to now that she might find love elsewhere, but I was struggling for an explanation. Affairs were always tinged with strangeness. This couldn't be. We still shared a wonderful loving life in and out of the bedroom. Could she really be having that kind of life with me if she was intending to do a bunk and be with someone else? That was nonsensical. Was our conversation this morning our one last moment together before her big goodbye, a goodbye that was inexplicable?

Realistically, Laura could have found somebody else. She met plenty of men in her job, and how many of them would be sophisticated, charming and good-looking? This beast of an idea began to roar louder inside me, as I began to consider the likelihood and implications of such a development. Why else would she have not come home? She loved home.

Something special would be needed for her to destroy what we had, probably something way better than the something not so special that had distracted me last year. Was that what it was all about? Was it that revenge thing that had gone through my head earlier? Had Laura not meant it when she said we had moved on and that I was forgiven? She always looked like she had. I dearly hoped this was the case. If she had that cold-hearted urge inside her, she had hidden it well for the whole of our time together.

I spent a couple of hours and several glasses of Jack Daniels musing over it all, thinking about what Laura's absence might mean. Every time I returned to the same conclusion. She wouldn't do this. She was actually incapable of this. It was utterly beyond everything that was important to her.

No, I emphatically reassured myself. If I knew anything about the woman I had married, this was not her. She would end the relationship first. She would always conduct herself in an honest and firm way. Laura wasn't the kind to cheat and do things deviously. If she had gone off me, she would have stood in front of me and would have wanted to do it all civilized, adult and open, with a strong declaration, closely followed by a wave of sympathy. That is how she had dealt with Joe, the bloke she had dumped a few months before she had met me. Skulking around was not her style. If I knew anything about her, I knew that.

I found the power to go to bed that night, although sleep was going to be elusive. I was thinking that everything might be sorted by the morning, that I would awake to something more positive and that Laura would have returned with some plausible and acceptable story. She would have something to tell me about some crisis that she had got herself involved in, that it had needed sorting, that her phone had run out of charge and that she was glad to be back and back to normality. At any rate, I switched everything off downstairs and went to bed.

TIME WON'T WAIT

The alarm sang as discordantly as always at six a.m., a series of horrendous high-pitched beeps that never failed to annoy. I looked around me desperately. Like an enthusiastic grasshopper, I jumped from the bed and onto the landing and into the bathroom. I looked out of the window, hoping to see that red car parked there, but my disappointment was ongoing. Now I felt that melancholy presence return again, so that my whole world was still covered in an ominous shadow and again I was gripped by vulnerability. In the shower, I silently and audibly cursed Laura for having not come home. Would she really have spent the night with somebody else like this? The affair idea had crystalized further overnight, as I could see no other reason for her absence.

I rang George and Lillian.

Lillian answered. "You mean she didn't come home? Are you sure?"

"Of course I'm sure. I was hoping she might be with you. She's not, is she?"

"Just give me a minute." I stayed on the phone while she was clearly conferring with her husband. It was unlikely that he would know anything that Lillian didn't, but not impossible.

Lillian came back on the phone. "I'm sorry, Dom. We've not heard from her. Neither of us. I'm sure it won't be anything serious. George thinks she might just be wanting a bit of time alone. Perhaps she wants to think about things."

I paused and thought about that, before realising this was George's attitude coming through loud and clear. "Come on! I'm not buying that. If she had asked me, she could have had some time alone. She didn't need to do a disappearing act."

"Don't speak to me like that.' Lilian had adopted a pained tone. "I don't know anything so don't take it out on me. It's hardly a disappearing act."

"Well, she's fucking disappeared, so is it an act or not? If it's not an act, what the fuck is it?" I knew I was becoming aggressive and that Lillian didn't deserve it, but I just couldn't help myself.

George was suddenly on the phone. "What's going on?"

"She's disappeared. Laura's disappeared."

"What do you mean, disappeared?"

"She was supposed to meet me. She didn't come home." I explained about the car.

"That's not right. That's not like her. Have you argued?"

"No. Not at all."

"Well we'll text her from here. Listen, Dominic, if she doesn't show up this morning, you need to go to the police."

"I know. I'm thinking I should do that now."

"I'd give it a bit longer. Try her work. Then you should report it."

"OK. I'm going to do that." I hung up.

I rang the art gallery. They paid her wages, so perhaps they would know more than I did. I spoke to Max, the manager. He knew nothing. "To be honest I was going to ring you. She hasn't shown up this morning and her phone's dead."

I had to ring the police. I had begun to worry about her safety. In waiting for me, had she become totally vulnerable and an easy victim for some sicko who chanced to go walking on Loxley Common that early evening. Was it he who had driven her car away, with Laura inside? On the other hand, should I have stayed on the common longer? Would I have discovered something? I just didn't know, and this uncertainty was suffocating. I didn't fully comprehend anything: what I had done, what I should have done, and what I should do now. Could somebody walking in that area have had intentions and the means of carrying out those intentions? That seemed unlikely, just like the notion of our relationship ending, but what else could this be? The only problem was that Laura had not been missing long. At what point would my concern be the concern of the police too?

I left a message on the school's answering machine saying that I had a stomach upset and that I wouldn't be in work that day. I had to make some kind of sense of it all.

My phone rang. Laura's parents again. George spoke. "We've not heard from you. Laura's not replied to anything. Have you found anything out?"

"No?"

"Have you asked around?"

"I've rung everybody – her work, her friends. Nobody knows anything. I'm worried about her. I think something bad might have happened."

"We're coming around. Don't go anywhere."

They both came. Lillian rang people, some of the same people I had rung, but she sensed, as did I, that they wouldn't know anything. Laura's disappearance was nothing to do with old school friends, the uncle in Manchester or Lillian's best friend. Laura herself had probably had a big say in what had happened although I hadn't a clue why.

George was imagining a similar reality to the one I had been enduring. "You have to phone the police."

"I was thinking the same thing."

98

"Well you need to report her missing. This is terrible. Where is she?" He looked at his wife with the same desperation as I had been looking at them.

"He's right," Lillian said. "From what you've said, something awful's gone on. Laura loves you. Ring the police. You can ring them while we are here."

"OK. But what if she's met someone else? What if she's with somebody."

George gave me a look. "Stop being stupid. Ring the police."

I picked up my mobile.

George and Lillian were staring at me as I phoned. As the dialing tone sounded, I was hoping that they wouldn't be thinking that this had anything to do with last year. In all truth, I was hoping it had nothing to do with last year. The only problem with that was that the alternative was worse.

"I want to report a missing person."

"Right, sir. Can you tell me the name of the person missing?"

"Laura Walker. She's my wife." As I said this, I felt a combination of shame and fear.

"Ok. When did she go missing?"

"Yesterday evening, about four o'clock."

"Is that when you last saw her?"

"Yes. I went to meet her at Loxley Common to go walking but she wasn't there."

"Do you go there regularly."

"Probably about twice or three times a month."

"Have you heard from her at all?"

I shook my head. "No."

"No note or letter? Perhaps an email or text?"

"No. It's just that she always comes home and last night she didn't."

I gave her all of Laura's details: her full name, age, address and job. She asked me questions about her state of mind, medical condition and the nature of our relationship. She asked me about our marriage and I told her that everything was positive, as I thought it was. I didn't mention last year. George might have wanted me to do that, but I didn't look in his direction.

"I think that's all I need, Mr. Walker. The information you have given me will form a missing person's report. Obviously, only a little time has passed since her disappearance so the next three or four days will be crucial. I know it must seem a lot to you, but these things often have satisfactory endings. Many mispers, missing persons, turn up within this time period, and I hope that will be the case here. I know this won't reassure you much, but it is highly likely."

When I put the mobile down, I felt like crying. I hadn't felt like this for a long time. I just felt so alone and helpless, unable to do anything to take away the pain of the situation.

"She'll come back," George said, although I wondered about what he was actually thinking. Did he really think that some harm had come to Laura? I welcomed myself to hell.

THE UNFAMILIAR

I woke up for a second time alone in my bed. It wasn't good. I felt possessed by emptiness, wondering what was worth getting up for. With the same desperate hope, I listened for some kind of sound downstairs, a sign that my life had had its normality restored, but there was nothing.

I decided to have another day off work. I made the phone call, spent a half hour on the computer, and sent the cover lessons off so that my students would have something to do for the reserve teachers.

I felt powerless, but I had to do something. Laura's parents had urged me to sit tight and wait, that she would be back. Lillian, always showing calmness and reason, said that her daughter might just need some private time and would doubtlessly return within a day or two. She had smiled at me as they left, whispering out of George's earshot, "She loves you."

Obviously, I was close to my mobile at all times. It was as if it was powering my heartbeat. I was still hopeful that I would get a text saying that all was ok, that she had needed some time out, that was all, and that she would be returning soon and we would be back on track.

There was no text. There was no reassurance. I didn't know whether she would ever be back or not. I hoped she would be. I believed she would be.

Then I remembered Whitby. She had wanted to tell me something, something significant. She had resisted, and I had left it. Perhaps I should have pushed her and pressured her into telling me what was on her mind. Maybe that would have answered the questions I was now asking.

STARING AT THE WALLS OF
HEARTACHE

Waking up alone for the third time was no easier than it had been the previous two mornings and it needed a decision. I decided not to go to work and to somehow try to address the riddle that I was now presented with.

Last night I had managed to calm myself. I had decided that one reason I had not to panic was the possibility that Laura had made herself elusive for one of two possible reasons: as a punishment, which I could partly understand, or she was involved with someone else, which was inconceivable and so much worse. In. either case, I could do nothing, so I was going to do nothing.

Today, under the sun's accusing glare, I decided that neither of these was the case. Something bad had definitely happened. I began to entertain notions that she had been taken against her will and that she was being held somewhere. What if somebody had seen her leave her car near Loxley Common and had the means to take her? If that was the case, where was she now? Where was her car?

As I sat there with the radio playing, I nibbled at a piece of toast, making little progress.

I knew what I now had to do. A phone call to the police wouldn't suffice. I had to go to see them.

At ten thirty on that Thursday morning, I was entering the main entrance lobby of Sheffield Police Headquarters, a place that had never impressed, but which seemed to be just some mess created by an architect. The chances were that they would tell me nothing of any notable importance. I was expecting some kind of vague reassurance and a clear lack of concern.

"How can I help you?"

"It's my wife. I phoned you a couple of days ago. She's missing."

I gave her the details and she studied a monitor in front of her. "Oh yes," she said. "Laura Walker. Can you confirm the name for me?"

"That's my wife."

Have you heard anything yet?"

"Not one thing. I think she's been taken by someone." I tried to sound calm.

"That's a bit of a leap. Do you have anything to suggest that?"

"Yes. It's totally out of character for her. She wouldn't do this."

"I have to tell you, Mr Walker, we have plenty of missing persons reported to us and to be honest with you, it's usually of their own free will. Do you have any evidence that an abduction's taken place?"

"Only my instincts. Can I see a police officer? Is there a detective I can talk to?"

"I'm sorry. Detectives only deal with these cases if there is evidence of foul play."

"OK. So, my instincts aren't enough then. Can I see a police officer then, somebody in uniform perhaps?"

"Take a seat, Mr. Walker," she said, in a reassuring voice that did anything but reassure. "I'm sure an officer will be available soon to interview you."

I sat there for too many minutes. Clearly, my situation wasn't as important to the police as it was to me, although I had expected that. Eventually, a stocky bald-headed man in a well-pressed white shirt walked up to me. He introduced himself in a distinct Welsh accent as PC Jon Evans.

He led me to a small, featureless room, just big enough to house two grown men, but which would never allow them to be comfortable. He entered what I presumed was his password into a computer and said little as the relevant information was brought up. "Right, Mr. Walker. I understand you wish to report a missing person. When exactly did she go missing?"

Twenty minutes later, I left the interview, somewhat deflated. He told me that in ninety per cent of cases like this, the 'misper' turned up after a few days and this was still within that time period. He was almost grinning when I told him about the circumstances of Laura's disappearance, as if walking in the woods was something out of the ordinary. However, he did add information to the notes on the computer, which made me feel that I was officially contributing to the situation, even if no investigation was taking place at this stage.

Once home, I went straight to the laptop on the kitchen table. I half-heartedly shouted, "Laura" up the stairs but expected no reply and wasn't surprised therefore when none came.

I sat there thinking about what the officer had said. For me it was a waiting game and I had to do some waiting. I needed to check for messages again. I pressed the button to activate the laptop. I looked down the list of deliveries in my inbox and saw something dramatic. There was a message from Laura's email account. Now I was terrified, with a heartbeat that made my whole body vibrate. I took control of myself and opened it.

Dear Dominic

I know that this will come as a shock to you and I am sorry. I have gone away for a while. Please don't think the worst of me. I needed some time to myself and decided that I didn't want to say a sad goodbye as I don't know when and even if I will be coming back.

The thing is, I never really got over what happened last year. I need some time to sort myself out, one way or another. What you did was pretty hard to forgive. I hope that in a not-too-long amount of time I can come to terms with it and we can move forward, but I want to be sure.

Please don't try to find me. You won't.

Take care, my darling.

L xxxx

I sat there staring at the words she had written. I didn't know whether to be relieved or burst into tears. I went through a range of emotions, mainly in the negative spectrum.

How could she? How could she do this? I went through everything over and over again, re-reading the email many times, and I was struggling to accept it all. This was a total departure from anything I might have expected.

Subsequently, I spent the rest of the day in a total daze, trying to come to terms with the idea that my wife had left me. I began to consider the notion that she had made a move away from me and might never return. This was all down to me. Why had I done it?

The house was eerily silent except for the dull tick of the kitchen clock. I spent the rest of that day and night just staring at the four walls, trying to extract meaning from the wallpaper and the furniture, trying to make some sense of her disappearance. That email. This seemed like the wrong final piece in the incomplete jigsaw, yet it was undeniable.

ELECTRONIC MAIL

I had printed out Laura's email. For no discernable reason at all, I printed out three copies, as if it was an important receipt or certificate that I was frightened of losing. George was holding it like it was an extortionate bill that he had paid that day. "I think this is pretty clear, Dominic. Laura needs some time."

"I don't believe it. I know it's from her email account, but it just seems so unlike her. It is not her."

Lillian was holding my hand. "I think you have to accept it, love. She wanted some time away. People sometimes need some time to themselves."

I shook my head. "I know that happens. But this is just so unlike her. She would have told me to my face. Having this out with me wouldn't have been a problem for her. I could accept this if this was what she was like, but it all seems so different from what she would do."

George passed the printed sheet back to me. "I don't know. She's not contacted us. We probably won't be happy until she does. But this is all your fault."

"My fault? I didn't make her go away like this."

"This is what happens when somebody does something stupid. She obviously needs to get clear of your stupidity and I don't blame her."

"George." Lillian reached out to touch his arm in an attempt at restraint.

"No, love, he has to accept this. He brought it on himself. She's gone because of the shit he caused." He looked at me, and I sensed the pain and anger that now preoccupied him, like it did me. "To be honest, I don't understand why you're questioning it."

'OK,' I said, wanting to tell him where to go but accepting in my head that it would be hollow, possibly wrong, since I hadn't done everything right and that this in actual fact could be seen as a deserved consequence. "OK. So I am the villain in all this. Why didn't she tell you beforehand what she was going to do? And why hasn't she been in touch with you?"

George paused and looked at me and then his wife for an answer that wasn't forthcoming. "Perhaps she will be in touch. In fact, she had better be. For your sake."

I told them about the text message and the piece of paper on the passenger seat of her car. "What were they about then? Read it!" I passed my phone to them with that most recent text message from her on display.

George spoke first. "Strange, but it changes nothing. That email shows everything for me."

"Could you see any other words on that paper?" Lillian asked.

"No. Just *please* and *meet.*"

George exercised his power of dismissal. "That could mean absolutely anything. Probably nothing to do with anything, I reckon. Sorry, Dominic, but the truth is in this." He held up the printed email and shook it gently. Part of me felt that he was actually enjoying this.

CAR

"Hello."

"Mr. Walker?"

"That's me."

"It's South Yorkshire Police, Mr. Walker. I'm just ringing to inform you that your wife's car has been found. You wanted to report her as a missing person."

"Where is it?"

"Well, this might or might not be good news. I don't know really. It was found in a short stay car park at Manchester Airport. It looks to us like she went away under her own volition."

Christ, so she wasn't even in the UK anymore. "Can you tell me which flight she boarded?"

"I'm sorry, but we don't have that information, as there's no evidence that anything illegal has occurred."

"I see. What happens to the car now?"

"It has been impounded but is available for collection when convenient. It looks like your wife's been a tad irresponsible. I'm afraid there's a charge."

That night Jamie drove me to pick up Laura's car. Clearly, Laura had left the country, but to go where? I had been impatient to get there, knowing that there was that telling piece of paper on that seat, a piece of paper that might disappoint and deflate, or which might raise questions and some kind of contradiction. I couldn't imagine what. It was like greeting an old friend when I got there. The red Audi looked exactly as I had last seen it, and I touched it affectionately before going straight to the passenger side.

Frustratingly, there was nothing there. Before I drove it home, three hundred pounds poorer for my trouble, I searched it for any evidence of anything. I searched the glove compartment, which contained wheel nuts, an old red lipstick and some shop discount vouchers. There was nothing of any note, with the car being immaculately tidy, as usual, and there was nothing that shouldn't have been there, nothing out of place. It felt very strange driving Laura's car home, almost surreal. As I parked up, I knew in my heart this would probably mark an end to me looking out of the window to see if she had returned. What was the point of that?

MALEVOLENCE

Pet people love their pets. People keep a beloved animal, they give it a life it would not have in the wild. They often show devotion and give up plenty of time to looking after these creatures and try to give them a life worth living. So many humans show so much care. I never understood it.

That's not me.

However, today I have departed from my normal ways. I have acquired a pet. My pet isn't so happy belonging to me, but my pet she is. She sits there, without a choice. Like many pets, she wants to go out and escape being my pet for a while but that isn't going to happen. My pet and I are creating a story and it is going to have the happiest of endings. Well for one of us anyway.

She is going to make me happy. Obviously, I have to make her totally mine, bend her to my will. That has always been the idea and it was always going to take some work. It won't take forever. She will weaken. Silly bitches like her are made to weaken. I don't expect to have to put her through too much before she does things right, makes the right noises and gives me everything I want. Of course, in time I will end her pain. Well, at some point.

Horribly, there is a strong unpleasant smell emanating from my captive companion, and I get a sense of being like a nurse in an old people's residence, and I know plenty about that. House-training may take a while. Ultimately, however, she will do whatever I want, make the noises I need her to make, think everything that I need her to think.

I am in control. It is necessary. She does need those toilet visits, but she has to earn them.

The room in which my pet lives is perfect. I spent some money, but I made it so brilliant – ideal for a captive. It is so safe. It is not totally soundproof, but not far away. Any cries or yelps won't have any impact, since sounds of panic or distress won't be heard. This is a case of welcome to my world, bitch.

The email should buy me some time.

SOLITUDE

I took a drive. The four walls were closing in, to coin a cliché, so I just picked up the car keys and decided to head out. I just needed to be away from the buildings, away from the painful reminders for a short while. I drove out of the city, and passed a sign for Chesterfield, Dore and Totley. I wasn't going as far as any of those places. I just needed a moment of sanity. Here would do.

I pulled up next to a long metal railing. This was Millhouses Park, arguably the prettiest and most well-maintained park in Sheffield. On a number of occasions, my mother had taken my older sister Kate and me on two buses to enjoy this park, which had a river flowing through it, as well as a boating lake and a pleasant café.

I got out and walked for a while. I took in the details of this peaceful environment. I could see hills on most sides and hundreds of houses that would all have views of the city and I wondered how many of the people in those houses had problems like mine.

Then I just let go. I had been tense and miserable throughout this ordeal and now needed to release those emotions, barbed wire in my mind. I immediately regretted this moment of weakness, so I rubbed my face impatiently, hoping that nobody nearby would notice. I was uncomfortable being visibly upset, and wanted to be much tougher.

The emotion wore off. I seized back my backbone. I actually felt strengthened by this release of tension and felt a sense that this was something necessary and advisable.

I unwrapped a packet of Silk Cut. I hadn't smoked for nearly ten years but this seemed to be highly appropriate right now. I normally despised the habit and criticized others for indulging in it but tonight health wasn't so much a priority? As I sat there inhaling clumsily and tipping the ash out of the window onto the grass alongside, I was thinking how life was going to go on.

Laura was gone. I decided there and then, as I watched a plane fly noisily overhead, that life had to continue. I wasn't going to be pathetic, yearning for the past or anything ridiculous like that. At the end of the day, I was far too selfish not to pick myself up and carry on. No, I had to still be a part of the human race, not only accepting what had happened but managing to put all of this behind me and somehow find some kind of strength.

Laura had left me. She had fucked up and had fucked me up. Now it was time to leave her.

MALEVOLENCE

She's not really my type. The women I tend to sleep with are a bit more formidable, a bit less full of themselves and not quite so pitifully weak. It's no fun for me trying to dominate a woman who thinks she is something special but isn't really, and this one clearly thinks she is something special indeed. I am showing her what special really means.

When I question her, the answers are just not coming out quickly enough so then I have to play rough. I don't mind playing rough, if that is how it has to be. She still has that look of extreme shock on her face whenever she looks at me and that amuses. I laugh out loud on numerous occasions every day. She has that small pitiful rabbit caught-in-the-headlights look on her face almost perpetually and when I remove the obstacle to her speaking she does nothing but squeal and shout, so then the gag goes on and the pain starts again. She looks at me with such understandable intensity and that look never alters, except in the few hours where I allow her to sleep.

I do need her talking normally, so I have nice moments that make her more relaxed and trusting. She asks questions, but I need answers. I get her to tell me about her life, her ambitions, her fears, take her away from her situation temporarily. I like to hear her speak, making note of the words and phrases she uses and how she says them. I record these moments and watch her closely. OK, so she isn't able to do too much by way of body language. She is secured after all, but I don't see that as a problem.

When she becomes awkward, when she has silly notions of having a choice in any matter at all, or when she thinks she can issue threat or warnings, I enjoy giving her pain. It is all I really have to give her, let's face it.

Disturbingly, that smell of piss coming from her seems to be getting worse and will only get worse. I guess I will clean her up soon, but it's just not my way of thinking at the moment. I'm doing nothing until she totally co-operates, and regardless, her life only continues while I allow her heart to beat. The more she purrs and the less she bleats, the less I despise her. She is going to give, and her giving will keep on giving.

STUMBLING

I sat there on a sunny Saturday morning cradling my cup of coffee like it was an important and valuable possession, looking out of the living room window at the flowers and the lawn. The grass had not been mowed this summer, so was in need of attention. I hoped to get around to that at some point. The flowers were interesting. Back in March, I had planted an assortment of bulbs, without any real sense of what I was doing because I was a total ignoramus as far as gardening was concerned. However, at random spots in the flower beds, I noticed splashes of colour and thought I'd not done badly.

Sitting on the sofa behind me, Jamie was looking through one of the travel brochures Laura had brought home what seemed like an age ago.

He was a surprisingly welcome presence. He had rung me to arrange something to get me out of the house and to distract me from the situation. I was in, although any arrangement would have to fit in with his adventuring on the dating sites. I was glad to hear from him, having been just about to contact him myself. It felt good telling him that I was feeling normal and that my life was going to roll on.

"You stay where you are, mate. I'm coming right round."

"But…" Too late. He had hung up.

He greeted me with a half-smile, wearing a new leather jacket that looked expensive and a copy of 'The Guardian' in his hand. "Hey you. Fancy doing breakfast. Wetherspoons is open!"

Now, some friends are useful and beneficial because they can show a real empathy and sensitivity, perhaps even offering an idea that can somehow help the situation. I did not expect that from Jamie Clover and, in all fairness, perhaps that was the best thing for me now I was trying to toughen up.

Within twenty minutes, we were sitting in a low-lit part of our local Wetherspoons pub away from the windows. I wasn't really that hungry, but had opted for beans on toast anyway, if only to be sociable.

Jamie was all questions. "Did you know she was going to America?"

"I knew she was going, but not till August. It was part of her job. To be honest, I'm not a hundred per cent certain that she has gone to the U.S. It just fits."

"What did that bloke at her work say?"

"Max knew nothing about her going early. In fact, she hasn't contacted him to say she was going, so it begins to look like she is playing fast and loose with her job, not just us. She's obviously gone early to clear her head or get clear of things, whichever way you want to see it. I guess she had to get clear of work."

"Will she lose her job, then?"

"No. Her boss is a sweet guy and I laid it on pretty thick about how she must have suffered some kind of breakdown. He'll support her, I'm sure. If she's gone to America, no doubt she will be in touch with him anyway."

"You're a sweet guy. I'd have let her rot. Let her lose her damned job."

"She probably will in the end." I felt better being with my best mate, like the old days, and two heads are better than one in most situations. We sat there for a couple of minutes without words. I felt myself becoming more like him by the second.

Eventually, he broke the silence. "Well, my old mate, what are you going to do?"

"I don't know. Get on with stuff. What do you think I should do?"

"I think you should live, mate. She's gone, and she's let you know why."

I still had some lack of acceptance in my mind, despite my determination to have a life. "OK, but the last thing I want to say on the matter. Deep down, this is not her. She wouldn't do it this way. If this is her, I never knew the woman."

"But she did, mate, and you probably didn't know her as well as you thought. She's gone. Maybe she will be back or maybe she won't. Time to get real."

"Either way, I'm out of it. When are we going out? Tonight good for you?"

There was little point us talking in any other way about my marriage and Laura really, since I knew that Jamie had never been in a situation like the one I was in. Apart from his two marriages, the deepest relationship he had ever had was with a bottle of double malt I had bought him as a present one Christmas. He had given that more long term serious affection than he had ever shown to any female.

He grinned. "Don't be daft. I've got two dates this evening."

"More recipients of the Trojan charm, I presume."

KATE

Jamie hadn't been gone long when the doorbell rang. When I opened the door, George and Lillian, both grim-faced, were there. "We need to talk."

Behind them was my sister, Kate.

This was something of a shock. We hadn't spoken for years, Kate and I. Totally unlike each other in just about every aspect of attitude and personality, I immediately wondered if her turning up here in her uniform, might be significant in our negative brother-sister relationship. I thought again. The half-smile she had displayed was her working expression, the demeanour of somebody who felt in some way superior, an aspect of her personality that had caused countless arguments between us as we had grown up and eventually gone our separate ways with minimal contact. As I looked out, it was apparent that they had all come in a police car, which was now parked on the front. She looked older than when I had last seen her, four years ago in a restaurant, where we had said brief hellos but that was all. I braced myself for a difficult conversation.

I had phoned them the night before to tell them about Laura's car being found. They had been reassured by this, as for them, like the police, it seemed to suggest that she had flown somewhere. We had spent several minutes considering where she might have flown when I had suddenly remembered about the forthcoming America trip.

"The thing is, I'm not happy about what you're saying." George chose not to sit down while I had already perched myself on the settee.

"What do you mean?"

"I mean, I have a daughter who is no longer here, god knows where she is, and you're here sitting pretty."

"Sitting pretty? What are you on about?" I wasn't a violent man, but utterances like these were not helpful. I clenched my hands together behind my back.

"Oh, you say that. Listen, I watch detective shows. I see what can happen with things like this."

I shook my head, disbelieving. I could see from the expressions on the faces of the two women, that he was going rogue here. "They said on one show that in the case of somebody who goes missing fatally, in a very high percentage of the cases, the partner is responsible. How do I know that what you're saying is the truth?"

"What the fuck are you suggesting? That I killed her? Don't be ridiculous."

"But is it ridiculous? You could have dropped the car off in Manchester."

"Of course it's ridiculous."

Kate wasn't saying anything and just sat there at the other end of the sofa. Was she here as a witness, or as some kind of expert prosecutor in my home-based trial as Laura's assumed kidnapper or killer? "What do you think about this?" We weren't friends, never mind brother and sister, had been even more diametrically opposed since the death of my mother, as Kate always thought my behavior made an unforgivable contribution to that loss.

"I don't know, Dominic. George and Lillian contacted me at work and they're anxious. I just want to help. I want to help you any way I can." She reached out and put her hand on mine as she said this. She had never done that and it was just plain weird. I had presumed she had come to back up George's accusations. To connect with me in some way was not even in my imagination

She hadn't come to my wedding. Perhaps she was thinking she might make my funeral.

"I need to ask you something, and I need to look into your eyes when you answer." George was standing in front of me, looking down at me. This was something I did not need. "Have you anything to do with my daughter's disappearance? My wife thinks you're genuine, but she's always been soft and I'm not. You turned Laura over for sex with that slag. Now I want to know what's happened to Laura."

Kate sighed. Clearly, she hadn't been expecting this and I guess it may have come as a real shock. She knew more than many that I could be a twat at times, so it should have been no surprise really.

Lillian had her hand on his arm in some feeble attempt at restraint. He turned to her. "I have to say this, Lillian. It's on my mind. He could have dropped Laura's car off at the airport himself."

"I think you would find that CCTV cameras there, and I imagine there are loads, would pick it up and identify the driver. Check that one out."

He hesitated before continuing. "And another thing. I've been on the phone to the airport for most of this morning. Laura didn't board any of the flights to America. If she's flown anywhere, it's not there, so you can stop presuming that. Her boss hasn't heard from her and neither have we."

This was something different. I thought before replying. "Perhaps she didn't go there, then. Maybe she flew somewhere else. Did you think about that? You just don't get it." I stood up and went face to face with the man. "I'm trying to cope with the fact that your precious daughter has fucked off. She's left me to sort everything out. You might be surprised to learn this while you are so busy treating me like some kind of dog, but life for me is no bed of roses without Laura. See this?" I pointed at my mouth with both fingers. "This is the brave face I put on for myself, you and the rest of the world."

At this point Kate gave me another surprise and moved up next to me and gave me the kind of hug I could never remember having received from her before. This was a bit emotional for me. Perhaps blood was suddenly becoming thicker than the water it had been for the past twenty years.

I think this show of warmth from the uniformed officer who, surprisingly to me, had a heart had an effect open the whole room. I sensed that my voice had become a weak pitiful whine and I also sensed that the hardness George had tried to display had faded. "OK. Let's say I try to believe you. Let's say she's just gone away for a break, however absurd that sounds. You know what will happen if I learn that you've done something. Even prison won't protect you from me."

Again, Lillian grabbed hold of his arm, this time with firmness but, judging by the way her eyes switched between her husband and me, I don't think she was totally convinced that this had been Laura's decision not mine.

"George, Lillian, if you think I have done anything here, you are so wide of the mark, it's unreal. The sad fact here is that I am stuck here still loving your daughter. I have to accept that she's left me and so do you. Go to the police, chat to a detective or two. Feel free, if you don't like my attitude. I would love it if they found her for you. The fact is, they don't even bother investigating." I waited for a response, but none was forthcoming. "You spoke to Max, then?"

"Yes. He knew nothing. I just don't get it." He had mellowed. "We are lying awake all night trying to work it out. I mean, there was that note you saw."

"Might have been nothing, that. Truth is, all we can do is get on with stuff and hope that she gets in touch with one of us soon."

As they left, Kate hung back. "Listen, if you need anything, my work and personal numbers are on this card, just ring me. I'm sorry, Dom."

"Me too, Kate." I gave her hand a reassuring squeeze.

"Perhaps we need a fresh start."

"Perhaps. I'll be in touch, Kate."

ALWAYS TIME FOR A GREEN DAY

These were strange days. I had rarely known a period of time like this one, when every hue and shade seemed to be unfamiliar. I was feeling like somebody who had taken off his Ray-Bans to deal with the harsh glare of the sun. I remembered going through the same process when my mother and father had passed away. Then, like now, I had known that life had to and would go on, that both my late parents would want that. I now had that same feeling, but this time I was more in control of things and it was obviously about what I wanted. I had to get myself going again. I went to work and did my job, just as I had always done. As a consequence of my change in circumstances, teaching had suddenly become central again, just like studying had when I had resumed university after each parental funeral. I was now working with a renewed passion and motivation, wanting to take whatever satisfaction I could from my work.

The actuality was that I became philosophical about it, imaginatively beginning to believe that this process was a challenge, sent to test me. A survivor by nature, I wasn't going to become suicidal at any point, and I had always seen myself as resilient, somebody who somehow gets through. I always believed and had proved on numerous occasions that I could cope with adversity and that is exactly what I was doing. Metaphorically, it might have become a landscape of rugged gloomy mountains and deep depressing rivers, but it was my rugged and depressing landscape and I was going to master it. I was not going to be about suffering and endurance, forever reaching into the past. At the end of the day, my life still had plenty going on. No selfish inconsiderate let-down of a woman was going to stop me smiling.

As a bonus, my Year Eights were enjoying the book we were studying. "Anyway, Lennie has gone. George Milton knows he's gone but won't say anything because he cares so much about his friend."

Joey Poole, a bright spark who always sat at the front said, "But why does he care so much about him, sir. He left without telling him. Why doesn't George think that this is a chance for him to look after himself? He'd be better off."

I sighed inwardly. If only I had possessed this boy's wisdom. "Well, think about this, class. If you really care about somebody, does that care end when somebody goes away? Should George really get on with his own stuff and not worry about what happens to Lennie?"

I could almost hear the cogs in their young minds whilst I fought off the subconscious workings in mine. 'Of Mice and Men' always provoked emotion.

Life post-marriage was about staving off dullness. To remove the intrusive quietness of the house, I played the 'American Idiot' album by Green Day and got as far as 'Boulevard of Broken Dreams' before I had to press the eject button. Too much realization.. It just made me become like I had never been, a man who was forced to keep realizing, however much I strived to move forward, that a part of me was still rooted in the past, especially my 'shallow heart'.

The battle would go on, however. I would win.

MALEVOLENCE

She has started talking. Well, she would. She's hungry, and she probably tires of the squalid stench she's creating. She has to think, maybe my life will get better if I play ball. She sees humanity in me. She senses that I'm not a total monster. Bless.

As she speaks in response to my prompts, I write down her answers, or at least any parts of her answers I feel might be helpful. I'm really keen on details these days, and the details she gives me tick boxes and ring bells. From her point of view, those details keep her alive, because I have made it clear to her that she is under the threat of a coming death that will be sudden and instant. There is something about holding a blade against someone's throat and saying evil words that is a real turn-on. Always has been.

She looks very pale. She keeps asking me why I'm doing this but I don't do much answering. I like her being anxious. She thinks, perhaps knows, that I am going to finish her off at some point. She just doesn't know how and when, so her speculation must be a prolonged agony. I don't want her to die too soon. Her demise is inevitable, necessary and obviously it's part of my plan. It just has to happen at the right time.

It is pretty weird having her here in front of me. I guess I could even take advantage of her if I wanted to, but that is too creepy, even for me. She does look pretty vulnerable. I will do anything, some pretty depraved things, but doing stuff with this one while she's tied up is beyond me, especially when she's so messy. I would probably become angry. Uncontrollable. Then she would die. If I was to become particularly wild, her death would be very bloody, I'm sure.

She can breathe for a little longer.

STAFF MATTERS

I found myself listening to some well-spoken man talking about cloud formations. He was going on about cirrus, towering cumulus and other stuff that might affect or represent the meteorological condition of the local area. I switched over to Radio Five Live. That was a live commentary of a golf event taking place at Saint Andrews. I switched to a concerto from Mozart. Was there nothing on the radio for somebody like me?

I had to go out. I had spent too many hours looking at four walls, trying to watch the TV and here I was listening to all kinds of meaningless radio outpourings. I was going to go insane.

My colleagues had arranged a night out on Friday, and I was reluctantly considering it. I didn't go on staff nights out. They were usually dull affairs overpopulated with young enthusiastic kids trying to be teachers who hadn't taught long enough to know what the job (or life, for that matter) was really about, yet were obsessed with work, like their whole lives depended on them thinking about teaching twenty-four seven. I always spent part of the night avoiding the boring ones, even if that meant going and playing on a quiz machine. I suppose they all thought I was a misery, but hey-ho.

It was less than a fortnight since Laura had left so I kept switching between weakness and strength, but the periods of strength were lasting for longer periods as time went on, yet I still didn't know exactly where I was and precisely who I was. Perhaps it was in a moment where I wanted to show some steel that I said that yes, I would meet my colleagues in The Forum.

Friday evening came, and I decided that I was definitely going. For all I knew, Laura would be out wherever she was, so why should I be a monk? I shuddered at the thought of what her lifestyle might actually be like these days so I had to do things and focus my mind on alternatives. I even bought a new shirt for the occasion, a red checked affair that I thought looked really cool. Others might have thought differently, but so what?

As I stood at the bus stop (which seemed strange, as I hadn't caught a bus for about two years), I couldn't help thinking that I was a single man again, and it wasn't exactly the shiny free feeling I used to know. Six years ago, I had enjoyed my single life, with all the laughs, drinking and women, but tonight just felt like a bargain basement version of what I had done to death as a younger man.

The Forum was at the top of Division Street in the centre of the city. A big noisy place, in truth, one of the reasons I had turned up at all was the location. I liked this part of town, always had, and liked the beer on sale here. For some reason, my arrival was a popular part of the night, maybe because they all knew what had happened the previous week, and people were all smiles. All the young ones were there so I moved towards Jim and Simon, two PE teachers who were always a laugh. They would take the piss out of me and I could cope with that.

"How you doing, Walker? I hear you had a stroke of luck."

I laughed, taking a serious swig of my beer.

I think I had been there an hour when my line manager, Samantha, a cheerful blonde woman who had always been supportive, especially so in recent weeks, pulled me aside with all the subtlety a woman now on the outside of several large gin and tonics could manage. She gestured for me to sit next to her. "Great that you could make it. Are you OK?"

"I think so. I just need a few of these." I held up my glass like it was a trophy.

Three hours later, much worse for wear, that same Samantha and I were sitting in a wine bar whilst, under the influence of too many drinks for me even to know which wine bar it was, I poured out my woes. We had left the others and I presumed she was feeling sorry for me as I must have given off the aura of a person not at ease with socializing. "Anyway, I'm getting on with my life. Nobody has the right to ruin another person's life. Nobody is going to ruin my life. I'm okay without her anyway. Everything is going okay."

Her hand was holding mine, and I felt quiet weakened by the booze. Consequently, when she reached across to kiss me on the lips, I didn't resist.

We had kissed for some seconds when I broke away. "I can't do this." It wasn't that she wasn't attractive. It wasn't even that I wouldn't enjoy the intimacy. This was all about what was happening inside of my head and what should really have been happening in hers too. It was about how I would feel that following day and at work. It had only been ten days since Laura had left. It even went through my mind how disastrous this would be if she returned and I'd had a play with the first woman who made herself available.

"I'm sorry. I thought you deserved it. I've always liked you, Dom. Just wanted you to feel better."

"Sex won't make me feel better."

"I wasn't offering sex, just a bit of female comfort."

"I'm sorry, Sam. If it wasn't now, I would have welcomed it. Don't feel single just yet."

She seemed to shrink a little. "I don't know what I was thinking."

"We were both probably not thinking. Both over-served at the bar."

She laughed, probably the same kind of deceptive laugh as I had done several times this evening.

MALEVOLENCE

Got to keep thinking. Got to keep concentrating and imagining now for a while. If I spend some quality time here, facing her, questioning and thinking, that will help everything to go the way it must.

I sit and look at her. She is not a pretty sight and won't ever be a pretty sight again. The only exit for her from this is the final one and our newly-established relationship is tragically terminal. On the positive side, she might be bleary-eyed, but at least she still has her eyes. Well, for now.

Since I cleaned her up, and gave her the needed toilet times, she has begun to tell me more stuff, so much that I need. She is becoming so co-operative that things are really developing. I'm not pretending that she really understands me — that would be too much to ask. No — she just has an acute sense of the danger she is in and thinks she knows what she needs to do to survive. Poor fool. This pet of mine should accept the inevitable. Good luck with the hope, though.

I need her to keep talking. I don't want one-word answers. I show her kindness when she talks. I pass her a biscuit or give her a drink and show her how serious I am when she thinks it's ok to just give me bits and pieces in response. The blows leave red marks on her face.

The fake kindness fuels her hope. Aren't women like this hilarious.

BIRTHDAY – JULY 26TH

I had been born exactly thirty-eight years ago. Weighing just over ten pounds, it could be said that I put my mother, bless her, under immense pressure from the moment of my birth (as all my early photographs testified) and my excitable and mischievious personality meant there was to be no let up for her in her time on this planet. Throughout my childhood, however, birthdays had always been special, involving parties, trips to the seaside and presents. My birthdays as an adult were also great, involving parties, trips to the seaside and presents.

Last year, the celebration had started with first-thing-in-the-morning sex, followed by a breakfast that was loaded with cholesterol, with Laura making the same effort on my behalf that I had grown up with. We had a wonderful early evening stroll in the grounds of Hardwick Hall and a proper birthday meal in town.

Today was the day of the 'Blood Moon', the day when our only satellite became coloured red by the sun's rays, when in my mind it was suddenly given the connotations of danger, death and change. This was no day on which to have a birthday, I sensed.

I woke up hung over, but forced myself to shower and put on clean clothes. I was determined to have a positive day today. There was no school for six weeks, so I had to get myself into a holiday frame of mind.

I checked my phone. There was a text from Lillian wishing me a happy birthday and an email from Jamie. I opened up the email to read *Happy Birthday you old sod. Let's have another drink soon. Have a read at my attachment.* I opened up the attachment, which turned out to be nothing to do with my birthday at all, but was some writing about some bloke meeting a woman and shagging her. Fancy sending to a bloke who was now getting no sex at all a piece of writing about sex. Bit insensitive if you asked me, but that was Jamie all over. Great mate, but no sensitivity.

It was only after I was into the fourth paragraph, with a reference to an Audi R8, that I realized that this writing was by Jamie and it was about himself. He had been saying for ages that he wanted to take up writing and here it was. I read it almost to the end, apart from two pages in all. It wasn't bad, apart from some dodgy punctuation. He and I were going to have to talk about this at the next meet.

As I put the phone down, there was a further beep to indicate another email. This was from Laura. With a clumsy finger, I pressed the button to read it, with my heart in transition. *Happy birthday babe. Sorry I'm not with you today but I hope you have a lovely day. L xxxxx*

I re-read this message several times, but resisted replying. On the one hand, she might have been thinking about me, having second thoughts, but on the other, she might have been doing that cat and mouse thing that women sometimes do. The 'I don't want you, but I don't want anyone else to have you' attitude. 'I really care about you, but I just can't be with you.' Both were utterly worthless. I refused to be emotionally affected by a mere email, understanding the intricacies of manipulation.

I pressed to close it. I wanted it removed from my sight. There would be plenty of time for me to read it again anyway, and this would probably happen the next time I had a substantial interaction with Mr. Daniels or Mr. Beam.

MALEVOLENCE

Her co-operation has become total. She knows how things are panning out and accepts what is going on. She has now realized she is to have her part in it although she doesn't know what that part is. From all of the sounds this bitch makes, they are the co-operative responses that display a greater willingness, and the nods and utterances signal acceptance of her fate. I think she even enjoys my cooking. Well, she's on one meal a day so I'm not surprised when she wolfs it down like it is everything. She looks pretty weak, has lost a few pounds, but that's understandable, restricted the way she is. Nobody thrives in chains.

I do not consider her feelings. When would she have considered mine, after all? Her future was mapped out a long time ago and I have reshaped the coming time period for her and me. I know that deep down she thinks I am evil, that I have done incredible harm to her, but so what? She has been tamed. That is all that matters.

For no real reason, sometimes I slap her, as I have from the beginning, if only to hear the sound. At times this is a single slap, a blow that makes her yelp, one that thankfully nobody else can hear. At other times, on those moments where she makes a mistake or becomes negative, I punch her repeatedly in the middle of her body and enjoy her yelps of pain. She knows I am in command.

Occasionally, and what is most effective of all, I drop the bomb of sensitivity in there. I give a sentence that offers hope, something dream-like, beyond possibility. That makes her tearful and hopeful, as if there is some way out of this. She's given plenty. She doesn't even know how much she has given and how helpful she is being. Her condition and the conditions I have placed her in mean she is constantly confused and afraid, I am sure, so that her permanent desperation makes her tongue looser each day.

Soon it will be time for her to return and shape the future. I hope she will recognize herself.

We have gone through photographs and some documents. I think I know everybody now and plenty of stuff about each. My knowledge of her needs to be as great as hers is and she is beginning to accept that. I never thought I was clever or anything like that. I didn't do well at school, although I always enjoyed reading and music lessons. But the thing I know most about is suffering, so I like causing some. The pain I have shown this creature has worked. It has given her a better understanding of me and, dare I say it, an acceptance, one that might comfort her in the gloom and danger of the place she is confined in.

Don't get me wrong, I knew plenty about her life and the people in her life before now, but I needed some specifics, a bit more flesh on the bones. In a typical life there must be ten million details, perhaps more, so I want to know as many of that ten million as possible.

This bitch is adapting. She is beginning to smile more. She is going along with my plan. She has a dream of survival and seeing the sun again but will only ever have nightmares about death and darkness.

AUGUST IS A WICKED MONTH

What a month it had been. There had been twists and turns, dullness and silliness and I was travelling along the road of life with my tyres only half-inflated, or at least that was how it felt at times. I wanted to get through, wanted normality. I was determined to move forward. It felt like enough for me to succeed, but was it?

I was just a man. Every day seemed to have at least one dark moment or sharp reminder waiting to pierce me and there were so many times when I asked myself whether actual happiness was ever going to be a possibility. That didn't mean I was going into depression. Thanks to my long-held selfishness and sizeable ego, there was no chance of that. It was just that everything wasn't as shiny and bright as life should be, continuing to be more dull and grey, with the odd glimmer of something better.

On many of these days, I found myself waking up angry. Who did she think she was, this cow who had deserted me and our life together? Anger would take over for a while, then give way to confusion. I kept asking myself, why? After all, the idea persisted that this was not Laura, not her style at all. Maybe this disbelief was the thing that stopped me totally moving on and enjoying everything and everybody around me.

I didn't want to be destroyed by my personal crisis. I started spending more time in the garden, helping Jamie with his writing, and watching horror movies. These were probably all I had right now, giving my existence some semblance of structure. These and other distractions took care of the daytimes while I just worked on the computer at night, often with my old mate Jack Daniels as support.

Curiosity sometimes got the better of me. I tried to access Laura's email account, tried her passwords, but none worked. She had even gone to the trouble of changing to a password that I didn't know. Why wouldn't she? We didn't have a joint bank account. We had talked it through and we had agreed that I would look after the mortgage and council tax while she would pay for the food and other bills from her account. This meant that there was no way I could check on the money going out of the account to see if that gave me any clues, but I anticipated a credit card bill coming through the letterbox one day and perhaps that would shed light on where Laura had gone. After all, she would have to spend money, wherever she was.

Facebook also yielded a frustrating nothing. The last entry in her newsfeed was the morning of her disappearance, when she had posted some witty slogan about rules for a successful marriage that was meant to be comical, but which now seemed ironic and hypocritical. I did wonder why she wasn't continuing her Facebook commentary, since leaving me the way she had did not have to mean an end to her online activity.

I paid a visit to her place of work. Maxwell had nothing reassuring to tell me. "She hasn't been in work all week. We're worried about her. She was due to fly out to America tomorrow."

"Has she been in touch at all?

"Only to say she's ill and staying with a friend."

Ouch. Friend obviously meant lover. She was definitely with somebody else, then. "You spoke to her?"

"It was an email."

"I didn't want to give too away in case there every to be some kind of resolution to this situation. "Did she say when she would be back?"

"No. She did say that she would still hopefully make the America trip. She asked me to email her the details in case she didn't make it back in."

I tried to keep a faint smile on my face, although this was agony. She was going ahead with a life without me. She had left me and there was nothing I could do but cope with it. I wanted to give Maxwell my mobile number, but had to resist, as that would give the game away. If she was playing away, which now most definitely seemed to be the case, I had to deal with it.

Most of these weekends, I didn't remember much. I would buy two one-litre bottles of Jack Daniels on the Friday night and the ensuing two days became forgotten pieces of my history, forty-eight hours I would never get back. More lost weekends to add to the collection.

The rest of the Summer, my feelings became much less changeable. I now believed fervently that she had left me for somebody else, that this wasn't a disappearance. I searched the house to check that key documents were here. Her passport had gone, as had her birth certificate. Also, some photos, mainly the ones where she was with family or friends. None of the photos taken with me on our various holidays or trips had gone, which told the story. She didn't want any reminders of me in her life.

MALEVOLENCE

I am preparing her for the big stage. It's not easy, but I never expected it to be. I put her make up on so carefully, like I'm painting a picture. Not going to do much about the hair, but I'll cross that bridge when I get there.

I want her to be dressed right too. Obviously, I have photos and ideas, things I have seen and know, yet everything has to work. This is the plan of a lifetime and it is going to work perfectly. So exciting. A smile in the mirror reassures and I carry on preparing in a way that I have never prepared before. If she looks right, then everything is on course for everything. Everything will be mine.

I look into her eyes. I see a contrast, but that does not matter. What must happen will now happen and nothing can stand in the way. Eyes don't need to show life or familiarity if they can show something else, something that gives something to somebody. These eyes will give.

At last she understands now what is happening. She has co-operated, but she had no choice. Now she has to accept what is coming, although I still see the terror in her eyes at times. She understands who I am now, who we are. I still enjoy the wide open mouth and the staring eyes. I have even filmed and photographed her like some model for a horror film. She now meekly accepts the future. She will never forget what she has gone through in this chamber of experience and longs for relief, that better time that will never come.

I am excited. My heart is beating like it has never done before and I know that this is how it was meant to be. It is not going to be long now. Whatever I have had to do to bring this about, I know it has been worth it.

WICKEDNESS

The following Saturday, I went out with Jamie. He was so positive and I guess it was infectious.

"Why do you still mention her every time we go out, Dom?"

"I don't know Maybe it's not as easy as I thought it would be."

"No, I don't suppose it is. Anyway, I've got a beautiful distraction for you, something wonderful. Got three chapters written for the book."

"Oh. Yes. The book."

"More of that stuff I sent you on your birthday. The best of my dating adventures; going to dress them up a little, make it a book for men about sex and the online stuff. Think it will be a laugh."

"Sounds like fun."

"We can do some research, you and me."

As if on cue, at that moment I noticed a woman glance at me and then look away. She was pretty, with long curly blonde hair, but I shrugged it off. Day One was still less than two months ago. "What do you mean?"

"Fuck off, Dom. You know what I mean. Let's get you back in the saddle."

"I don't really know if I'm ready for that yet. We've not been that long separated."

"Come on, Dom. We're blokes. We get over heartbreak like machines. Some of these women I've met have been split up from somebody for two years and not had a shag. They go on a dating site after two years celibate. Unbelievable."

"I can believe it…" I paused. The sexy blonde had glanced at me again, this time with a faint smile on her lips. "I think we should get another drink here, mate. It's a nice place."

"Another double JD. That will be your eighth."

"Oh, bollocks. Who's counting?"

Abruptly, I was woken up, not by the glowing sunlight, but by noisy bedsprings, which were accompanied by grunts and piercing sighs from the next bedroom. Looking around, I realized that I was under a blue duvet in Jamie's spare bedroom with a mess of blonde hair on the pillow at the side of me. I couldn't remember much, but some of the details were obvious. I studied the details. The woman at the side had her face away from, me, still with her make-up on judging by the smudge on the side of her cheek, with a black handbag on the bedside cabinet. I did a three-sixty and noticed her black dress and tights strewn on the floor at the side of Jamie's spare bed with my stuff on a chair next to the door. Had I actually performed? Judging by how little I actually remembered, it was clear that I couldn't have been much more than barely conscious at the end of last night. At any rate, I felt severely poisoned this morning. Well I guess physically it wasn't impossible that I managed to do something, since I hadn't had any sex for a few weeks, and Shakespeare once remarked how the body was capable of anything when the need is great, or something like that. I couldn't remember anything.

I didn't feel good. Sharing a bed with someone didn't feel right. While she slept, I sneaked out from under the duvet and put on my clothes, hearing some kind of big finish happening in Jamie's room. I wanted to get home. I wanted a bath. I was sure that I smelled of her perfume, Calvin Klein Euphoria, the same one I had bought Laura the previous Christmas.

This was too soon to be back in the saddle. At home, every morning as I awoke, I thought of Laura, and today was no exception. This woman, whoever she was, was gently snoring as I closed the door behind me. I didn't know whether she was attractive or not, and was back home before there was even the chance of me caring.

JD CLOVER

For the rest of a month that passed so slowly, I didn't do much other than work, drink, watch the occasional television programme and listen to music. On some nights, Jamie would send me some of his writing and I would help him with it. To be fair, it wasn't very good, but it was funny. He had plenty of stories to tell about his online dating and it actually distracted me from my miserable state of being, so much so that I actually looked forward to getting an email from him with some depraved, woman-baiting chapter attached. I wasn't comfortable with the sexism, but really enjoyed the humour of it. Certainly, editing and laughing at his writing was better than being a miserable bastard, and it prevented me drinking heavily.

This went on for weeks. I had had an unwelcome liaison and did not want another. I guess I had suffered a setback in my quest to become a happy single man again, and was finding it wasn't that easy to move on from the love of your life. Deep down, whatever I told myself, I still wanted what I had had, although I would have preferred to see everything differently. Life had to be about now and the future, not the past.

I changed nothing in the house. I don't know if this was out of laziness or because I wanted to preserve everything. Perhaps subconsciously, I still wanted to wake up and find it all a dream, although deep inside, I knew the reality. Laura was out there somewhere. She would have come back from America by now. I wondered if the next contact I would receive from her would be an official letter from a solicitor, wanting to arrange a financial settlement and make the separation legally permanent. How would I deal with that?

Every time I thought of that kind of contact being made, I winced. The prospect was so far from what I had planned, what I thought we had planned. I spent much of this time in a haze of confusion and uncertainty about the future, with spells of defiance and asserted independence, when I would go drinking with Jamie.

It was a Friday night. I was returning from a game of squash with Jamie. He was all excited about his writing and bought the drinks that evening to thank me for helping him. We had worked together on creating what was becoming a manuscript and had laughed out loud so many times. Obviously, I assured him that what we had written was a fantastic piece of work (it wasn't) and that it had actually helped me cope so much (it had).

"Shall we include a chapter about you and your stuff, just as a sub-plot?'

For some reason, I found him irritating and refreshing at the same time. Maybe it was the basic way he expressed her disappearance, his failure to grasp perhaps what it meant to me. He was my best mate, yet he was a world apart. "Don't you even think about mentioning me or my shit. You've got loads more interesting things to write about."

"And I'm still doing the research, mate. I need to meet a psycho now."

"What, worse than the one who got you into trouble at work."

"Yeah, I guess so, as long as she doesn't kill me…Are you drinking much?

"A bit."

"Well, keep on top of it." He pointed a finger like a stern parent. "Otherwise it will be on top of you."

"Of course."

BOOMERANG

Why does so much of humanity like a warm sunny day? In this fading summer, the sun was smiling down on me like it knew something I didn't as I stepped out of the car.

On this day, my seven hours at the school had been a game of two halves, with three easy pleasant lessons in the morning, but tougher classes with surly and lazy pupils in the afternoon. Work was often like this. Nobody, teenager nor adult, cut it quite so well after lunch and the controlled chaos of football, sex, make-up and mobile phone usage were strong in the minds of the awkward teenagers. In all fairness, the same things might also have occupied the minds of their teachers. Of course, the job couldn't afford us the honesty to ever admit that. I guess the hypocrisy of being a teacher was half the fun.

Anyway, dreams can't trump reality on most occasions, especially in the classroom, so conflict was as inevitable as the passing of time. In every classroom I had ever entered, the teacher had to show himself as a confident defender of education, whatever that was worth these days, and we had to promote working hard in lessons like it was the greatest pre-requisite in life. One day they would make kids who could do a full day without their batteries of concentration and effort wearing out halfway through. Such were my thoughts as I made my way home. I concluded, as I turned into our cul-de-sac, that I probably needed some alcohol and to do some more work on that dirty writing of Jamie's to stop me being the ultimate bore.

At least it was a Friday, with a weekend ahead of doing whatever I wanted. Consolation was divine, but it was a long time coming. The Friday feeling meant waiting for the golden dawn, herald of the weekend's glories, that three o'clock brought with it and the promise of abandoning the body clock for a couple of days to spend time with JD or some of his lesser alcoholic cousins.

As I left my car top walk up the path, I waved to Joan and Arthur, an elderly couple who had moved in when we had, at number six. They were just leaving their house.

I put the key into the lock.

I stopped.

There was a noise.

It was the sound of a chair being scraped across the kitchen floor.

There was somebody in my house.

A burglar?

I continued to listen.

There were no further sounds.

Forcefully, I turned the key then pushed open the door. Any burglar was going to regret picking my house, and if it was the same burglar as last time, he would get a little extra for his trouble. My fists were clenched and I was ready to fight. At that moment, I didn't care if he killed me. The shit I had been through over the past few months, he was going to feel the full force.

As I approached the kitchen, her back was facing me.

Her back.

It was a back full of meaning, but the meaning it had lacked clarity.

She turned to face me. "Hello, Dom."

I felt the express trains of conflicting emotions crash inside my mind. I was standing there and I just stared. It was all I could do. Intensity brought with it a paralysis. Anger was at odds with relief, whilst surprise and shock twinned themselves and met up with anxiety. This was real theatre for an onlooker.

But there were no onlookers. There was only me. Only her and me.

This should have been deep unprecedented joy. Back in July, that would have been the case. There was no way I could feel delight, however. Not now. I couldn't allow that. There was too much that was inexplicable. Plenty that was unforgivable.

"I'm sorry."

I stood there. What the fuck did that mean? I was still staring. Sorry for what? Sorry that she had come back or sorry that she had left. Maybe she was sorry that I had been through so many shades of hell. For some seconds it was as if I was hallucinating, that she was some kind of created image, or a hologram, manipulating my mind. I couldn't speak.

"I've been through the mill a bit.".

I didn't move. I couldn't. Not even my lips. For now, I was gripped by an inability to respond and didn't even want to breathe particularly. I was taking in the woman in front of me. My wife was before me, looking quite different, but still my wife. She was still beautiful, the same eyes, the same figure, but this time with hair that was streaked blonde and wearing a red cotton top and faded jeans. I wanted to take in every detail. She looked paler than I remembered and I could see uncertainty in her eyes.

Eventually, I came to life. "Laura. Where… Why?" I would have a thousand questions to ask her but those two would do for starters.

She moved purposefully towards me. "Dom, I've been very ill." Her voice was different, more nasal, but this was my wife come back, so that was small potatoes.

I held her in my arms for some seconds before gently pushing her away from me. "Ill? How?"

"Well, it's a pretty long story. I got myself hurt."

"What? When? When you left me?"

"Not straight away, if that's what you mean." She looked into my eyes imploringly, but I felt as hard as tempered steel.

"Hurt?" I'd been hurt. "You left me, remember. I had no say in it. Left without a word or a good reason."

"True, I had to leave for a while. I had what I thought were good reasons."

"Yeah. Reasons that good that you couldn't tell me about them."

"I know. I'm sorry. I needed to sort my head out."

"I never realised there was anything wrong with your head. I thought we were both happy."

"I needed to think about the future, what I wanted from it. I needed to make sure that my head was clear for our marriage and had to have some time on my own for that."

"And where did you go for that?"

"Manchester."

"Manchester? Why the fuck Manchester?"

"It's a big place and I wanted to lose myself. I thought Manchester would be good for that…I was there for a couple of weeks. I was going to come back. Then it happened."

"What did?"

"I got mugged – near the railway station. Near Piccadilly. I think I must have fought back and he tried to strangle me. In the end, he settled for smashing my head against a wall, I was told. I woke up in hospital not knowing who I was and with no

153

ID on me. Nothing. Not even my driving license. It was all in the purse that he took."

"Amnesia? You're kidding me?"

"No, Dom. I spent days not knowing anything about anything. The doctors and nurses, and the police when they visited, kept asking me things but I was useless. All I know was that I was laying in a bed not right. All In was fit for was watching television and sleeping.

"How long did this go on for?"

"Over two months. Nearly three. Eventually my memory started to come back. My voice has suffered, as you can tell, but the doctor said that might not be permanent. I hope so."

"And the hair. Didn't you always say blonde streaks were chavvy and desperate? Or have you forgotten that as well."

Laura laughed, touching her head. "No. I did this before the attack. Just fancied a change, I think. I was in a strange place."

"Are you here to stay, or have you come back to recover?"

"I want what we had, Dom. I want our happy marriage back."

"Of course you do. Why wouldn't you?"

I went and made myself a cup of coffee. As the kettle boiled, I turned to her. You are going to have to give me time to get up to speed. I've been through the ringer a bit."

"I know and I'm sorry. If it's any consolation, I wanted to be back here within days of my going but what happened in Manchester spoiled all that. "Some people are so evil."

"Did they get the bastard?"

"No. And I never got my purse back either. I'll have to apply for new cards. A kind nurse gave me ten pounds so I could get home or I would have had to beg or walk the whole way here."

"He didn't take your key then?"

"No. The key was in one of my pockets, so I suppose he had to rush off. Just the purse and my phone. I expect he was in a hurry. By all accounts, I was discovered pretty promptly or things might have been much worse. I could have died, Dom."

I couldn't say much after that. We just sat there drinking beer in an atmosphere that was far from comfortable, although we were holding hands, whatever that meant. I asked her questions and she asked me some, since her memory had not been fully restored after the attack, she said. "I need to catch up with some things. Please forgive me if I have to be told things that happened. I can't help it."

There was a surreal awkwardness about going to bed that night. After all the time that had elapsed, it felt like we were two people who weren't really in a relationship anymore, two friends, perhaps, who found themselves having to bunk up after a night out in unfamiliar circumstances. It was noticeable that Laura took her nightie to the bathroom, which was something totally new. Normally, she had been comfortable stripping off in front of me. However, I didn't give it too much thought.

The sad thing about me was I still would have had sex with her, if it had been on offer. Turned on after such a tragedy. How shallow and one-dimensional was I?

She seemed to be smiling awkwardly as she sidled into bed alongside me and kissed me on the cheek before cuddling up to me. I put my arm around her. I wasn't sure what my feelings actually were deep down. To think that I had yearned for her return and now that it had happened, I was left in a state of numbness, wondering perhaps whether it was me now who needed to go away to think things through. At least I was going to sleep on it.

The next morning, I awoke to find myself once more in a half-empty bed. With last night's events still surrounded by a haze, I quickly shook off the dullness I felt, springing out of bed, wanting to see Laura's face again. The uncertainty faded. Realisation returned. Subconsciously, I was yearning for more than this, which might have been more of that male selfishness. Perhaps the reunion might have meant a passionate morning before rising, but that would have to wait.

Because of all the circumstances in this, my feelings at this point were paradoxical. I wanted to hold her in my arms, yet didn't feel the kind of closeness that made that appropriate. The basic man in me would have got to grips with her, no problem, but the state of mind of the husband in me, more sophisticated and thoughtful, needed to be freed from doubt and resentment.

I ventured down the stairs. In the kitchen, Laura was on the laptop.

"Hi, babe. You're up early."

She looked at me with an appreciative smile. "I know. I need to buy a few items of clothing. You know what I'm like. I'll need some money, babe."

"So has your taste in clothes changed much?"

She swung the laptop round to reveal a row of tops I had seen her wearing countless times. "Hardly. I still like good clothes. I probably still like the same foods too."

"But you didn't fancy staying in bed today? It's Saturday, you know."

"Must be the attack, babe." She got up and poured the dregs of her coffee into the sink. At least her figure hadn't changed. Just seeing her moving across the kitchen made my stomach knot though, just like it did before. In this particular situation, however, I calmed myself by anticipating that the actual sex would have be very disappointing, either a ten-second job or a pressured impotence. There was too much emotional history here, way too much commitment. There was still that massive elephant in the room, an elephant that was seated and seemingly implacable, and until I was happy with her reasoning and story, Nelly and her trunk were going nowhere.

I looked at the empty dishes on the floor. "Have you fed August?"

"No. Where is he?"

"Is he still outside?" I went to the back door and he came bounding in, looking up at Laura, probably still as astounded as me that she'd returned. He went underneath one of the chairs, looking up at her. While he did that, I filled his bowl and he sidled up for breakfast in true relaxed predator-fashion.

"Have you reacquainted yourself with him?"

"I gave him a cuddle and a stroke yesterday afternoon. I think he's forgotten me." She was accepting this with a fatalistic expression as if it was only to be expected. It probably was.

"Well, I'm sure that will change. You know how tight you and he were."

"Of course."

"What are we doing today?"

"Today?"

"It's our first day back together. Let's do something special. I need to know you again. We need to get back on track, you know. Relaxed with each other."

"Such as?"

"Well, we could drive out to the seaside, after we've visited George and Lillian. They'll be dying to see you."

She took hold of my hand. "I want to talk to you about this. Everything is a bit big for me, a bit immense, to tell the truth."

"It is for them too."

"I know. Do you mind if we leave seeing them for a few days though, while I get my bearings."

"OK, but they will be desperate to see you. They'll think I'm keeping you to myself."

"You've not told them, have you?"

"No. I thought that was your job. That was what you said last night."

She looked at me. "Oh yes. Oh, and Dom, the trips. Can you let me get used to being back before we go on any journeys anywhere? There are plenty of times when we can go to the seaside."

"OK. The beach can wait, I suppose." I sighed. I realized that normality in this house was not going to be any time soon. "But George and Lillian will still be dying to see you."

"Let me just get comfortable today, Dom. I think I need to speak to them on the phone first anyhow. They're old, and the shock of me turning up might not be healthy."

"They're not that bad." I wasn't going to argue the point, although both George and Lillian were good health personified. "So we just chill out here today, then." This felt like treading water to me but she might be right. Obviously, I wasn't going to bully Laura into hurrying to our normal relationship if she didn't want it yet. That would have to come from her. I would try to be patient, although partly I resented the way she seemed to be controlling everything.

"Well actually, babe, I need to go out this afternoon."

"Great. I'll come with you." I was doing my best to be a paragon of patience. Besides, doing some shopping together or visiting would be right on all levels.

"I need some me time, Dom. I have some shopping to do. Woman's stuff."

"Fair enough."

"Can I have your bank card? Believe it or not, the number is one thing I can remember."

She left the house early afternoon. I spent this time fiddling with things and reading bits of books, then reverted to watching a documentary about the Moors Murderers on TV. This was not the blissful Saturday I would have chosen, but I so wanted her to totally recover from her ordeal. Clearly, it was within the realms of possibility that she was still suffering some after-effects from that despicable attack. Who knew what an experience like that could do to somebody?"

She came back at eight o'clock. I stood in the living room doorway and had a prevailing sense of relief.

"I'm making a drink. Do you want one?"

"OK. Did you have a nice afternoon?"

"Just mooched around the shops and stuff, nothing special. To be honest, I did some thinking."

"Thinking?"

"Thinking about how horrible it must have been for you. You weren't to know anything. I wasn't much of a wife to put you through so much worry. I hope I can make it up to you." She filled the kettle and I watched her putting the coffee carefully into the cups. "Things will get back to normal in time. They will return to how they were. I'm sure of that. This marriage is everything to me, Dom. Manchester taught me that."

NOT QUITE PARADISE

The next day, things were weird. The bed was again empty when I awoke, although this time, when I went downstairs, she wasn't there. I heard some noise at the back door, and it became clear that August hadn't been let in or fed. Where was she? Did she think it was fair to go wandering off without telling me, after all that had happened?

A normal Sunday for me prior to Laura's return would have been to go to the pub and have five pints and a Sunday roast but now she was back, this pursuit seemed redundant so I decided to tough it out at home till she returned. I started by phoning Jamie. I hadn't spoken to him and he had listened to me for all those painful hours in my wifeless suffering. Now Laura had returned, and he should know.

"Hi Jamie. How are you?"

"Fucking fab. Been writing away, mate. This is going to be a fab book. You ever been in a clap clinic?"

"No! I'm not that careless. And anyway, for your information, the place is called a GUM clinic now." I was very knowledgeable when it came to sex it occasionally and was very vocal when it came to going 'bareback' without knowing her level of integrity. Jamie knew that.

"For your information? You're a twat sometimes. You don't fancy going to a clap or GUM clinic and getting tested, do you? Research for the book?"

"Bollocks to that. You can do it."

"OK, I will. Are we doing Sunday lunch?"

"Mate, I can't. I have to tell you, there's been a development. Laura's come home."

"What? You're joking!"

"No. She's here."

"What, she's at yours now? Let me welcome her home."

"No. She's not here right now. She's gone out, but she is home."

"That's incredible. Well, I'm made up for you mate."

The positivity did not feel right. "It's not that good. Got mixed feelings about it, to tell the truth. It feels strange, though I hate to say it."

"That's normal, after what happened. Where's she been all this time?"

I told him the story Laura had told me. He didn't respond to any of it apart from when I told him about the attack, when he just swore emphatically, although I wasn't sure he was accepting Laura's version of events. It was a bit far-fetched. His interest in my situation, however, was at odds with his writing aspirations. "You'll still help me with the book though?"

"What else have I got to do? Of course."

Laura returned home at about half past four, saying she had been in Meadowhall, and from there had gone to Castleton to have a long inspiring walk. "I wanted to enjoy some countryside. I just need to restore myself."

I had waited for her to return at any moment like a pathetic puppy dog. I was never comfortable with subservience, so this pained me. I had spent six hours today trying to be independent and not wanting to be dependent on this woman who, after all, had left me.

When she came in, I pretended that I had been busy doing what I wanted to do and did not betray any sign that my day had been influenced by her, laying out a relaxed smile and giving her an affectionate kiss on the cheek. I felt that if I conceded that I was dominated by her, I would regret it.

I was hoping that things were going to pick up soon.

BAN TAA

The politeness of staff in Thai restaurants is second to none and I always thought that civilisation could learn a lot from Thai restaurants and how they had everything sorted. Unhurried and smart, they tended to be, like I wanted to be too, although I always failed miserably in that area. Messy and stressed were terms that suited me more.

The Ban Taa Restaurant that we now found ourselves in was consistently pleasing. Laura had always referred to it as the Barn Tart, which I suppose reflected her sense of humour more than mine. Whenever we had eaten there, we had always found the food to be first class and service was always with a smile and that level of politeness and respect that sometimes we forget is important. Consequently, the place was always busy and to find yourselves at a decent table, you always had to book at least twenty-four hours in advance. The Thai artefacts and art and the staff all dressed in traditional Thai attire only served to add to the ambience. The toilets (always important, as far as this customer was concerned) were immaculate too.

Laura had been back home for several days now and those days had been quiet ones. She hadn't talked much in the house, which hadn't been much, as she had always been out driving somewhere, or visiting someone or somewhere, alongside almost daily trips to Meadowhall and Crystal Peaks for shopping. I initiated most conversations. Apart from the television and the computer, and the new iPhone I had bought her, she didn't seem to show any interest in anything, although I did catch her listening to some classical music, which was a new one for me. "Mahler is brilliant," she said.

"When did you start listening to classical."

"Always liked it."

"I never knew. You never even mentioned it before."

"Never told you."

"Perhaps we should go and listen to an orchestra sometime? Do you fancy that?" I sat down next to her on the settee.

"Shouldn't you be off now?"

"I'm not going. I've phoned in. Pulling a sickie, my sweet. We can do something together."

Laura had pulled a face at this news. "Why are you missing work, though? That's not good, Dom."

"I thought we could enjoy the day. Things haven't been all that good for us so far and they won't become good again unless we start trying. And that's both of us, not just me."

Laura had hung around for an hour, then had gone out. It was as if she had sneaked out, since I had only realized she had gone when I had heard her car engine starting up.

I had stayed away from work for nothing, hanging onto some desperate feeling that everything was going to be ok, that the planets of the universe were going to align themselves at some point soon in my favour. Love would conquer all eventually. However, doubts were building. Would Laura ever regain her old self so that things could be on course again? If not, we were in real trouble.

Perhaps tonight would be different, with that delicious Asian cuisine. It was a cold Sunday night, the kind of evening where a couple might rekindle old emotions through a familiar experience indoors. We had located ourselves in the corner in what was an intimate alcove.

I had a glass of JD and coke in my hand as I gazed into Laura's sweet eyes. Her hard-to-get strategy was really very sexy, I had to admit and at least we were together this evening, unless she suddenly decided to rush off somewhere, that was. Thankfully, Meadowhall was closed now. How good it would be to have her back properly, I couldn't help thinking. I had worked hard on schoolwork that day to free up this evening. "I'm having my usual. I don't need to look at the menu."

"I'm going to have duck." She gazed up at me, flashing that smile of hers.

"It's another change."

"How do you mean?"

"From the chicken and water chestnuts. Divine, you said last time."

"Well, you know, life is about variety, babe. I'm back, totally refreshed by my crazy amnesia. Ready to taste some of that variety that makes life interesting. I guess the reset button has been pressed."

"Sounds good to me. You know what I feel about variety." I tried to give her a flirtatious smile and she smiled back but she didn't seem like the Laura I had known. Perhaps I needed to press the reset button too, hopefully not repeatedly.

She closed her menu and placed it flat on the table in front of her like a novel she had just finished and took a sip from her glass of sweet white wine. She took her mobile phone from her handbag. "How long do you think the food will take to come?"

"I don't know. Usually takes about twenty minutes."

"You don't mind if I go through my Facebook do you? I don't want to seem ignorant."

"You back on it then?"

"Of course. You can't keep a good woman down. You don't mind?"

No, babe. Feel free."

I looked around the restaurant. What was I searching for? There were a range of couples and groups of varying ages. There were people laughing, having serious conversations, a couple looking into each other's eyes.

"We're usually like that."

"Like what, babe?"

"That couple. So into each other."

"Listen. I'm only on Facebook. I'll be all yours in a few minutes. I promise. Don't fuss so much."

"Hey, don't worry about it. After losing you for those months, I can cope with a bit of Facebook." Clearly, I was pretending, but sometimes pretending was crucial. Tonight it definitely was. I had to think more on the lines of test match cricket or chess and drop my football mentality. Patience and timing were the keys now, not passion. I wasn't sure where love was in all of this. I suppose it was waiting in the wings.

After about twenty minutes, not that I was counting, Laura put her phone away. She smiled disarmingly and within about two minutes the main course arrived. There were no words spoken during the meal and at no point did I remotely feel like the bloke in that cosy couple, but so what? My wife was back at least. The gap had to be bridged at some point.

When we got back to the house, I was all excitement and dared to anticipate. Would we consummate the return of our marriage? Would she come over all tender and needy, sexually demanding, like she used to be? I deeply hoped so.

Inside, Laura took her coat and mine and placed them on the coat hooks.

"I'll make us a couple of hot drinks." I said.

"Great. We can take them to bed with us to help us to sleep."

My heart sank a little. Clearly, passion wasn't that high on the agenda.

I brought the drinks to the bedroom. Laura was already in there. She was in a curled-up sleeping position, demonstrating how she wanted to nod off rather than develop things physically. Body language can be so tough. I placed the hot mug of hot black coffee on her bedside cabinet and got into bed. I couldn't feel anger, although I so wanted intimacy.

Within seconds she was out of bed. She had the red satin nightie on, the one that had never stayed on for long two months previously. "Bathroom".

She was in there for a while. When she came back, she placed her cup on the cabinet and got into bed. I immediately placed my arm around her.

She looked into my eyes and I knew the worst. "Let me sleep, babe."

* * *

In the morning, when I came down I discovered that Laura was going through papers relating to banking and credit cards, kept in a large red storage box behind the living room sofa. She calmly put the papers back. "I wanted to have a look at our finances, babe. I have something to tell you." I stood there, keen to hear what she had to say, praying that it was something positive.

She gestured to me to sit at the kitchen table. "I'm quitting the job."

"What?"

"I don't want to do it anymore."

"Why ever not?"

"It's just not me. Another reset change."

"But they've always been good to you and you've been so good at it."

"That's not always enough. We only have one lifetime."

"Why resign?"

"I want to do something else. It's boring, not me anymore."

"But we need the money. We can't keep this house, our lifestyle, without your money." That was definitely the case. Laura worked on commission, and because she was so good at selling paintings, she often made more money than me. That was a key feature of our relationship. The money she made was vital, funding our weekends away, as well as clothes and luxuries.

"What will you do? This is your profession."

"That's just it. I don't know."

"Well, don't resign yet. Have a long think about it."

"It's too late. I sent the email on Friday. I've finished, Dom. I'm not going back in."

"That's ridiculous. How are we going to live? Send another email, or go and see Max. He knows about your problems. He'll not want you to resign."

"I'm not going there again, not for anything. It won't be for long." She was wanting me to look away and show some acceptance. "Don't worry."

DAUGHTER DEAREST – A FAMILY PORTRAIT

She had put it off for several days. She just wasn't ready. She made an emotional phone fall first, to help her overcome her nervousness, she said. I could hear the loud expressive sounds from the other end of the line and it was arranged for Laura to go to their house the following evening. George had wanted to see her then but Laura had put them off, saying how tired she felt. She asked that I drive her there, which was unusual, but she expected to have an alcoholic drink and didn't want to risk anything. I had work to do for school and Laura's idea that I would drop her off suited me. Surprisingly, she said she would feel under more pressure if I was there as well, which I didn't fully understand but I went along with it.

"They'll appreciate you being back. He's been a mess without you. Just like I was." I stayed in the car long enough to see her knock on the front door. Why hadn't she just opened the door and walked in like she usually did? When I started up the car, she was being lovingly embraced in the doorway by her father with her mother behind him. I drove off feeling quite saintly.

Thirty marked books and four prepared lessons later, I heard the key in the door and Laura stepped into the hallway. She had a satisfied smile on her face as I greeted her with an offer of coffee. "Did it go well, then?" I asked her.

"Yes, babe. Very well. It was so good to see them. Their house too. I mean, their house is looking better than ever."

"Well, they do spend a lot on it. It was a palace when they bought it."

"I know it was."

"Was George pleased to see you?"

"Yes. Dad was delighted. Mum sort of was, but didn't show it as much as he did."

"She's probably holding back for your benefit. Lillian's usually as emotional as he is."

"I know that. I'm not an idiot.

A MOTHER'S RUIN

It was eight o'clock. I had just sat through the misery and predictability of Coronation Street, waiting for those dreary provincial closing titles when there was a knock at the door.

I encountered a perturbed-looking Lillian on the doorstep. "Why didn't you just come in? You don't have to knock."

"I need to talk to you."

"You do? Laura's out. Meeting up with an old school friend."

"I know. I texted her. It's you I need to speak to."

What was this about? I wasn't in the mood for any kind of reprimand or warning. Yet, that was more her husband's style than hers. Lillian always tried to keep the cart on its wheels. To be fair to her, Lillian had always given me the benefit of the doubt and, if the potential son she never had was putting it too strongly, she always seemed keen to keep me in the family.

"It's about Laura. I wasn't sure, but I had to come and see you."

Bewildered, I was all ears. "Please sit down. Would you like a drink?"

"No. I just need to talk to you."

This was very dramatic. I sat on the chair opposite her, feeling a tad uncomfortable. She was clearly nervous and I noticed she was trembling. Was it bad news? Had somebody died?

She looked at me, as if she was probing me for something mutual, for some sign of something that I couldn't figure out. "Laura…Well, she's not really Laura is she?"

"What do you mean?"

"Surely you've noticed. She's totally different. She was at ours for half an hour but that was enough for me."

"Half an hour? She must have been there longer than that. She didn't get back to mine until half nine."

Lillian raised her eyebrows slightly. "She must have gone somewhere else after. Her friend picked her up."

"A friend? Which friend?"

"She didn't say. She just said it was a friend."

"She never even mentioned a friend to me. I thought she was getting a taxi back to ours."

She's changed too much."

"Of course she has. She's been through a pretty bad ordeal."

"It's not just that." The grave expression wasn't going away, like this was the worst thing in the world for her. I wanted to help her in this, but at the same time I was curious.

"What are you thinking, Lillian?"

"That's not Laura. That's not my daughter."

I laughed. I knew from her deeply-troubled face that I shouldn't have done, but I always did the wrong thing at the wrong time. "Of course it's Laura. Who else could it be?"

"Dom, she's not right. Just not Laura. Everything she does, says and reacts to is different. It's as if she's a very good impersonator, but not quite the real thing."

"Come on. So she's a bit changed. It's hardly supernatural."

"There are too many things. The words she uses, the way she moves, the things she says. It's all not her."

"Of course it's her."

"No, Dominic. In fact, she says so little, when it comes down to it. She says the minimum."

"What does George think?"

"He just sees Laura. That is why I've come here. Do you not sense something?"

"It's her. I know she's different but we all know why. A brain injury can do terrible things to a person. Fred West became a mass murderer after a brain injury. All the things you're querying are down to that bloody attack."

"Yes. She told us about that. I'm not sure about that."

"We just need to help her on her road to recovery. She will get better."

It was like she hadn't been listening to me. "I was suspicious from the first second. She hugged me like a stranger. Differently. Call it a mother's intuition if you want. Just don't call it the demented hysteria of a mad old woman, because it's just too uncanny. She seems to remember so little from before her time away and everything she mentions or asks about is different, it seems to me. She walked in our house like she had never been here before."

"Again, that would be the amnesia. She's different. I will give you that. I'm having to deal with some changes myself but I think we just have to help her. It might take time, but we all have to help her to find herself. If I can do it, then surely you can."

She leaned forward. "Listen. I've known Laura from the day she was born. I know her totally, utterly, comprehensively. That's not her." At this point her eyes were as wide as they could be, like a facial exclamation mark.

"What do you mean from the day she was born? You adopted her from an agency. She walked into your arms."

Lillian was suddenly sheepish. She had said too much. I waited for her to continue and she knew she had to say more. She paused, then took a breath. "That's not the entire story. In fact, it's not the story at all. We adopted her from a woman who didn't want her. We cut some corners."

"What corners?"

" George knew people back then."

"What do you mean? Organised crime?"

"Yes, I suppose so. He had some pretty powerful friends who could arrange things. Most of them are dead now, but back then…"

"How did you get away with it? The hospital people would have had something to say, surely?"

"I delivered her. I even cut the umbilical cord myself. Her mother was really a kind of surrogate. She didn't want a baby. Was a bit of a low life, and we were desperate. George sorted out the paperwork, or lack of it."

I thought, then took a breath myself. "Well, I'm sure you've never regretted it."

She was staring at me, searchingly. "Do you really think that's Laura with amnesia or some mental condition?"

I nodded.

She looked at me as if I was somebody foreign, saying words she didn't understand. She paused for a while before speaking. "Ok. Hear this. I started talking to her about our holiday in Poole, the one when she was a teenager. I knew how much she loved that holiday and always regretted that we never went back there. I wanted her to mention the donkeys in the neighbouring field. They made a big impression on her."

"Yes, she told me about them. She named them after Disney characters."

Lillian laughed gently. "All she did was try to change the subject. In fact, she made several attempts. She didn't give me any of the memorable details of that holiday, the one she always said had meant so much to her."

"She's just forgotten stuff, Lillian."

"Yes, and that was when she got up to go. Her friend's car was outside. Said she had to go. Funny!"

That holiday in Poole was something she always liked to talk about. Laura must have become quite ill. It must have been some bump on the head.

A TRYING TIME

A week on from Lillian's unexpected visit, there was a gentle breeze today that refreshed, while the temperature was friendly. We had had what I thought was a wonderful early evening walk, and I tried to put the mother's notions behind me. It had been the same as it had always been. It was clear to me that that romantic connection we had had for so long was now returning, and both Laura and I were smiling as we returned to the car.

More than ever, I knew that Lillian was wrong in her struggle to accept the circumstances relating to Laura's return. My wife and I had held hands as we walked around the Dam Flask like we always had and I sensed that this was so much the Laura I knew and loved. I felt so sure that things were on the way back to how they had always been. I don't know much about psychology, but I was convinced that time would heal Laura's emotional wounds and her mother's fears would prove groundless. Emma, a former colleague of hers, had picked Laura up at her parents' and they had gone for a coffee before she had returned to mine. It was good that she was renewing acquaintances, a sign that she was returning to normality, even if she felt the need to go out very day and enjoy the city and its surroundings. A normal marital relationship was something that could not come soon enough for me.

In both my heart and head, I knew things would ultimately be resolved to everybody's delight. I was ever the optimist when I wasn't drinking.

"I'm going to take a bath. It's so muggy. I feel dirty."

"Shall I sit with you? We can talk about stuff."

"As long as you bring me a large vodka and orange."

While Laura sat back and soaked I sat on the toilet and we discussed plans for the weekend. " 'Mission Impossible' and Chiquito's it is then."

Laura, with her eyes closed, said, "I feel like a holiday."

"We talked about this before you went away. Where do you fancy?"

"I don't know." She looked so relaxed and at peace. "What do you think?"

"Sorrento probably. Loved that place."

"Why? That hotel was miles away from anywhere. And then there was the fight you had."

"What?"

"The fight you had." She paused. "With that German."

"What? I'm sorry, babe. I had no fight with anybody. What German?"

"The one who pushed in front of you in that queue."

"Where did you get that idea?

"What?"

"I think I would have remembered fighting. And with a German."

Laura paused, and kept her eyes closed. "Perhaps you were drunk. Perhaps you don't remember."

"No. I didn't get drunk that holiday. Not at any point during the ten days. Fighting with a German? You must be thinking about World War Two."

"I suppose I dreamed it."

I was puzzled. "You must have. You do have some interesting dreams, though. Have you had your recurring dream recently?"

"No. Just the normal ones."

"They're a funny thing, dreams. You wake up remembering what you dreamed about, but if you don't write them down, you often forget them. Perhaps you've had the dream but you've been forgetting it."

"Which one?

"The one. The killer one."

Laura sat up slightly. "No, I've not had that dream. In fact, I've even forgotten the details of it. Will you remind me?"

I told her the various details that she had told me and she had her eyes wide open. "It's just like you were saying. Dreams are easily forgotten unless you write them down. Refill my glass, will you, babe.

"My favourite holiday was Venice. I loved the buildings and the food. I thought it was superb. Anyway, why am I in this bath on my own? Get in with me."

After we had bathed together for long enough, chatting away like old times, we got out. I wrapped a bath towel around her and started to dry her. Straight away, she kissed me. Only a peck on the cheek, but it was enough. I gently pushed her out of the en-suite towards our double bed and she appeared to be welcoming it.

"What are you doing?"

"Making love to you. What do you think?"

She put her arms against me. "I'm thinking no way, not now. I don't want to."

"Why not?"

"Do you not understand anything? After all I've been through, I need time out. You have to give me more time, babe."

"It might help you though. It will help us. Make us both more relaxed."

I felt her eyes probing mine, looking for an answer. The only answer I could give her came from my sex drive. I was so turned on and she couldn't be unaware of the fact. "Go on then," she said. "Lie on the bed."

I lay down on the bed and watched as she dropped the towel and sat astride me. Before long she was gyrating vigorously, looking down at me as she did so, with aggressive contortions in her expression. She was squeezing and digging her nails into my upper arms and it was hurting but I wasn't going to let her know that and spoil this moment. She increased the speed of her movement and it was over for me very quickly. Straight away she jumped off me and hopped back into the bathroom to clean herself up. The whole thing had probably lasted no more than one and a half minutes and throughout it, Laura had made no sound.

There were now bloodstains on the duvet from what she had done to my arms, which were now featuring deep cuts that would need treating. I went down to get some plasters and antiseptic from the kitchen and applied both. It felt weird, plasters after sex.

She stayed in the bathroom for an hour. I got into bed and switched on the television to watch 'Stranger Things'. As the programme finished, Laura came into the bedroom and lay down as if to sleep, facing away from me.

"Do we need to talk about it, babe?" I asked.

"Yes, we do, but in the morning."

The sun was shining through the curtains to announce another warm day when she poked my arm, which hurt from the crazy sex the previous night.

"We do need to talk."

We were lying in bed, our bed. "What about, babe? I'm all ears."

"Sex."

I held up my wounded arms. "Do you mean these?"

"Well, yes. I'm sorry about that, but we need to talk about sex generally."

"What about it?" At this point I was full of hope that she would say the right things, give me something that would explain and assure.

"I'm not ready, Dom. Just not up to it at the moment. I think it's some kind of PTSD linked to the attack."

"OK. I see. But you have been back nearly two weeks."

"That's hardly any time. You need to be patient. Do you need a doctor to tell you this or something?"

"No. Of course not."

"It will pass, hopefully, but just not yet."

I shrugged my shoulders. "Babe, like I said, I can wait." Inside my heart was sinking. I was desperate to make love to her again, this time for a longer duration, more normally and less painfully, and I was praying she would feel the same way, knowing what she had been like before. I hadn't lost my intent to recapture past glory with this wife of mine, although I supposed timing was important. These things could not be rushed. Perhaps that was what we had done last night. Tried too early. That was why the whole thing had been so…different. That was why Laura had been upset in the bathroom for so long and why my arms were cut and bruised this morning. Or was I just fooling myself? Had everything been destroyed in Manchester?

"Anyway, I have some good news for you. You can do something good next Saturday. I'm going out."

"Oh yeah. Where?"

"A school reunion."

"Another one?

"Yes. Got a message on Facebook today."

"Ok, babe. That might be good for you. You need something to get you back on an even keel. Where's it at?"

"Some place in town. It's just a few of the people from school. Will probably be boring, but hopefully not." She looked so happy at the prospect, albeit nervous, as if she had been unsure about my reaction.

"Ok." I would go out too that night. Jamie would be receiving a text from me and the delay in Laura's return to normality would be softened for me by an alcoholic session with my budding author friend. I had some more of his chapters to talk through with him and he had a parcel for me. This time it wasn't a CD; it was a book about amnesia. My secret buying days were over, however, had been since her disappearance and remained so now that Laura had quit work. She had applied for several jobs, she had assured me, and was just waiting for news of an interview.

"You can have a free night. Have a drink."

* * *

It was early morning when Laura stepped into the bedroom. I had intended to wait up for her, but had fallen asleep watching 'Newsnight'. I had stayed in after all. Jamie was out on another date so hadn't been available. I had no other mates, and didn't want to go and sit in a pub on my own.

Groggily, I glanced at the clock. It was four thirty. I faced her as she undressed. "You're late. Where've you been?"

"Enjoying myself. I think I deserve it. Met up with some people I haven't seen in years. Dawn's pregnant and full of it. Gillian and Tracey were reminding me about this maths teacher we had who had a crush on me. Then there's Leoni. She's sweet but under a lot of pressure."

"Pressure?"

"She's lost her job, like me. Struggling to pay the rent."

"You didn't lose your job. You quit."

"Same difference. Anyway, I had a fantastic time. Went dancing."

"That's fab, babe. Just what you need."

MALEVOLENCE

Two things I have often tried to avoid. I don't have much time for male company and I've never liked computers. I have used them for this project quite a lot recently so I suppose I'm learning to live with them. I could never live with a man, with the stupid clumsiness and dirty habits. They're about one notch above dogs when it comes to sophistication and have all the imagination of stranded starfish. They are made to be taken advantage of then done away with in whatever way.

I'm typing a credit card application. It is my third this afternoon. They aren't in my name, of course, but a person like me is always on the lookout for more spending money and these should do it. This application is from a woman who died last week – I got some good information off a contact and can pick the card up from her empty house. I can do some excellent power-shopping then bury the card deep. No damage done.

As far as the big project goes, the bitch tried to wreck my plan by giving out a fake truth. A fucking German? Why did she say that? Pretty stupid, when you're at my mercy. If she was within reach right now, I would make her pay for that.

I see that that bitch Lillian has been stirring it. She was a problem from the very beginning, but I don't see her being a problem at the end, in all certainty. Something needs to happen though. I was thinking that she would be easy to overcome but perhaps I underestimated her. Perhaps I need to solve that problem soon.

REVELATION

I had met Jamie in the Wetherspoons near the hospital. He was in such high spirits that he might have floated over the hospital roof if I didn't keep him grounded. "Anyway, I'll be sending you the last three chapters in a few days. Once you've gone through my crazy prose, I'm going to publish it."

"Publish it? How?" I had helped Jamie with his writing, but thought it was just for fun, not for anybody else to read.

"Just have to send it off. Three hundred quid and I've got a cover. Professional too."

"Well, in that case you'd better send the whole lot back to me. I'll go through it again. If other people are going to be exposed to your filth, it's got to be written properly."

"People are going to want to read this in their droves."

"How are they?"

"Through Amazon. It's dead easy. I'm talking to some woman in America. 'Absolute Too Much', coming to your internet sometime soon."

"Wow. Big time or what!" I laughed, then paused. "They weren't from a fall." We were in the corner of the Crosspool

Tavern, which was busier than usual, as there had been some kind of cricket match on. Jamie and I were sitting in the corner and I needed to talk to someone.

"What?"

"You asked about the bruises. They weren't from falling."

"A fight?"

"Not exactly…Laura."

"You had a fight with her. Fuck off! You're kidding me, right?"

"Not a fight. Sex"

He grabbed my arm and pushed up my polo shirt sleeve. "Fucking hell, mate. They're terrible. I know you and she are kinky but you're a bit cut up there. Sex?"

"It's not right, is it? It's not normal."

"How did it happen?"

"She just grabbed and dug her nails in. She's stronger than I remember."

"I once got my hair pulled by a woman but nothing like that. You look like you've been savaged by a leopard."

"Things are bad. Laura's changed."

"How do you mean? A tiger in bed?"

"Not just that. Everything is just so empty. Everything good has gone. Half the time she doesn't speak. She sits opposite me at the breakfast table, but there are no words. I thought things were getting better last week, but in the past few days, everything's become so miserable."

"Perhaps she's not a mornings person anymore."

"I come home at night and it's the same. Most of the time there's no sex, not even any love and when there has been sex, and that's just the once, on that one occasion since she came back, it was ridiculous. Violent and hurried, like I was doing it with a violent psychopath. She ran away into the bathroom straight after and I didn't see her for an hour."

"That's hard. I guess she's been affected a lot by what happened."

"I was thinking the same thing, but now I'm not so sure. It's just so not right. She's not the same woman I married. Her mother thinks it's a different person."

"That's crazy. How can that be?"

"It can't be. It's Laura. When we go on our walks, she's the same as she always was. It's when we're at home. It's like she's changed some. Not her fault, but it's horrible. It's left me feeling so uncertain and I thought I'd been through the worst. Horrendous. All I do is pretend all the time that everything is ok and make pathetic excuses."

"Has she got a new job yet?"

"That's another thing. I don't even think she's looking for work. It's all bollocks. She even had me pick up her things from the gallery and I had to explain to Max, who was well pissed off. She's not even had the decency to speak to him, and he did so much for her. He was such a friend to her, gave her a job initially when he didn't really need her and trained her up. She's just stabbed him in the back. Just like she's stabbing me in the same place."

"What you going to do? The D-word?"

"No. Of course not. I can't end the marriage. It's everything. Things just need to change. I just don't know if the marriage can continue indefinitely with Laura like she is."

"What then?"

"I've got to just hope and give it time. I guess this is some kind of test. I still love her but I'm finding it so hard to like her the way she is right now. Besides, if I don't stick by her, who will?"

"She has her family."

"That's another thing. She doesn't. Lillian is already doubting her. She doesn't even think she's the real Laura, which is absolutely ridiculous. If she isn't, it's one hell of a doppelganger."

"Or else she has a twin?"

"No. Lillian adopted her at birth. She actually delivered her."

"She delivered her? How does that work? Deliver a baby and it's yours?"

"It was a bit of a back street adoption from the way Lillian told me. She and her husband paid a woman to be the surrogate but it was all done unofficially. Load of bollocks really. Could never happen now. Social Services would be all over it. Lillian doing the delivery meant that the baby didn't become official until Lillian filled in some forms and reshaped Laura's world with the help of her husband's influence. He used his connections."

"Connections?"

"He's fucking shady. Always was. He's so well-connected and can fix stuff. I think it's Freemasons, or something like that. Mobsters. He's painted for all those rich folks. They all have portraits by George in their best rooms. That's how he got that big house."

"Weird, if you ask me."

"I'll tell you something else that's weird. Poor August."

"Your cat?"

"Yes. He and Laura were bosom buddies before all this. Would you believe, I was actually jealous of that cat, with all the affection and cuddling it used to get. Now, she doesn't feed him, won't even have him on her knee. Work that one out. Says she's developed an allergy. How does that work?"

"Again, a bit weird."

"A bit weird? How can someone who loves animals turn against her pet?"

"What are you going to do?"

"Don't know. Probably just keep waiting for the old Laura to come back. Just hope it's not hopeless. It has to be worth it, I keep telling myself that. I can't count how many times. I think I'm just a soft bastard. Last night didn't help."

"Why?"

"We went to the Botanical Gardens. That was always a good place for us. It was a lovely night so I drove us up there. She didn't want to go, but I have to admit I pressured her. It seems like I need to pressure her more and more to do anything these days. She was talking about watching the TV, but I guess I made a bit of a song and dance about us being a couple who went out and did things, so she relented.

"Well we got there and we were walking down the main path. You know, the one that runs down the middle of the park, with all the benches running down the sides."

"I know where you mean. I had a date there a few weeks ago."

"Anyway, we were walking down there, towards where the squirrels all hang out, when this bloke ahead of us, to our left, supposedly reading a newspaper, sits up and says, 'Well fancy seeing you here.'"

"To you?"

"No. To Laura. Now Laura's reaction is the strangest thing. She immediately comes over all faint and tells me she needs to go back to the car. This is not part of my plan but this is my wife, so obviously I'm getting her back to the car. We turn around, and are on our way back. Behind me, I hear the bloke on the bench shout, "How are you doing, Jo Jo?" and she grabs at my hand to pull me forward with her. She wants away from there in a big way."

"That sounds a bit weird to me."

"A bit? Well, we're in the car and Laura goes all strange on me. I ask her who the man was and why he seems to know her, but she says he doesn't, that it's mistaken identity and that we should go home."

"Did you go home then?"

"Did I fuck. I had the car keys in my hand and nobody was going anywhere. I was back in the gardens and down that main path. She was calling after me, making a bit of a show of herself, but I wanted a word. The gobshite was already on his way towards the bottom entrance but I caught up with him.

"I was powered up, and he knew it. Out of breath, I was. "How is it that you know my wife?" I asked him.

"He laughed and said there was no way Jo Jo was my wife. I said she was my wife and her name was Laura. He went a bit coy, but I insisted, and he reckoned that Laura, my Laura, was Jo Jo, a prostitute in the Chesterfield area who hustled blokes. He told me he had spent some time with her and she had tried to rob him but he had been wise to her and had stopped her."

Jamie came alive. "Fucking hell! How did you react to that?"

"I asked him when he had known Jo Jo. He told me it was about three years ago, but she hadn't changed much. I knew that was impossible, since Laura and I had been together all that time and she wouldn't have had the time to go to Chesterfield. And as a prostitute? Well."

"Ridiculous. Did he say anything else?

"He asked me if I knew Lulu, Jo Jo's partner in crime. Obviously I didn't, as who the fuck was she? Laura has no friend by that name. He reckoned that the Jo Jo and Lulu he knew were well known in that town and not for good reasons. The idiot had become irrelevant.

One other thing. He said that Jo Jo, whoever she was, gave a great blow job and liked to dig her nails in, so I suppose in that way it could have been Laura."

"And what do you think, now. Mistaken identity?"

"Definitely. I was relieved on the way back to the car, glad that he hadn't known her this summer, because that would have really rocked my world. Laura looked scared when I got back, there, was waiting at the top of the path. Told me she was frightened that I was going to hit him."

"A bit weird."

"A bit weird."

LEONI

Surprisingly, I could hear voices as I entered the house.

This had been a tough day. A teenager had run out of one of my lessons with a knife, a very unusual occurrence at my place of work, and police had had to be called in to the school. It had left me somewhat stressed so I really wasn't too bothered about entertaining. I was wondering whether Laura had applied for any jobs. Money would be tight this month, with no second salary coming in, and we needed both of us working or my credit card bill was going to grow in an unhealthy way. I still couldn't help feeling sad that she had given up her job at the gallery. I was struggling with the whole idea that she could see a better alternative and why she would have wanted to quit a position like that, especially since she had loved that job so much for so long. Why leave a gift horse without even looking it in the mouth?

In the living room, Laura was sitting with somebody I didn't know. "Babe, this is Leoni, an old school friend of mine, the one I told you about."

I smiled at Leoni, taking in the important details, like her smile, her neat petite figure, brown curled hair and the pale face that suggested she needed to perhaps get out more or recover from some kind of illness. Then I remembered that this was the woman who had had it tough, losing her job and wondered if she wasn't eating properly. She was very attractive, I concluded, as any man would whose woman had denied him that essential pleasure for three months. She also had a familiar look about her. I had seen her somewhere before.

"Hello, Dominic. Pleased to meet you. Laura's told me all about you."

Was she wonderful or awful? She spoke in a high-pitched voice with a North Derbyshire accent and I felt almost like she was searching for answers to questions, but only for a short duration, as she scrutinized me before ultimately returning to a magazine she had resting on her lap.

I couldn't figure out where I had seen her before but knew I had to make this work. "I can't help thinking I've seen you somewhere before."

Laura broke in. "Leoni does gym where you go playing squash."

So that was where I had seen her. "I hope you're going to have a meal with us, Leoni," I said, as positively as I could muster, thinking that being kind to this woman might make me feel less bitter and frustrated about my domestic circumstances. Also, Leoni needed some support, by all accounts, and that smile she displayed suggested a nice, kind woman and I was usually a good judge of character. Another reason was that it would get me Brownie points with Laura, which had to be positive in the strains of our incomplete marriage. I had never even heard of this friend of Laura's before last week.

Leoni looked at Laura then agreed to stay. I offered to go and cook spaghetti bolognese and got up. As I left the living room, I heard a giggle behind me. I wasn't sure whether it was Laura or her new old best friend and I could only imagine what was so funny. Still, if Laura was amused by something, that wouldn't do her recovery any harm. Vainly, I thought it might be some sexual innuendo that would be helpful, but felt compelled to cast that idea aside as I went to cook.

An hour later, we were gathered round the dining table and tucking into food alongside what must have been a third bottle of Shiraz. I tried to keep the conversation as light-hearted as possible, if only to distract our visitor from her problems. "So what was Laura like at school? A typical teenager?"

Leoni looked at Laura before speaking and few seconds elapsed before words emerged. "She was just normal really. We were into fashion, make-up and stuff like that. Laura was good at lessons, always beat me in tests and exams."

"And were you there when she had the accident?"

Laura interrupted, looking at Leoni. "The car accident that gave me two broken legs. You missed that. Leoni didn't arrive at our school until Year Ten. It happened in Year Nine."

Leoni said, "We were together in art lessons. Even then, she was too much when it came to drawing and stuff like that. I guess that's how she got the job she had."

Laura was looking at her intently. I guess she didn't want the art gallery mentioning, as it was such a sore point as far as I was concerned, and she knew it. "Dom, tell Leoni about Sorrento and how good it was."

At that point I gave something of a monologue, with occasional support from Laura, who seemed to remember much more about this one of our holidays. "Pompei was a mega place. It just takes you back a thousand years to how the Romans lived and what their houses were like."

"And the skeletons, Dom. The corpses."

"Yes, they were quite moving, especially the ones at Herculaneum, where there are really sad skeletons of people who had died waiting for a boat to pick them up. And the brothel! It makes it crystal clear how sexually orientated they were."

Leoni spoke. "That would be just the men though. Dirty bastards. The women would be victims."

"I don't know."

"It would be. And it's not changed much. Women are still victims. Men are still the problem."

"Not all men, and not all women." I looked at Laura, hoping for a positive response or a reassuring smile at least, but all she displayed was deadpan. Sit on the fence if you must, I thought.

"Most." Leoni had a serious look on her face. "Most men, anyway."

I wasn't going to debate the subject. I felt some discomfort towards her now, though, so I tried to change the subject. "Do you think this wine is OK. It was a two-for-one deal." I wasn't a big fan of the red stuff but didn't mind it so much when pasta or spaghetti was involved. Funny how eccentric the taste buds can be.

The wine was ok. Leoni stayed for a couple of hours after, and I left the two of them playing CDs and chatting about stuff while I went upstairs.

I heard the living room door close. I suppose they needed a confidential chat. There was a time for girls talk and this was probably it, especially with the problems the two women were having. Perhaps they would both encourage each other to find work. Leoni had been a director's secretary for a large paint manufacturer and had said at the dining table that she was looking for a similar post somewhere else.

It was nine o'clock. "Dom, Leoni's leaving."

I gave her a hug and told her I was hoping to see her soon.

"No doubt you will," said Laura, with an ominous smile at Leoni as she ushered her outside and closed the door behind her. She must have seen Leoni to the Uber vehicle that would have been waiting outside. Laura was a caring woman and this was her friend.

There was no doubt about it though. Leoni's voice would be irritating with prolonged exposure.

MALEVOLENCE

I watched a bird picking at a slug yesterday. I watched intently as the beak pulled away at the outer covering of the creature before piercing the body of the tiny repulsive being, whose slime trail could not save it on this occasion. Does a slug have feelings? Does it have a right to feelings? I found fascination in it all. I loved how the bird felt around for a while, testing the environment, before it pushed its beak further and further into the soft meat of the dead slimy creature that was so soft to the touch of the hard pointed mouth of the predator.

That's the trouble with prey. They are always too soft. All my victims, ever since I was a teenager, breaking hearts and ripping off arseholes, forging signatures and stealing wallets, with the occasional attacking and killing, have been soft and stupid. They sometimes pretend not to be vulnerable but then have no real way of fighting back or resisting. There are too many who try to show a strong side but too often it is just a thin covering for their need to suffer. I hate veneers. Take the tortoise. It looks like a really tough creature with its supposedly thick shell, but that covering counts for nothing when the eagle takes it high then smashes it on the rocks, before satisfying its hunger and feeding its babies.

This Dominic is about as soft as any slug or tortoise I have ever seen. His stupidity is legend. The new Laura has him all over the place and he is so deluded and accepting that she can basically get away with anything she wants. She won't even be sleeping with him anymore by the look of things, so things for him are going to become even more desperate. He just can't take it. Sadly, his decline is proceeding and the end is coming. I'm shortening the timescale of this project. It's boring.

Not only that. What happened in that park the other night also suggests that my timings have to change. This is not going to run and run, as it is more risky than I thought. If I am honest with myself, my aims in all this have shifted. My aim initially was to settle for a while, gradually building things up, but now I'm not thinking that. I'm too impatient. I reckon money-wise I can be sitting pretty much more quickly. I just have to carry on thinking, and strike at the right time.

UNDERSTANDING?

Things carried on. For the past week, things were pretty dull. I arrived home from work every day with the same anxiety that was my life these days. Sometimes I returned to an empty house and would while away my time in a solitary fashion, usually trying to create an upbeat mood with music. I would try to enjoy songs, for me all too often the deep emotion of Noel Gallagher, the assertiveness of Eminem or the singalong rebellion of Green Day, while nursing a cup of milky coffee or something stronger. I always wanted to find a positive mood then hold onto it.

At other times, I would find the television to be dominant. Laura, on the rare occasions when she was home, might be sitting on the sofa eating nuts or crisps. Actually, I found these arrivals home more difficult, since she was showing all the signs of somebody without direction, like she had no interest in anything anymore, including us. I was pushing myself to remain unselfish, to keep the sympathy and empathy going while there was a chance of recovery but this was becoming so much the long shot, requiring much more in the way of patience than I had ever had. Affection, energy and sex were staples for me and, however much I tried, I was kidding myself if I thought I could become Mother Teresa or Gandhi. I needed more! I had always been seen by fellow university students as selfish. These days, I was biting my tongue, gritting my teeth, strenuously pushing the physical and emotional frustration out of my mind.

Of course, the big question was, could a man survive without affection or intimacy, and for how long? Laura wanted so little of the former, and none of the latter, so what was I going to do? However, I also realized there were things worth fighting for, things worth holding onto as they were necessary to our lives. Things like trust and shared experiences. Deep down, I felt I could go without some stuff for a while if it helped. I hoped Laura would do her bit too.

On this occasion, I could hear a tap running in the bathroom so, realising that I wasn't really going to be able to relax totally downstairs, I decided to sweep up the leaves outside. The summer was over and nature was now littering the landscape. As I swept and mused about things, I watched as the familiar blue BMW entered the cul-de-sac and parked outside.

I waved to them and went into the house. I shouted up the stairs, "Babe, your parents are here." More than ever, I wanted Laura and Lillian in the same room. I wanted to see the dynamics when they met again, especially after what Lillian had said.

There was a delay in replying before she said. "Tell them I'm busy in the bath. I'll see them at the weekend."

"Can't do that. Your dad will think I'm being manipulative and controlling. No chance."

"Shit. Don't be a twat!" Her voice was as sharp as a steak knife, like she felt I was hurting her so she had to hurt me back.

"Just throw something on and get down here. I'll be the hospitality for a few minutes, then you can take over."

As they came in, Lillian led the way, furtively indicating to me that I wasn't to mention her last visit here.

I'd figured that anyway. "Would you two like a drink?"

"Cup of tea will be nice for me," George replied. "We're just here to see how Laura is. Wanted to check that she was OK."

We had been sitting in the living room for about ten minutes when Laura finally emerged, hair still wet, clothed in a black T-shirt and blue shorts. "Hi," she said with apparent confidence, with a broad smile on her face that contradicted her earlier reaction from the bathroom, as in turn she hugged her father then her mother. I noticed that the latter kept her arms firmly at her sides. Lillian still doubted then, even if she was wrong.

"How are you, girl?" George was all smiles.

"Getting better, Dad. At least I hope so. That's right, Dom, isn't it?"

I nodded, but I wasn't sure why. Things were pretty shit, if I'd had the guts to be honest.

"And how's the job hunting going? Dom told us you quit the gallery."

I watched, as Laura went on the defensive. "Jobhunting's going ok. Not found the right job yet."

"You don't need me to tell you this but I'm going to say it anyway. Perhaps you should have carried on working until you found the job you wanted."

"Oh, really? Well you're not me, Dad."

"Have to say, it was a bit of shock. Thought you loved that job."

"No. Not anymore."

Lillian wasn't saying anything. She was just looking at Laura, tension etched on her brow, studying every reaction, probably every detail. Her scrutiny was making me uncomfortable, never mind Laura.

August made an appearance. He sprang up onto the sofa and made his way onto Laura's knee. In front of all of us, Laura abruptly swept him onto the carpet, probably making the poor fellow feel unwanted, and in a way that I knew was the total antithesis of how she used to be. I loved August and I loved Laura, so what could I do?

Lillian looked at me, with her eyebrows raised, but only for an instant. She turned her attention back to Laura. "I have to tell you about Mrs. Kelly."

"Who's that?" I asked.

"Laura, tell Dom about Mrs. Kelly."

Laura made an evasive hand gesture. "Dom doesn't want to know about Mrs. Kelly."

"Of course he does. She's funny."

"Well, I don't want to talk about her. The last time I spoke to her she wasn't nice."

"When was that?"

"About a year ago. Outside her house."

Lillian carried on. "OK, Laura, do you know, for a moment there you reminded me of when you had that tantrum over school uniform? Do you remember?"

"Of course I do. I went mad. School uniform is pretty horrible though."

"That's interesting. Laura, you never had a tantrum over school uniform. What's going on here? Mrs. Kelly died in an old people's home last week. Her daughter told me. She's not been anywhere near her house in eighteen months. Alzheimer's."

Laura scowled. "I've got amnesia, for fuck's sake. I don't remember things properly."

"Laura!" I think George and I spoke at exactly the same time.

George reacted first. "You can't speak to your mother like that."

202

"I'm just trying to explain myself. Can't I do that? Against the law?"

"You're being mean. After all we've done for you."

"What you've done for me! What I've done for you, you mean. Got yourself a neat little daughter that you virtually stole."

"How can you say that? How can you speak like that?" George spoke with such a pained voice, like his soul was being ripped apart by a daughter I didn't recognise as my wife. I actually felt for this man who had been so hostile to me, justifiably, for over a year.

"Well, I can't remember a lot of things and you're not helping. Especially you, Mum." She looked across to me. "Support me here, Dom."

I could barely believe this. "What? Why don't you just explain things without being horrible?"

"Well, fuck you too. I'm off." With all the petulance of a teenager, behaviour I had never imagined before in this house, she grabbed her car keys and left the room, shouting as she went, "And don't come here again unannounced like this. Fucking winding me up. I'm not having it. Stay away till I'm better."

"Within seconds, from the silent living room, we heard screeching tyres and Laura was out of the cul de sac before George had reached for his jacket. I had never seen him looking so affected, so much so that any previous animosity on my part had dissipated, and I wasn't sure whether his wife was puzzled, angry, miserable or a combination of all three.

TIMES-A-CHANGING

We didn't speak again that night. I had tried to cope with the strangeness of it all and had wanted to bury my head in the pillows to find unconsciousness as soon as possible. It hadn't worked. I was too disturbed by the evening's events and was wide awake when Laura returned sometime in the early hours of the following morning and, with discretion being the better part of valour, I decided to let her mull over how ridiculous she had been. I pretended to be fast asleep. It was just as well that I heard her settle in the guest bedroom, so that I could mull over everything.

However, the following evening, Laura was surprisingly defiant. I was in the bath trying to relax when she walked in. She plonked herself down on the toilet seat and looked ahead at a spot somewhere above my head and below the ceiling. "I'm making a request and it's important. I'm saying it because it's vital if I am going to be well again. First of all, I don't want my parents at this house again, not until my memory properly comes back. I need to recover, and they don't help."

I felt forced to respond, defending a couple who perhaps might not have defended me quite as much. "That's not fair."

"You have to tell them, or I'm leaving tonight. I'll sleep on the streets if I have to." She pointed a finger towards the outside and towards an imaginary street. "You'll never see me again."

"You were so out of order, though. You didn't have to speak to her like that."

"She pushed me. She went too far. She's jealous of Dad's feelings for me so she wants to make me seem false and worthless."

"Well, I think you managed that yourself. You've some apologising to do."

"It will be a cold day in hell."

"Well, hell will be what you're left with if you don't realise how important your parents and I are to you. For God's sake, we're the only people who deeply care about you."

"Why are you bringing yourself into this? Why is it always about you? Why is everything about you?"

"Nothing is about me, clearly."

"What does that mean?"

"Well, babe, you aren't much of a wife to me these days. We hardly talk or go out and all too often I don't even know where you are."

"Are you bullying me again? Last time we were in this bathroom together you were a bully."

"Bullying you? How?"

"Wanting me to have sex and sulking like a five-year-old because I'm not up to it. You've got to stop this. This is abuse. I could have you removed from this house if you abuse me like this. I can go to the police."

The way she looked at me was shocking. "But I'm not abusing you."

"I'm fed up of this shit. And I'm fed up of you." For the second time in a few days she decided upon a dramatic exit. I heard a door slam and the Audi was on the move again.

She came back a couple of hours later. Having bathed, I had chosen to dirty my insides with a few JD's, probably because of the stress, which was what usually happened with me. I was always partial when any kind of emotions were involved, negative or positive. I was sitting in my Wednesday dressing gown when the car pulled up outside.

Laura sat down close to me on the sofa and faced me.

"I'm really sorry, babe. I don't know what came over me. I think it's loneliness and frustration at not getting better, but I have an idea."

"I'm all ears."

"Let Leoni move in for a while."

"Leoni? Why Leoni?"

"She's good for me and she needs somewhere to live. She can sleep in the spare room."

"What? Aren't I company enough for you?"

"It's not the same. Not right now. Besides, Leoni's in a bad situation. We'll be helping her."

I sat and thought for a whole two minutes. "No, Laura. That's a step too far. Things are hard enough for me as it is."

"In that case I'm leaving tonight." She stood up, staring down at me with a severe expression cutting through her face. "And I tell you this. Once I've gone, I won't be coming back. Not ever." She left to go upstairs and I heard the sound of a suitcase being taken down from the top of our wardrobe. I sat there thinking. How had things come to this? We had gone from total love and kindness to defiance, threats and a growing number of puzzling details.

I was in no doubt that she would carry out her threat to leave. She was ill. I would be here alone again, confused and miserable, pitied and probably ridiculed behind my back. I would be drinking heavily. I hadn't been happy recently but that was because I was trying to cope with her illness and how that illness was affecting things. Things would spiral out of control if she left now. I went upstairs to our bedroom, where Laura was purposefully filling an already half-packed case.

"OK, she can stay, but just for a couple of weeks, while she gets sorted."

"Thanks, sweetie." She dropped a jumper onto the bed and put her arms around me. "Things will work out in the long term. I promise. Have no doubt."

I was very doubtful.

MALEVOLENCE

After three weeks of the project going live, I'm starting to enjoy myself. I actually think this whole thing is making me smarter, calmer and more calculating as I work things out totally to my advantage. Of course, I don't have to be that smart to outsmart this dummy, who knows as much about people as I know about nuclear physics. Like any pushover, he deserves all he gets.

There are a few loose ends. They need sorting. Arrangements have been made.

Actually, it has all gone better than I expected. I expected the occasional slip-ups or hitch, but there have been none.

As far as this jigsaw of mine goes, I have just a few pieces to put into place and then the plan will be complete and I'm taking everything. I was prepared to give him a chance, see if he could function under the new circumstances, but he clearly can't. All he does each day is make me despise him more and that will never do.

Oh, and I'm fed up of that fucking cat.

A CAT'S TALE

"What's happened to August." I was concerned. I loved that cat like I hadn't expected to do. His food was still there from the previous night and it was early evening. Normally, the cat had a healthy appetite and never missed a mealtime.

"I don't know." Laura was sitting texting on her mobile phone. She didn't even look up at the thought of her beloved August not being around suddenly.

"Did you feed him yesterday?"

"Probably. I think so."

"When was the last time you saw him in the house?"

"A couple of days ago. Is this an interrogation, Dom?"

"I'm just worried. It's not like him. And this is not like you… Have you looked for him?"

"Hardly. I'm allergic to him. Remember?"

"He's still our pet. He's for life. You always used to say that. Remember?"

Laura waved her arm dismissively. "He'll come back. They always do. They're like bad pennies. He'd have to be dead not to."

For some reason, I felt a chill up my spine as she said that final sentence. I detected a total lack of care or concern.

Laura looked up from her device, suddenly discovering a conversation topic that was meaningful to her. "Leoni's moving her stuff in. I'm going to pick her up at about nine. Make an effort."

"What do you mean? Moving in today?"

"Today. Pretty soon."

"I thought it was in a week or two. Shouldn't we have talked about this first?"

"Yes. We should. But we didn't, and she's coming. Make her feel welcome. You know how you say you love me. This is how you can show it." She gave a knowing smile. "You never know, it might make a massive difference." She winked at me.

Hours later, I was still thinking about August. I went down the garden and called him. Normally, he was very good at responding to being called. It wasn't usually straight away like it would have been with a dog, but he usually appeared within a couple of minutes.

I shouted his name repeatedly. The trees in the next garden looked down contemptuously and the fence was unmoved. There was no sign of him. I went around the front of the house but again it was to no avail. Where had he gone?

* * *

Leoni had two grey suitcases with her, which she took upstairs to the guest bedroom, barely muttering a hello to me as she effectively intruded on our privacy. Laura was with her for the rest of the evening, and they came back down and into the living room while I was in the middle of a police show on one of the American Channels. I was ensconced on the end of the sofa and they filled the rest of the long seat.

They were quiet, but the tension they brought into the room with them made me uncomfortable. I sensed they were instantly in a conspiracy against me. Was I being paranoid? Maybe I was, but I couldn't help feeling that Leoni moving in wasn't going to help my deteriorating marriage in the slightest. I had been a fool and wondered how much worse things were going to become.

I decided I didn't need to find out who the killer was and stood up. Significantly, I now knew that I was better off somewhere else, that being up close to this pair and this toxic silence would only make me irritated and uncomfortable. Yet neither of them had actually said anything untoward. Perhaps it was their lack of communication that communicated everything. The Laura I had loved would have held my hand.

At this moment, there was one thing I knew. If Laura threatened to leave a third time, I would agree to it. A costly divorce was preferable to a crap home life, which was exactly what had happened to my circumstances here. Pretty much total shit.

A latecomer to the party, I would have to be tougher. Much tougher.

REMEMBERING

Jamie was excited as he sat across from me in our kitchen. Laura had answered the door and I had heard the two of them laughing as he had come in. This was more like the old days. Weird! If it only could have been a sign that things were going to improve, that I would once again find myself in a relationship worth caring about. I was skeptical.

On the other hand, my mate was really excited about his writing these days. I was enjoying helping him, if only as a positive distraction, and although it was hardly quality writing, it would be quite a fun read for the right kind of reader, I thought. Between us, we had certainly put in enough jokes.

"It's coming on fine," he said. "Just written a bombshell of a chapter, all about Amsterdam. You're not going to believe it when you see it. It just needs few of your master writing touches, but it already looks like a strong part of the book."

"So it's a book now, not just a manuscript?"

"It's always been a book. Thinking big, mate. It's just about complete."

"Complete already?"

"I've put in loads of hours. I was up all night two nights ago. Besides, some of the chapters just write themselves. Recounting my adventures."

"It can't be much good if it's almost complete. They always need rewriting a few times."

"Give over. It's a right laugh, man."

We both laughed simultaneously as Leoni walked into the kitchen and Jamie stopped. His body language changed and he was immediately puzzled and clearly ill-at-ease. He had looked at her intently, then at me. My first thought was that he fancied her. I had been through this with him so many times, so I therefore did the necessary introducing. However, I wanted to continue talking to him about the writing. I wanted to find out more about how he was going to publish the damned thing,

He didn't. His eyes were fixed on her as she filled the kettle and spooned coffee into two. He seemed to be relieved when she'd gone back into the living room.

"What's she doing here?"

"She's living here at the moment. Going through a rough time. She's been here a week"

"Why?"

"Weren't you listening? She's Laura's old school friend."

He looked at me in disbelief. "Don't you recognise her, dafthead?"

"Recognise her? From what?"

"You pulled her."

"What?" Was he delusional?

"That's right, bucko. You pulled that woman."

"What do you mean, I pulled her? When?" In my mind, I was scanning through all the women I had been with in the past thirty years. The image of Leoni never appeared.

"She was the one you were chatting up, you know, in Jester's when you were wasted. Was it six, seven weeks ago? Blonde hair, more make-up and she wore glasses then. She was the one you shagged at my house. Don't you remember?"

"Not really. I was wasted that night."

"She was the one who came onto you big time. She wore a lot of make-up that night, had blonde hair, spoke posh then, but it's definitely her."

"It can't be. Not possible."

"Listen, Dom, I wasn't drinking like you that night. I know who we pulled. This bird, Leoni. You definitely were with her that night."

TENSIONS

Of course, I didn't sleep. I had got into bed facing away from Laura and had just dwelled on things all night. I just had to lay there, waiting for the daylight to return. I would be exhausted at work the next day but there was nothing I could do about it.

After that bombshell of a conversation, the shock had stopped me enjoying Jamie's writing endeavor. My horror continued to grow after I had shown Jamie out through the front door, and we both knew as he turned to go down the path that he was leaving me in something of a predicament. If Leoni had been with me that night, what the hell was she doing now living in my house? Clearly, there wasn't much left of our marriage, it seemed, but this threatened to finish it off totally. Pretence seemed to be encompassing the entire house now. I probably wasn't the only one acting.

I had made a point of looking Leoni in the eye as I spoke to her about me cooking something special the next day. She didn't flicker, no sign of concern or anxiety at all. It made me think that nothing had happened between her and me, unless she was just one cold, calculating bitch. On the other hand, she might have forgotten the night we had or hadn't had, just like me. I couldn't remember anything, and certainly had no idea of the condition she had been in.

If Leoni let Laura know what had happened, she would leave me, I was sure. Things were too strained. That time last year, we had been stronger, more together as a couple. However, would I really care if she got up and left? That was difficult to ascertain, since all my positive feelings were now rooted in the past and there was so little now for me to feel hopeful about. Separation now seemed to be inevitable. I had been hoping that things could return to how they were, but that was becoming some kind of pipe dream. Sex had gone. Love was in its dying embers. Any belief I had was fading. All I really wanted now was control over things, but Leoni's presence here threatened that.

Could Jamie have been wrong? I didn't remember Leoni and, surely, even in a drunken state, she would have made some impression on me. He had had a drink or two as well, after all, so perhaps his memory wasn't hundred per cent reliable. I still found his claim disturbing and was unable to dismiss it totally. In a city the size of this, was such a coincidence possible, or was something much more sinister going on? I had read books like this, too many of them, and had read no end of conspiracy stories, as well as watching crime shows on TV where a woman links up with somebody outside the marriage, followed by devastating consequences.

Stop it, Dom, I told myself. My imagination was starting to run away with itself. Before I knew it, in my mind they would be planning my assassination and the subsequent cover-up. This was hardly going to be a body-under-the-patio situation.

Two days later, I went into the kitchen, where Laura and Leoni were seated next to each other, both with mobile phones in their hands and both intent on their screens, with Leoni clearly playing some kind of word game. Possibly not her only game, I thought.

As so often happened, I felt a clear change in mood as I entered. They smiled at me, but I felt they were very much adapting to my presence. I wasn't sure what to make of it, but I was sensitive to the difference. Was Leoni being here at all related to the fact I had slept with her and, worse, did Laura already know about it? As if in response, Leoni looked up at me and it was as if she had never seen me before. This might mean I was in the clear as far as exposure was concerned. If I really cared.

The following night, I emerged downstairs from a much-needed shower to find Laura and Leoni sitting next to each other on the settee watching one of those wildlife documentaries that they were both into. They were always together. I noticed that Leoni's feet were resting on Laura's and it seemed a bit intimate, but they were women and their gender was always more touchy-feely than men. Anyway, what would I have gained from questioning it? Again, I sensed that they became alert and aware as I walked in. Like so many times before, I felt like an unwelcome intruder in my own house.

I picked up my laptop, opting to prepare lessons rather than watch some lion having a zebra for lunch. As I did so, I couldn't help noticing the two women glance at each other and my paranoid state made me wonder what they were communicating to each other. Were they agreeing that I was a nerd or geek or worse? Were they expressing disappointment that I had come into the room? I had no idea really. I was beginning to wonder about their connection to each other. I was realizing more and more that I needed an exit strategy from this horrendous scenario.

I looked up at them from the defensive wall of Hewlett-Packard and shot a bolt across the bows. "Where exactly did you two first meet?"

"History," Laura said. "We sat next to each other."

"You both seem pretty close. Did you spend much time at each other's houses?"

"No," Laura replied. "Leoni lived quite a distance away from me. We only saw each other at school."

"Yes," Leoni said. "I was a bit of a loner at school to tell the truth. It's so lovely that we are able to spend time together now, and I'm grateful to you for that, Dom."

"Actually that's great. I'm doing some work on perspective with my Year Ten class. You two can help me. The kids love anecdotes. I want you each to write me the story of your friendship. The history of you knowing each other. It will be fantastic for my students to read how two people can be separated yet return to become brilliant friends."

"What?" Laura said.

"I would love you each to write about your history with each other. I want to use it in a lesson."

Laura's face became contorted. 'We're doing nothing like that. What are you thinking?"

"It's a great story. Let's write it."

"I guess we could put something together, with us both putting our memories together. I guess we could do that. Leave it with me, babe."

That was the first time she had called me 'babe' in Leoni's presence. It even seemed to come out awkwardly as she said it. "No." I smiled, although I hoped there was no mischievous glint in my eyes. "Do it separately. Could you do it now? We have two computers. Or would one of you prefer a pen and paper?

Laura's face had reddened. "Why don't you write it, Dom? Write your own fucking lesson. It's your job."

"But it would help me, babe."

Her face had hardened again. "We're writing nothing. School for us was ages ago and memories have faded."

"That won't matter. In essence, it will be true."

"Essence be fucked. Whatever we write won't be as it was." As she said these words, the charge of emotion seemed to be overwhelming and the anger that lit up her face was disproportionate. She nudged Leoni, and, simultaneously, they left the room. Then came the repeated thuds of them heading upstairs.

I had touched a nerve. I needed to talk to Lillian.

A STEADY UNFOLDING

It was three in the morning when we were dramatically awakened by some sharp knocking on the window of the front door. Laura's space in the bed was empty. I had heard the front door open at about One, so I presumed she was in the bathroom, or even downstairs with her modified body clock and new passion for twenty-four hour television. Upstairs it was pitch black, and when I turned on the light, I felt like I was being attacked by the painful stabbing glow of the light bulb.

This was silly o'clock, hours before even the birds would be making their feelings known. Bleary-eyed and half-awake, wondering what this was about, I clumsily made my way downstairs, and I could see the outline of somebody in a uniform outside.

I opened the door to let the cool autumn breeze into the house.

"Hello. Is this the home of Laura Walker?" A man in a raincoat with a grim expression on his face to match his deep voice was standing there with a youngish woman in a police uniform alongside him. The thought hit me straight away. Someone had clearly died or was badly hurt.

"It is. I'm her husband. Can I help you?"

"Is she here?' I'm Detective Sergeant Richardson, South Yorkshire Police. This is my colleague, WPC Hawkins. We need to speak to her urgently, I'm afraid."

Reluctantly but necessarily, I was about to rush up to fetch her, but she was already arriving at the bottom of the stairs, as awake as I had been, and I sensed that the wonderful Leoni was irritatingly not too far behind her, like the appendage she was.

"What is it?" she asked the detective, and at that moment neither officer looked as if they were capable of cracking a smile without their faces falling apart.

"I'm afraid we have some bad news. Do you have any strong drink in the house?"

We ushered the officers into our living room. I allowed Laura to take over, since it was she they had asked for. The sweet Leoni sat on a chair, watching for the bad news like a morbid spectator. I was developing an urge to strangle her that grew day by day but I was so far managing to control that impulse.

The officer spoke and looked at me and repeated himself. "If you have any, a whisky or a brandy might be a good idea."

"I guess so. We have JD in the cupboard."

"Well, would you please pour a couple of drinks for your wife and yourself. We have bad news."

With drinks served, the officer stood next to the fireplace while the WPC sat in a chair. I looked at Laura, who had Leoni leaning against her like a dependent child. "I need to confirm that your parents are George and Lillian Stewart of Cleveland Rise, Mansfield?"

"That's right," Laura replied. I could see fear in her face.

"I'm afraid I have to tell you that they were found dead in their car in the early hours of this morning. Well, yesterday morning."

"Dead? How?" Laura clearly couldn't speak. I moved next to the end of the sofa to hold her hand.

"I'm afraid it's foul play. Everything suggests that they were murdered. They were found on a country lane on the outskirts of Mansfield with multiple stab wounds."

I was stunned. This was unthinkable. Murder was a rare occurrence, and even then, it was usually undesirables killing undesirables, often with drugs or robbery as the motivation. I had always felt secure and safe in our part of the world. The UK was relatively safe. George and Lillian were hardly undesirables, even if he did have some shady connections. Was it about money?

Yesterday morning? I had been heavily asleep alongside Laura, and it seemed ironic that I could sleep so solidly while they were being slaughtered.

He continued. "They were on this lane and it was there that for some reason they stopped their car and were killed. I'm sorry to have to tell you this. Obviously, this is now a murder investigation. I have to prepare you for the inevitable, I'm afraid, as far as the media is concerned. Also, this is going to be a news item within the next two hours. I'm afraid those wheels were set in motion the moment Lillian's brother identified them."

Laura couldn't speak. I could. "Who will have done this? What kind of scum would kill people who harmed no one."

He looked at Laura first, then at me. "At this point, we just don't know. Don't get me wrong, I'm confident we will find the killers but it always takes some time, I'm afraid. We just need some information from you people."

At that moment, I realised that I'd actually liked that couple, that my negativity towards George had been misplaced, since all he had done was be a caring dad, the kind of dad I was going to be one day, the kind my own father had been. I spoke and tried to sound like I was up to it, since I knew Laura would be too devastated to say anything. All she could do was sit there staring into space and I knew I would need me to be strong for her. I made my attitude clear to the detective, saying, "Obviously, we'll do anything to help."

The questioning took place without formality and we sat together while each of us replied. All the detective could do was ask some questions about George and Lillian's lifestyle and their acquaintances and associates. Leoni remained there throughout in that way she had of being where she wasn't wanted, well, at least unwanted by me. The policeman revealed that George and Lillian had been robbed, with an empty wallet being found on the floor of the car and tell-tale marks of jewellery being removed from Lillian, and how that may have been the motive. He did reveal however, how that lane had not been the location for any crime for the past fifteen years, which I felt was significant. Somebody knew the area perhaps.

After about an hour and a half, the police had gone. None of us returned to bed. Leoni annoyingly accompanied Laura into the kitchen. I wanted to show solidarity with my wife so I gripped her hand and told her I would help her through this. Her reaction was uncomfortable and hesitant, and for a moment I wondered if she thought I had had something to do with their deaths.

In that kitchen, silence overpowered. It was a silence that I didn't really comprehend. I had expected hysteria, confusion or a sense of being in denial, but there was none of that. In fact, I sensed nothing at all. I sat there looking at Laura, expecting her to open up in some way, but she stayed silent in a world of thought and contemplation, just staring into space, looking at her watch from time to time. Leoni was a reflection, just sitting opposite Laura, looking at nothing particularly and saying nothing particularly. It was as if they were waiting for something, but for what?

I felt like a spare part, which was weird in my wife's hour of need, so I told Laura that, should she need anything, I was only upstairs in our bed and would welcome being woken up if it would help her. She was my wife, after all, however estranged we were becoming. To be fair, she smiled appreciatively, and I went upstairs, where I could only dwell on how somebody would murder somebody as sweet as Lillian. I felt guilt at having wanted to do something bad to George on occasions, maybe punch him in the face or trip him up, which was bad enough, but she was a sweet old woman, who had always been kind to me and who was always charitable in her nature. In fact, I felt very aggrieved while I lay awake in bed and hoped the twat or twats who had done this would be captured soon and given plenty of years in prison.

While lying there in my strange solitude, I couldn't help replaying Lillian's doubt about Laura. I wished she could see her now, clearly devastated about the death of her parents, suddenly a hollow mess of a human being. Lillian had been wrong about Laura. I knew that now. I wasn't much of a Christian but supposed that Lillian could see that now, wherever she was.

* * *

The veil was weird. Everything else at the funeral service of George and Lillian, held on the outskirts of Mansfield, was as anybody would have anticipated but Laura insisted on wearing a black veil for the whole of the proceedings. The service, as you would expect, was a sad affair, and the detectives at the back of the church were indicative of the tragic and brutal nature of their deaths. Would the murderer or murderers turn up here? Only if they were known to the victim, I concluded. Hardly likely, in either case, I felt.

The whole service was shorter than I expected. I expected more speeches to celebrate their good deeds and selfless work for charity. I knew for a fact that George had given away paintings to raise money for a local hospice and that Lillian had helped out at a soup kitchen in the town. These things weren't mentioned. The vicar, a friend of the couple, did, however, speak quite sincerely and emotionally about the kind of people they were as far as the church was concerned and how they had done so much for the parish and had apparently made regular generous donations towards the restoration of the roof.

Things weren't right. I had glanced across at Laura several times, but could see very little in her facial expression, with the veil covering up her eyes like a blindfold. In all the time I had known her, including at least three funerals prior to this one, this had not have been the kind of look she had gone for, not the way for somebody who could never care less if her emotions were on show. She was always totally frank and open. On the contrary, I had sometimes felt she was totally lacking in self-consciousness. She was a woman who wore her heart on her sleeve, hiding nothing, and that was one of things that had made me fall in love with her.

When she had said to me that she was going to wear a veil I had initially laughed. After all, who would wear a veil for their parents' funeral? Laura had scowled but my reaction was unchanged. I could understand a bride wearing a veil, perhaps to suggest romance or vulnerability but for this event, surely open emotion was the order of the day.

"I want to wear a veil because I don't want to hang out my feelings in public like a drama queen. I hate people who do that."

"Drama queen? Your mother and father have been murdered."

"But they weren't."

"What?"

"They weren't my mother and father. For a real mother and father, yes. But I'm adopted. Yeah?"

I was struggling here. At no point ever had Laura ever devalued George and Lillian in this way and how she could decide to cheapen their parenting after their brutal death was beyond me. I could see why somebody might claim that natural ties were stronger, but this was ridiculous. They had worshipped her.

"So you are saying this about people who loved you and would have done anything for you? Really? What the fuck has happened to you?"

"Nothing. Perhaps it's you who needs the reality check."

"Do you think I need you telling me about reality?"

"Probably you do. They weren't that good. He didn't even like you anyway." She had an expression on her face now that I hadn't seen before.

"Weren't that good? How good did they need to be?"

"Listen, Dom. I never told you this. I should have done. He…he did things." The way she dragged out the last word added a sinister intensity that made me uncomfortable.

"What things did he do?" I knew what was being insinuated here but didn't believe it. I wasn't George's biggest fan but this was ludicrous.

"He was a bit weird sometimes. He liked to touch me… inappropriately."

"How do you mean?"

"Couldn't stop touching my bum. Ran his fingers down my back all the time. It was very creepy."

"Fuck off, Laura. What the hell is going on here?" I looked into her eyes, but all I saw was a fixed expression, like this was the absolute truth and she was standing firm.

"I'm saying it because it is true. He was nothing better than a pervert and Mother was in denial about it. It's hardly rocket science. You know about Me Too, Dom! You read the newspapers." There was drama emblazoned on her face and I thought she was going to strike me. Who was this woman living in my house? How could somebody so sweet become so vile?

"So Lillian is at fault too?"

"She let me down many times. When I needed her when I was growing up, she was never there for me." She bowed her head.

I didn't know what to think. It was as if we had all moved into a parallel universe where everything had changed beyond recognition.

* * *

Several times over the next few days I tried to break down the barrier that Laura had created, show her how stupid and unreasonable she was being.

"I don't want to talk about them."

"But you have to talk about them."

"Watch this space, Dom. See what happens."

This wasn't right. Two caring people who had died under horrific circumstances shouldn't be treated like this and Laura would have known that more than me. However, it became clear that she wasn't prepared to talk rationally about her late parents. Obviously, I had no choice. For the first time ever, I was now emotionally connected for the first time ever to a violent crime and to say I was utterly shocked would have been something of an understatement. It was just so much weirder, so totally inexplicable that my wife and I couldn't be of the same mind.

"I think we should talk about what's happened."

"I don't."

This went on a number of times. On the third day, she decided she wanted to talk about them. I was just coming out of the shower when I heard her on the phone. "Hello, I wish to speak to Geoff Forbes. He's handling my parents' estate." I continued listening as Laura showed more than enough interest in what was happening with the financial legacy of the dead couple.

I was waiting for her call to end, noticing that emerging impatience that I was seeing too much of these days, usually in my direction. "So when will it be concluded then…And I can expect to receive payment by when?"

What was interesting about this was that Laura had a positive animation about her that I hadn't seen since her return. It was really significant that she was now engaged in some money chase.

I continued to wait as the phone conversation continued. "Six months. Why that long? They died last week…How long does it take to sell the house? So, what's the earliest I can expect to be paid? I have lost my parents, you know. I don't want the whole thing dragging out. Do you know how painful this is? I want to get past the stress so I can appreciate who they were and what lovely people they were."

I felt myself becoming cynical. It seemed to me that Laura had no feelings at all for the people she had lost and was in fact only bothered about being legally reimbursed. The woman who had packed in work and who now had a life of idleness wanted a massive handout, which I thought was both callous and repulsive. It all was becoming totally depressing. I was starting to despise this woman, the woman I had loved beyond anything.

Of course, I didn't believe her accusations about George and Lillian. Had her mental breakdown made her into a compulsive liar?

THE RETURN OF THE POLICE

"Sorry to bother you again like this, but we need another conversation with you, Mrs. Walker. We've got more information."

"Oh, right." Laura and I had been eating in the dining room, where things were icily uneasy, even without the increase in tension that came with a police presence. Leoni was out of the house, fortunately, visiting a sick relative. Uncle Sid was pretty poorly, although Laura had put her hand over her mouth and looked away when Leoni had said his name so pitifully.

Laura showed them into the living room and I followed, focused like a private investigator looking for clues. At least it wasn't after midnight this time. Aside from my marriage and its dysfunctionality, I had my fingers crossed that these police officers had news of the killer being caught and wanted the secure knowledge that he was now behind bars.

"Here's the thing. I told you we suspected that this was a car-jacking, that they had gone for a drive for some reason and been stopped by the assailant. Evidence now suggests something different."

"What do you mean different?"

"Essentially, that the assailant was in the car with them. A few seconds of CCTV footage, that's all we had, but just enough to see a figure in the back seat of their car. A hooded figure, unfortunately so we can't make out who, I'm afraid. We don't know whether they were driving under duress or not, but that hoodie? Does that sound like anybody you know, Mrs. Walker, or any acquaintance of your parents you know?"

Laura sat there thinking intensely, then shook her head. "No. As far as I know, they don't know anybody who walks around with a hood up. We don't know anybody who wears a hood, do we, Dom?"

She had a point, and I shook my head.

"Are you absolutely sure? It could so easily be someone they know. Most violent offenders are known to their victims."

Laura shook her head. "They were in their fifties, you know. A teenager, or somebody young, do you think? Do you think my parents might have been murdered by a druggie?"

"At this stage, we don't know. Still gathering evidence. Of course, what we want to know is, how did the killer select them as victims? There was money in the house and plenty of valuables, but, as far as we were able to assess, and as you may know, nothing was taken, and there's no evidence that the assailant was even in the house. It would have made more sense to rob them at home. We're having trouble working out how and why they were selected in the first place. What the killer gained from this is baffling us, to say the least."

PAPERWORK IN NOVEMBER

I held it in front of me like it was a still from an unwatchable horror movie. In actual fact, it was far worse, even for this miserable Sunday morning. Beyond belief, it left me shivering with incredulity. This was a horror beyond all horrors.

Six weeks on from Laura's re-emergence, I had decided to find our marriage certificate. I don't know why I was even bothering, but I wanted to hold it in my hand and use it as some prop in a dramatic attempt to remind Laura who she was or, more importantly, who she had been. It was probably silly and immature, really, but a desperate man is prone to that kind of urge. Something had to wake her from this strange persistent dream she was trapped inside or, if not, I would rip up the document and that might trigger her to leave which would bring an end to the weirdness. She could leave with the parasite Leoni, and perhaps they would venture into a golden sunrise, or Leoni would go in search of another mug. We would be finished forever. Of that I was sure.

While I was looking for a solution to the confusion that prevailed, I thought I would try to kill two birds with one stone and locate a few money-related documents that might be important so I could stash them securely. Two of them were endowments I was paying into, whilst another was my latest Premium Bond statement. George and Lillian's murder, which I still found difficult to accept or understand, had made me feel a tad insecure.

I had positioned myself on my knees in our dining room, consigning to the bin pieces of paper that merely reminded me that I paid an electric bill two years ago or had completed my Council Tax payments eighteen months ago. I found the life insurance papers that I had wondered about in a big white envelope. Unfortunately, my password sheet, a pre-requisite in our modern digital society that I had been looking for, was there too.

Suddenly, there was something I hadn't seen before. At the bottom of the drawer was a larger brown envelope with the words 'medical documents' written on it in black felt tip that seemed so out of place. It wasn't in my writing, and it wasn't labelled in the way Laura normally labelled things. She was normally much neater, and never used block capitals unless it was on an application form.

Normally, I would have ignored an envelope like this, but today, I decided to look inside. There were several items. I held a bank card in my hand, gleaming and new, and in the joint names of Dominic and Laura Walker, with an expiry date in October 2022. Why was this so unfamiliar to me? Alongside it was a folded-up piece of paper. I unfolded it to reveal that it was from the vet.

It was a bill for termination, although the vet's name was unfamiliar. It announced to me the details of the death of August and explained his disappearance. The cold, factual details gave a clear explanation for why poor August was no longer around. I was shaking.

A third item in the envelope was a council tax letter for an address in Chesterfield, which related to some property on

Wolstenholme Street, which I had never heard of. This I tossed to the side, with the details of this barely registering, since the vet's bill had been explosive.

When I heard the front door, I went straight to the hallway, holding the bill in my hand. "Why didn't you tell me?"

Laura, closing the door behind her, looked at me, seeing the bill. She paused. "I would have done, but I didn't want you to be upset. I thought the idea of the cat disappearing would be kinder. August was ill, Dom."

"How ill? He didn't look ill to me. Last time I saw him, he was the healthiest cat ever. He was climbing that fence." I pointed in the direction of the garden.

"I'm sorry, babe. The vet said he had a tumour, that he was in pain most of the time. It was the kindest thing that could be done for him.

"Which vet? Our local vet? Curtis? The one who's treated August since he was a kitten."

"No. You obviously know that. I took him to a different vet. One in Crookes."

"Why would you do that?"

"Truth is, I've never liked Curtis."

This was news to me. "Since when?"

"He just charges too much and then charges some more. I don't like being robbed, but I just never told you."

"So what happened to August?"

"Isn't it obvious. You saw the bill."

"I mean to his body. Did you bring him home?"

There was a telling silence.

"You had him cremated there! Oh my fucking God. "We always agreed...Well, you remember exactly what we agreed."

"What did we agree, Dom?"

"We agreed that when August died, we would bury him on the back somewhere. I was going to dig up a section of the lawn and replant the grass afterwards. Surely you remember that?"

"I remember, of course I do, but that would have only messed up the garden."

"So what? This was August. You were supposed to love him."

"I did the best thing for him, Dom. And for us. You have to believe that." She had that imploring look on her face that I had seen several times since her return.

"And what about the bank card? What's going on there? You don't even have a job."

She screwed up her face. "Oh, for fuck's sake. I just wanted some independence. Do you think I enjoy living off you and depending on you all the time, like you're some fucking god. Well I can tell you this, mister, I don't."

"But my name's on the card. I signed nothing!"

"Babe, I did that for you. It seemed easier. I think it's the way I've been feeling recently. Needed something to perk me up."

"How are you going to make the payments? You have to make payments on a credit card."

"I'm sure I'll have everything sorted soon, so paying the card off won't be a problem." She had a wry smile on her face at this point, like I was some kind of imbecile.

"This is all a massive problem. Your behaviour and attitude have become ridiculous. I don't recognise you. And what the fuck is that council tax letter all about?"

"What council letter?"

"Some road in Chesterfield. Wolstenholme Street. What has that to do with you?"

At this point, she lost it. "I think this is abuse. Don't you know, you can't do this. I could have you thrown out of this house for the pressure you're putting me under. You are going to make me ill." She paused, and just gave me that stony stare. "And I just might do that, if you don't back off and stop being a total arsehole." She left the kitchen and I heard her go upstairs and a door slam. The last words I heard, shouted down at me, were, "And for your information, the council tax letter is Leoni's. She wanted me to help her get a refund. Is that ok with you, knobhead?"

Wearily, I pulled out a chair and sat at the kitchen table and, not for the first time, I had my head in my hands. Eventually, I just got up and took my jacket from the coat hook in the hall and left. I needed a drink.

Everything was quiet and pitch black downstairs. I had had plenty to drink for a Sunday. I supposed the best thing would be for me to quietly make my way to bed and get in without any fuss and try to find sleep as soon as possible. That would be the smart move, avoiding any confrontation. In the pub that evening, while I nursed the JD and coke, I had decided that things could not go on the way they were. The bottom line was that I was no happier with Laura in my house than I had been when she was away, so what was the point? It was time for an ultimatum, and in the morning, an ultimatum would be issued. I had been accommodating for too long. Perhaps that was the problem. Maybe the new Laura needed a man who was no pushover, like I had been since her return. It was even possible that my malleability was making her worse. Was I part of the problem rather than the solution?

I think I was in that state where you're not quite asleep, but not really awake, a period of time that lasts less than a minute but which can be a period of realisation. My eyes opened and I suddenly wondered where Laura actually was. Even in my inebriated state, looking out of the window, I saw our two cars outside the house, so she had to be in the house.

I got out of bed.

I went across the landing to the spare bedroom. I refused to call it Leoni's room out of principle. I listened. They were talking. Being not quite sober, I clumsily opened the door and switched on the light so I could see inside the room.

"Fuck off, Dom."

"Why didn't you fucking knock," I heard Leoni say, in that broad dialect of hers that I might have been able to endure if it wasn't Leoni. At this moment, however, it was as if I was the lodger here, and she was the mortgage payer. How I wanted her to leave. Come to that, how I wanted to live in this house on my own for a while.

It was worse than that. They were in bed together. Not only that, but with all the flesh on show, they were at the very least, topless. This was disturbing, but at least I understood much more now that they were closer to each other than Laura was to me.

Then there was the giveaway. On the duvet in front of them was a sex toy.

"No! What the fuck is going on?" I don't know why I said this. I was now instantly sober and it was clear that I no longer knew my wife in any way.

They stayed where they were, the two bitches lying there like nothing was wrong. There was no "It's not what you think". Not even a, "You caused this." All that came out was, "I want a divorce, Dom. This is nothing to do with anything. We need to get a divorce."

I was in total agreement.

MALEVOLENCE

This is all turning out quite different. I guess my needs have grown with my plan. I started off and all I wanted was a pay-off. Now I am going to have a much bigger pay-off and sooner than planned.

Also, I'm discovering real hate. It's an aphrodisiac, hate is, and it provides real drive for what I want to do now. Things are getting much messier than I thought they would and I intend to make things much tidier.

There's a big inheritance coming my way. It certainly pays when rich parents get murdered.

If the dickhead and the bitch divorce, the bitch gets a load of money, probably half of everything, but the wimp could make a claim of his own. He could even claim off that wonderful inheritance. That is not going to happen. After all, I have gone to a lot of trouble with this, and let's be straight, the whole of everything is a lot more than half. I redrew the plan, this time with a different ending.

This amounts to millions. I can do a lot with that kind of money. I can actually disappear, find myself in a place where nobody knows me, where I have no history and where my future can be under a new name and with a new identity. Luxury for the rest of my life.

JD ON DIVORCE

In this shitstorm of a life, I needed a rock. Like in that film, 'The Shallows', where Blake Lively stays on the rock to stop the huge shark devouring her. That rock was her security. My rock knocked at my door before letting himself into my house as I stood in the hallway to welcome him. "Hi mate," I said, in the cheeriest voice I could muster. "Would you like a drink?"

"OK. I'll have a brandy and coke. Do you have that here?"

"We can do whiskey and lemonade. Will that do?"

"OK. I'll have that." He paused. "Where are they?"

"Fuck knows. Laura goes nowhere without her little sidekick."

"Does she know you shagged her?"

"I don't think so. I don't think I did shag her. Either way, I don't know what Laura would say if she found out. It's all becoming irrelevant, basically. We're moving farther away from each other as each day goes by. Leoni's not the issue."

"So what is?"

"Everything is wrong. So fucking wrong. We're getting divorced."

"Are you sure about this?"

"That woman I call Laura is not the woman I thought she was. Her parents get violently killed and all she thinks about is the money she'll inherit."

"What?"

"Exactly. And that's not all. Our cat August disappears and I find out she's had him put down with some bullshit tale of him being terminally ill."

Jamie was horrified. "August is dead? That's so fucking mean."

"And you've not heard the best of all. She's shagging Leoni."

"No!"

"I know. Who could have seen that coming? I want out mate. Big time."

"Lesbo? How do you know?"

"Caught them at it. Well sort of… Don't fucking laugh. It's not funny."

"I'm not laughing. Fuck, Dom. What the fuck is going on? Has she become a total bitch?"

"Yeah, Jamie. Ticks very box. She says she wants a divorce. I definitely want one."

"Well, that does sound like she's doing you a favour. Every cloud, Dom."

"I knew you would think that."

"Well, I would." Jamie had had two disastrous marriages. "Look at me. My first divorce got me well shot of Mrs. Lethargic. The second saw me waving goodbye to a money-hunter who just wanted a meal ticket in her life. I wouldn't mind, but they were both crap in the sack."

"That is not like what is going on here. This is just so much weirder. Your two marriages times ten. Something very strange is going on here, even stranger than all the disturbing details I've just told you. You can help me."

"What do you want, mate? Say the word."

I paused, then I knew what I wanted to happen. "I need you to follow her for a while. She's hiding something. You might find out what."

"Doesn't sound like she's hiding much."

"Well she disappears for long periods of time. I don't know where she goes when I'm at work, but she's never to be seen on the security camera and her car is hardly ever outside the house. She's always evasive or gives me some bullshit when I ask her about her day. No, there is something out there that I don't know about, and it might be the key to a lot of this."

"That's dodgy, Dom. Following someone is a criminal offence, you know. And this is my holiday, for crying out loud."

"I know, but I have given you loads of help with your book."

"OK, I do owe you, but it is still stalking."

"But you're not stalking. You're researching. Any problem, I'll take responsibility."

"I'm not doing it, Dom. It will seem weird. Like I'm some psycho. She could end up phoning the police and getting me prosecuted. People get jail for stalking."

"As if I'd let anything as bad as that happen."

Within ten minutes we were in Butler's, a massive electrical store, buying a tracking device. For all his protests, Jamie had come around to the idea. He was becoming excited about trying his luck as a private eye, and he wasn't working for the next seven days. "It's simple, Dom. You put it under her spare wheel in the boot of the Audi. You can do it when she's asleep."

I went to the guy at the counter. "Is there any way two people can have access to this thing at the same time."

The bespectacled bearded assistant looked at me with a knowing smirk. "Well sir, for that you will need to buy two trackers, obviously."

FOR BETTER OR WORSE

The house was empty. Upstairs, the only sound was the slow hum of the sweeping hand of the bedside clock, whilst downstairs the television was making the only sounds, and the only signs that there was life within these walls.

Obviously, she was still spending virtually all of her time with Leoni. I had tried to console myself with the idea that this was what she needed, that this was essential for her recovery, but now I was scrutinizing it with a new more critical eye. At the end of the day, this woman had dropped me, had dropped her parents before their untimely deaths, deaths that I could not ascribe to her as he had been asleep in my bed while they had been slaughtered or I would otherwise have looked very hard for a link.

My ringtone sounded. "Dom."

"Hi mate. How's it going?"

"Well, your lovely wife certainly likes driving. She drives fast too. Without the tracking device, I would have lost her. A real speed queen. She drove from yours this morning to Chesterfield. She parked up on Manor Hill for fifteen minutes and then drove off to the town centre, where she picked up that sexy Leoni bird you know so well and from there she went to Costa at the M1 services. She stayed there for an hour." I knew most of this, as I'd been watching stuff on my phone, but I let Jamie enjoy his Sam Spade moment.

"Are they still in Costa?"

"Yes. She and her dodgy mate are downing enough caffeine to cope with you, it seems."

"Oh, thanks for that. Well, you carry on what you're doing mate. I'll help you with your next book as well as this one."

"You'd better. I'll ring you later."

* * *

"Dom."

Hi, Jamie. Did they leave Costa?"

"They left Costa."

'Where did they go?"

"They separated, mate, briefly. I followed the car, obviously. She drove to a road full of massive houses and private medical establishments. She ended up parked in the car park of a residential home. Sunny Vale, it's called. Caroline got out and has gone into the place while Leoni's staying in the car."

"What the fuck is she doing there?"

"I don't know, Dom, and I'm realizing that I'm no detective. You need to get somebody more savvy to find out what's going on."

"Just find out what you can."

MALEVOLENCE

I have always been very independent. You cannot be otherwise if you are me and you can't imagine me unless you have walked in my shoes.

Like any predator, I am a survivor. I have this weird ability to sense danger and a similarly strong sense when someone unwelcome is close, which as a faculty sometimes comes in handy. I once sensed that I was being followed home from work by two likely characters and had to deal with them. They didn't enjoy the meeting. I have always been good with a blade and I'm sure neither of those misguided cretins will ever pleasure a woman again this lifetime.

Anyway, I'm just leaving this place, heading to my car when I learn that there is a threat to the plan, that a risk is emerging. It's not a nice feeling. Nobody anywhere likes that feeling of being vulnerable, so why would I? The only difference is that I'm not just anybody.

I see him, some distance away. It's some bloke in an Audi, could be a private detective but more likely it's that prick's mate, that knobhead who thinks he's hot with the ladies. I have to think. The best thing I can do is think.

Naturally he follows. It is pretty clear that the arsehole has told him to watch and see.

There is some driving done before he stops alongside the factory. Well, it used to be a factory but now it's just an old building, a ghost of bricks and mortar.

Of course, he is an idiot. I sense he's a total buffoon, writing a book about his sexual doings and thinking he's all that. Well, we will see about that, I say to myself.

Pretending to be dumb, I have brought him to a part of town I am more than familiar with. I look the place up and down. I know this place well. You could call it the neighbourhood, and it has the two fabulous qualities of being convenient and risk-free. I have done plenty in and around here and don't mind the dirt or the rats. He is stuck in the strands of a web, but he doesn't know it.

Out of the corner of my eye, I see that the Audi has stopped. My move. I walk. I push open a decaying door and am in what was once a warehouse. I am ready to strike again, out of sight from this dead fool.

This is now a waiting game. I am waiting and I am alert. I am hoping to hear footsteps. I am believing that he is stupid enough to leave his car and come looking. This is the time. He is no James Bond, just some dumb ass doing his idiotic mate a favour. Well, that is going to cost him some.

The footsteps come. I know he is going to at least try the door. He won't come into the factory, I suppose, since even he will sense danger. But he will wish to check what the lovely Laura is up to. I hear the handle turn. Old, there is the squeak of rusty metal crying out.

The door opens. I see his arm as he pushes the door.

I strike. I bring the blade crashing down. I hear his squeal of pain and that is music to me. I bring the blade down repeatedly and his arm falls alongside him and he is kneeling on the floor when I move on top of him. My fingers find his eyeballs and I strike with four fingers and he is blinded, permanently. At this point he is mine. He has lost himself. He is just a massive scream.

I make the most of possessions. Here is a new one.

MALEVOLENCE

Well, he is looking different now. Gone is the swagger, the Mr. full-of himself stuff. He now sits there in the seat of doom with all that blood. His woman-chasing days are over. That's for sure. He's going to die soon, and the sighing and swaying behind his gag tell me that time is coming soon. Even I have no say in that.

Torture. Should I or shouldn't I? I think I should. I think I should show this jerk what happens when you are unlucky and in the wrong place at the wrong time. Got to show him that being too close to a fire brings a terrible burning. And the lovely man has written a book. Well, here is his final chapter.

THE DISAPPEARED

I was outside his front door, going through my key ring for the key to this flat. Jamie had given it to me six months ago, with the understanding that it would be there for him if he ever lost his and so that I could look after things during his times away. I had fed his goldfish, Herbie, while he had been away in Spain, but apart from that, I had never used the key.

As I arrived there, the first thing I noticed was that his precious Audi wasn't in his parking space. Had he left today, or had he never returned?

Two days had passed since Jamie's last contact with me, when I had tracked Laura to a road in Chesterfield, not far from the City Centre, the road where Leoni had lived, Wolstenholme Street.

Now, the signal had stopped inexplicably, and there was no sign of him, which was pretty close to unbelievable.

Two days had been too long. I let myself into Jamie's, which was situated in close proximity to Sheffield City Hall and about fifty pubs. The room was in a dingy dusty darkness, with the curtains closed, so I rectified that and let the sunshine in, allowing an immediate invasion of light, although that wasn't refreshing.

With the light on, the flat was characterized by cluttered untidiness. There were a couple of empty cans of Carlsberg on his coffee table and an opened parcel revealing what must have been about ten copies of his book, 'Absolute Too Much', that he had been so enthusiastic about and so proud of. I picked a copy of the book, read the blurb then returned it. This was not time for this. I needed to find a clue for what had become of this man.

There was no clue. There was nothing.

* * *

"When did you get this?" Looking across at me was one of those police officers who had seen everything and who had probably lost the edge that was needed to make him good at his job. Perhaps this desk sergeant, a greying man in his fifties, was counting down the days to a cosy retirement and was finding people like me irritating. Either that or he had just taken an instant dislike to me and was determined to disappoint. Either way, I was going to put up a fight. Jamie's life was at stake.

"Two days ago. Just before he disappeared."

'Do you have any idea where Sunny Vale Nursing Home is?"

"Yes. I googled it. It's near Chesterfield."

He paused for what must have been a full minute. "I'm not sure this helps us in any way. To be honest with you, it doesn't really suggest anything. It's not as if he's going to be in that nursing home, is he?"

"But this was one of the last places he was before he disappeared. Surely that suggests something. His disappearance is linked to that place in some way." I couldn't tell the police about Wostenholme Street, since that would give away the fact that I was tracking my wife. I was not going to be prosecuted for stalking, not while it was still possible that Jamie was OK and just keeping a low profile. After all, I wouldn't put it past Jamie to be with a woman somewhere, holed up in a love nest. He'd done that before.

"Well, I'll put it in the report, sir, but I don't think it gives us anything."

I wanted to hit this policeman. That would have been no good at all, as it would have just had me behind bars and powerless to act, but the frustration was overwhelming.

MEMORIES

Reluctantly, I had arranged to meet Laura in Costa out at Meadowhall to talk about the divorce. I was already there, seated in the far corner, with a clear view of the car park and the doorway and today I wanted an edge, since being given the run-around just wasn't working for me. I needed some kind of advantage, because being a gullible fool, waiting for her latest outrage, was just becoming ridiculous. I need to make some developments of my own, and give her things to react to. I wanted to take control.

When she walked in, she looked like a knockout, wearing a long black dress that she had worn several times before her vanishing act, but usually for restaurants or trips, not trips to the local coffee shop. She had a half-smile on her face as she approached the table. As usual, I sensed heads turning around me, which was Laura's usual effect on a room full of strangers. Why was it that all I now saw was ugliness?

I kissed her on the cheek and went to order her a drink. I wanted this meet away from home to go my way.

"Do you remember Whitby?"

"A little. The sea was nice."

"You had something on your mind there. What was it?"

"What do you mean?"

"You kept saying you had something to tell me, but you never said it. Don't you remember that? I often wondered what you were on about while you were away. You had something big on your mind but were being quite evasive. Was it that you wanted a divorce?"

She had opened her purse and was fiddling with the contents, as if counting her loose change and checking that her cards were still there. "Probably about that job, or how miserable I was."

"What? You said you were so happy because of the job, as well as being with me. The job was something you loved."

"I was living a lie. Now I don't have to."

"I don't believe you, but even if I did, you never had to. You know you could have made the same decision, but without the strange suddenness and over-reliance on me."

There was a pause between us. I knew I couldn't continue going down this road without inciting a conflict, which would probably result in her storming out. I wanted to find out her thoughts, however. I wanted to learn something. Had the old Laura been totally destroyed by the assault?

She broke the silence. "The other day. Was that anything to do with you?"

"What?"

"Some creep following me, like a stalker."

"Followed? Why would that be anything to do with me."

"Well, it was your mate."

"Nothing to do with me," I said. "He said nothing to me. I think he was curious about Leoni more than you."

"Oh yes? Why would that be?"

"Look there's something I have to tell you about Leoni. Your lover."

"What can you possibly tell me about her?"

"The thing is, she and I had a moment while you were away."

"A moment. You mean you shagged her."

"Yes. I think so. I was drunk, but I think so."

"When?"

"Before you brought her into our lives, Probably, well more like possibly."

Laura got up to go. She was laughing. "Well, don't worry about that. And I'm not going to worry about your friend Jamie."

"Why? What happened?"

"Let's just say we had strong words. I've cured that curiosity of his that was...irritating."

"You know he's gone missing?"

"Has he? He said he was fed up with it all when I spoke to him. Perhaps you pissed him off like you do everybody else. I did warn him off pretty strongly so perhaps he's done a runner for a while. I'm sure you and he will be in touch soon. Don't worry."

"But that's not like him. He's not the kind of bloke who runs away from stuff."

"Well I only spoke to him. I told him to fuck off and stop following me if he knew what was good for him."

"Is that all you did. All you said?"

"What else? What exactly are you accusing me of?"

"I don't know. The truth is that I just don't know you anymore. And then there's what happened to George and Lillian."

"What the fuck! Why are you connecting that with me? That's well out of order!" She got up abruptly, with the sound of scraping chair legs attracting further attention from other coffee drinkers. I hated Costa really. I don't know why I had chosen to meet her here, since it was never going to end well.

And we hadn't even managed to talk about the divorce, anyway, so nothing had been achieved. So much for taking control.

SUNNY VALE

This was leafy. I had been to Chesterfield on a number of occasions but had never been in this part of the town. It was a long tree-lined road, where signs were on display every fifteen yards or so. I had always thought that the place that people called 'Chessie' was a bit run-down, with that silly spire that needed fixing but which would probably cost too much, and all those dodgy nondescript areas where crime rates were high. I had always felt that its people were never sure whether they wanted to be in Yorkshire or in Derbyshire but were happy to reap whatever benefits were going from both counties. I didn't blame them really.

My body was trembling with anticipation, but of what? My brain was all over the place. Within those walls ahead of me was something that might provide the answer to everything that was confusing about my marriage. Then again, it might provide nothing, and I would just be making a total fool of myself. I had never been any good at handling embarrassment. I parked my car in a spacious car park lined with bushes and flowers and sat for a couple of minutes composing myself, preparing myself, so that, if there was anything to learn there, I would learn it.

Ready to try my luck, I shook myself out of the car and surveyed the well-maintained flowerbeds as I locked the car door. I sauntered over to what was clearly the main entrance, trying to muster confidence, where a green sign with white lettering announced that all visitors were to report to the reception.

I pushed open a glass door like I knew where I was and as if I had a sharp sense of purpose. Once inside, I did a quick three-sixty and took in plenty of white décor with well-placed photographs showing a range of elderly smiles, a large vase full of mixed flowers that looked like some petrol station had been raided last night and noticed plenty of comfortable seats next to the walls of this reception area. There were no people in this area, although I had no idea what that meant. Essentially, I was in an airy, light, not unpleasant area with a big desk straight ahead, a bit like something out of a budget hotel, woodwork lightly varnished, and, like in a cheap hotel, the whole thing was about attempting to be classy but not quite managing it.

I noticed that a large woman in her mid-fifties was sitting at a computer side on to me as I approached the desk, looking at some kind of spreadsheet. She had black hair, probably dyed, that was swept back neatly under a nurse's cap.

The lady, whose tag said that she was called Michelle, turned to face me and smiled disarmingly. "Good afternoon. How can I help you?"

I had already got it all worked out. "Hello. To be honest, I don't know whether you'll be able to help me. It's just that I'm trying to trace my wife and I think she may have called here to see a friend."

"Sir, we have fifty-six residents in this home. Who's your wife?"

"Laura…Laura Walker."

"I'm sorry. I don't recognise the name. I'll just check the

visitor's book in case she called here before my shift started...
No. Nobody called Laura has visited. There's a Mrs. L. Field.
Could that be her?"

I shook my head. I reached in my wallet and took out a
passport photograph of the two of us and held it in front of
her. "This is her. On the right, obviously." I grinned.

"Oh yes. It's Caroline. Is Laura her middle name?"

"Yes it is. She doesn't use it often." I had had to think
quickly. Who in God's name was Caroline?

"Caroline Lawrence is your wife then?"

I thought quickly. "Yes. That's her maiden name. Who does
she visit here?"

"Judy, her mother. She's been here a number of years. A
well-established member of our little community." She stopped.
"Hang on. Don't you know that?"

"Of course I do. I just didn't know her name. I'm preparing
a surprise for Caroline and I want to let her mother know so
she can attend. Residents are allowed to attend parties, I hope?"

"Of course. We do encourage family contact in all its
forms."

"Can I see her? With you, of course."

A few minutes later, I was standing inside the room of a
woman called Judy Lawrence, a woman who looked elderly but
who apparently had developed early onset Alzheimer's, which
I had always thought to be the cruelest infliction that can ever
happen. She had lived here for fifteen years. The room was neat,
with a few ornaments, pictures, including two of Laura, and
useful gadgets all neatly arranged, although whether that was
due to her or the staff of this place, I couldn't say.

Michelle was with me. She had declared that it was more
than her job was worth to let me talk to Judy alone, although
two twenty-pound notes had somehow made things easier. "Hi
Judy. This is Dominic. He's Caroline's husband." She gestured

255

to me to smile. I complied, although I hadn't a clue what this was all about.

"Hi, Judy. I'm planning a party for Caroline and want you to attend. That's why I'm here."

"Caroline's lovely. She looks after her mother. When she comes here she brings things for me and she's a good daughter."

"That's good. Every mother needs a good daughter."

"Yes."

"You must feel so good, having a good daughter."

"I do. Not like the other one."

My senses sharpened. "Which other one?"

"The one who went."

"She went?"

"The one who never comes here. She went. Went long ago."

"When did you last see her, the other one?" Here came the revelation.

"Not seen her since the first day. The day the demons took her." I heard Michelle sigh behind me. "I try not to think about her."

"And why would you?"

Judy looked at me. "How would you feel, mister, if one of your daughters never even talked to you? I don't think you would like it. Not one bit."

"Which one of your daughters never talks to you?" I was learning quickly.

She stared ahead of her, as if the cream paint on the wall held a strange fascination for her. "The one I didn't keep, the one who doesn't even know Caroline. The twin."

JOGGERS LANE

The view from the top of Joggers Lane was always good for me. Ten minutes from the residential build-up that is Sheffield, at various times in my adult life I had found sweet solace in parking my car at the top of the hill and gazing out at the idyllic and stunning countryside. All you can see when you look down is a wonderful greenness. In fact, looking down from the top of Joggers Lane, I always felt totally refreshed.

I needed to be at one with nature and get my head together. What I had learned in that residential home was a game-changer and I knew that when I eventually arrived home, it was going to kick off big style. I was in some danger now and at some point I would need to involve the police. Nothing would kick off up here right now, however. This was the epitome of tranquility. There was no better calm before the storm.

Should I go straight to the boys in blue with my suspicions? I started the car three times but each time I switched the engine back off, dejectedly. Going to the police might not be my smartest move. They had been pretty resistant to me about Jamie's disappearance, and they were hardly likely to believe this

story. "Of course, Mr. Walker. I'll just write down the details."
Yeah, right.

No, I was going to confront Laura. Confront Laura? If only. In actual fact, I was going to confront Caroline. My confusion about my wife had to be cleared up now. This was not my wife, as I had supposed for far too long, but some evil bitch born at the same time, to the same mother, somebody who had grown up and stolen her identity, probably brutally, and who was living a lie, taking on a role that clearly did not suit. The big question now was, would I be content with questioning her, or would I kill her? Here I was, at the top of Joggers Lane, trying to work that one out.

MALEVOLENCE

He always had to die.

It wasn't always this way. Long before this started I was somebody else. I was somebody who liked to sit and play with the few toys I had and read things. I can't exactly remember, but I suppose I must have been somebody who had hopes and dreams, although they might have just been grey clouds. Sitting here on this settee, with Mahler coming out of the speakers, I look back on what was and what no longer is.

One memory I hold pretty dear is of a boyfriend my mother had. Friendly guy, well at least to her. He gave her cuddles, and bought her bunches of flowers from time to time, and always greeted her with a smile and some warmth. From what I understand, he looked after her physically too, with all that cooing in the bedroom.

His friendliness to me took a different form. I worshipped him. He was a great father figure in my young mind, taking me to toy shops, funfairs and, later, giving me lifts to parties and buying me nice presents. I guess I saw him through rose-tinted glasses. He was somebody who gave me much-needed security, who made me feel that I was a normal child, not an urchin with a hopeless individual as a mother, but somebody who actually had a family.

One night, when I was thirteen, the friendly stuff took a whole different direction, one that changed things.

Mother was out of the house. I was in my room, listening to music, Kylie's latest album, I think. Anyway, he came into the room. He knocked first, of course, and sat at the edge of the bed. I guess he had had some drink as his breath smelled of alcohol. I had never drunk alcohol, and still don't drink much, but he had. To cut a long story short, he put his hand on my leg. He left it there.

I looked into his eyes, pleading with him to move it away, but he had a look in his eye that told me this was not going to end well. I was innocent and wimpish back then, young and stupid, but innocence and my peace of mind disappeared as he became forceful, and he knew what he wanted. Within seconds I was underneath him and silently losing my virginity in a way that I did not want. I remember lying still as he buttoned up his trousers and left the room, without any words while I was wiping up blood off a sheet at midnight and suddenly understanding how the world had turned.

Mother could always pick them. If they weren't doing stuff to me, they were knocking lumps out of her or her bank account, cheating on her big time. I hated them all. And so many rows and fights. Home was just a place of misery and nastiness. I don't know whether she liked the dodgy relationships deep down and enjoyed the suffering, because she never learned from things. She needed my help so often.

I caught up with my mother's boyfriend some years later. He had left my mother after a blazing row over his drinking. I expect I was long forgotten when I bumped into him at that bar. I reminded him somewhat and talked him into taking me back to his place. His place was pretty dingy, but it was ok. Tomato ketchup on the table and a pile of unwashed dishes needing attention would not affect things much. I only wanted his dick and balls. With one quick unexpected movement of his kitchen knife, that aim was achieved. I carried them out of the house while I laughed at his agonised screaming. I had his tackle in my hand all the way to the canal where I threw them so there would be no reconnection, knowing he would always be reminded of our time together.

I never enjoyed home. I hated the fact that she rarely washed my clothes, smoked so heavily that when I went to school, the other kids thought it a good laugh to give it to me in the playground and I was a magnet for bullying and all the shit that kids inflict on each other as they grow up.

Obviously, in time I dealt with the bullies in a way to make up for stuff, but that wasn't the point.

The point was that life was pretty shit.

When I was thirteen, we were evicted. At that point, Mum was so into the booze and pills that all her money went in that direction and I found myself begging on the streets until I found a better way to earn money.

Sex came along. I didn't like sex much, but it liked me. I had a friend called Jilly who earned two hundred quid a week doing stuff in cars and made another friend who made the move with me into doing tricks. She had had a shit time like me. With her the abuse was from both her mother and her father, and had been physical, and she had spent time in the care system where things had been even worse.

The thing about two of us becoming workers together was that we could look out for each other. Occasionally, a punter would become violent, so we acted as each other's protector, always within earshot of each other, never servicing a punter at the same time.

Of course, we both got into some bother. A bloke in a blue Ford Focus was refusing to hand over money before I gave him a blow job, and then had the nerve to hold me there, demanding a freebie. There was no way I would do it for nothing.

To this day, I don't know which came first. Did I bite first or was it the crack on the head from my friend's hammer that made him cry out. I'll never know.

Police must have been close by, and I guess they took the view that the biting was an accidental reaction and it was my friend who got sent down for GBH. With the hammer, she'd reduced the guy to a virtual vegetable and she ended up claiming that it was self defence and ended up with a seven year sentence. She was out in four. I was glad, because life was riskier on your own in that game.

I had the sense to put money away. I managed to use my looks to set up something good with a rich Bengali guy who owned five restaurants across Derbyshire and into North Nottinghamshire. I guess his wife wasn't doing much for him and he had plenty of enthusiasm when he met up with me.

I suppose he became emotionally attached. That was how I was able to make a breakthrough. I got some photos of us. I was really nice to him about those photos. I told him I didn't want to send them to his wife, his wife's family and the local mosques, but I needed a flat. He was angry at first, and I took a slap or two across the face but that changed nothing. I let him sleep on it.

Within six weeks of his sleeping on it I had a flat on the smart side of town. It was no penthouse suite or anything like that, but it was better than the hovel I had rented since leaving home.

I think it was about fifteen years ago that Mum became ill. I didn't love Mum too much. She had let me down too many times and her stupidity had caused me to have a totally crap childhood so I was resentful. However, she was my mother, so I took over her house when she was moved into a nursing home.

I didn't visit her much. Sometimes I hated her and could not be in the same room as her. Other times, I felt an attachment that I didn't really understand, so on those moments I might go along and spend ten minutes there, taking her some fruit or a magazine. It was boring as hell, and often I changed my mind and turned around. She didn't deserve visitors, but she did have early onset dementia and, obviously, she couldn't make decisions to hurt me anymore.

Two years ago, on a cold December, I had popped along to see her. It was then that she had said she had something to tell me, something important. She said she wanted to tell me before she lost her mind totally, which would have been okay, except she had no mind to lose. She'd never had much of a mind.

I remember just sitting there in shock. I could not believe what I was hearing. I walked from the home in a daze. That daze became anger, bitterness and in my head came thoughts and ideas, none of which were nice. That's when my project began.

CONFRONTATION

"When were you going to tell me?"

"Tell you what?"

"About your mother."

In the style I had now become accustomed to, she didn't take her eyes from the television, with its riveting images from some daytime drama that was much more important than being totally rumbled and found out. "I don't know what you're talking about."

"Oh yes you do. And more to the point, where the fuck is Laura?"

"I don't know what you are on about. Are you losing your mind?"

I remained standing and was looking down at her and was having to control myself, as I knew that if I didn't, I would strangle this evil bitch, and what would that achieve? The bottom line was that she was going to have to tell me where her twin was, the long lost twin she had replaced and who hopefully was alive somewhere. I wanted a resolution. "I just need to know, Caroline. Or is it Jo Jo?"

"What is wrong with you? Have you lost your mind?"

"I know the story, Caroline. You're the bitter and twisted sister."

"I'm sorry. I think you are going nuts. Do you know what I'm going to do? I'm going to have you sectioned. And when you get out, we'll get something more permanent organised."

She left the room and went upstairs. I followed her, cautious, but determined.

"But you killed Laura."

"Oh come on. Why would Laura kill Laura? No policeman would ever believe that. Why would I kill somebody totally dumb?"

I ran at her, pushed her onto the bed, and had her neck in my hands. I was going to end her life. My life did not matter, as the only important thing was that this vile witch did not go on living after what she had done. I was on top for her and I could see that I was finally winning. Grotesquely, she was choking and I was thinking that that this was a fitting end for her.

I heard a squeal behind me, then a sudden rush. All went black.

ENERGY TIME

"Time to wake up." The words sounded cloudy and vague. "Time to wake up!"

Blearily, my eyes opened. I could see that Caroline, if that was her name now, was standing over me like a predator. I was lying on the bed and couldn't help noticing that she had a gun in her hand. It was a Glock, I observed. Not that I was an expert on guns, just that it was the same one Michael Caine had used in 'Harry Palmer'. He'd used that to blow away a drug dealer, I seemed to recall, and here was the same weapon pointed in my direction.

It all came back to me. I became gripped by a very cold fear.

"I have to tell you, you've not got much time left to live. In fact, I'll probably kill you when I tire of this conversation or when I get fed up of holding this." She waved the gun light-heartedly. "Whichever happens first, obviously. Welcome to the wacky world of Caroline. You won't be the first and you're unlikely to be the last."

"You killed Laura!" I tried to free myself from my terror. If I was about to die, my only chance at all would be if I showed no sign of fear.

"Laura! Are you talking about the little chicken who cries like a two-year-old. Do you mean that Laura? Do you mean this Laura?" I could only watch as she picked up a mobile phone from the top of the chest of drawers and faced the screen in my direction. "See how she cries."

The screen showed Laura, at least I presumed it was Laura, tied to a chair, and looking beaten and crying. If this was my Laura, the thought came to me that this might be the last time I saw her. She was wearing the same clothes, disheveled now, that she had been wearing when setting off to work on that fateful day that seemed an eternity ago. Caroline placed the phone back on the chest of drawers, out of sight.

I began to sit up.

"Down, boy. Just you stay horizontal, or your life ends now, not in ten minutes."

"Is she dead?"

"Put it this way. You won't be seeing her again. Is that good enough? In fact, I won't be. I don't want that bitch polluting my phone for much longer, either." Her voice sounded different now. It had an accent. Her words now made me think of Derby or somewhere in that region of England. "If you ask me, she was never really alive. Not with that shit existence, married to you."

"Why?"

"Why what?"

"Why would you do this? When all is said and done, she was blood to you."

"Well, sometimes, that just isn't enough." Her callousness was loud and clear, and I was beginning to realise that my situation, like Laura's, was hopeless.

"You don't have to do this. This is ridiculous and you need help. Put the gun down and I'll help you." I was going to help her all right – help her to an early grave.

"Don't fucking move. And for fuck's sake, don't offer me help again or it will be ker-blam, and you won't have a head anymore."

I was shivering with fear, but trying desperately not to let her know it.

I heard a sound from downstairs. Somebody had entered the house. Leoni? Perhaps there was some hope there. "Leoni. What will you tell her?"

I heard footsteps as she ascended.

Caroline spoke loudly. "The question is, what will Leoni tell you?"

Leoni came into the room, and the lack of surprise on her face told me that she was part of this. They kissed intimately, all the time with the gun fixed on my chest. Caroline turned to me. "I think you know my fiancée too well."

Leoni stared, disdain gripping her face. "While I'm here, you were a lousy date, even for a man. And you really shouldn't drink so much."

I could have replied with something witty, sarcastic or insulting, but that Glock was too much on my mind. I was as cowardly as ever. I looked at Caroline. I wondered how I could have mistaken her for Laura. "So you knew all along. Or did you put her up to it?"

"My idea, shit face. Just needed information for my... let's call it a project. That's it. A life-changing, life-ending project." They both laughed. I started to think that if roles were reversed, I would just shoot her whatever the consequences were. I was filled with hate and it was going head-to-head with my fear. I considered whether a quick movement of attack by me could avoid a fatal shot, but there was no chance. That was why she was keeping me horizontal. I remained easy pickings

"You did give away plenty, pissed up like that. The problem with you is that you like this stuff too much." She picked up a bottle of Jack Daniels that had been in the bottom of my side of the wardrobe. She slowly and methodically passed the gun to Leoni, who took it from her smoothly, as if she had been handling guns all of her life. "Hold this. Keep it pointed at his heart. That's the big stupid thing he keeps about there." She pointed at my chest. "If he makes any movement at all, paint the walls red."

I watched as she took the top off the bottle, placed it about a foot above my head and poured the contents onto my face and into my mouth. I began to wonder if her plan was to burn me alive and present it as an accidental death or death by misadventure. "I hope you enjoy this, your favourite drink, and this sort of sums up the respect I have for you.

And by the way, while you're all ears, what was that about, sending that hopeless fuck to stalk me? Not one of your best ideas."

"Have you killed him too?"

"Put it this way. He's an even bigger twat than you. And he's not very tough at all. I didn't film this, unfortunately, but I did have him crying for his mama. Did a bit of an Ian Brady on him. Did some finger snapping while he bled to death with no eyes." She looked back at her fellow bitch. "I'm wasted in this life, Leoni. Should have been in the Gestapo, pulling the fingernails from spies and traitors."

Like a coiled spring and fully awake now, I so much wanted to get my hands around the throat of this monster. However, I had no chance with two of them here and a gun pointing at me. I didn't want to die. I hated being powerless. I was at their mercy and that was a feeling that was intolerable and frustrating, partly because my existence was coming to an end, but also because she had killed the people closest to me, yet was still arrogantly alive. "Of course, you'll do life for these things you've done. I don't think you'll like permanent imprisonment, separated from Leoni forever. You need to have a rethink."

She had a smug grin on her face, while Leoni just looked at the floor. "No rethink needed, sonny. You attacked me in the marital home. I defended myself with the only weapon at hand, this kitchen knife. Here it is, ready and waiting." She reached and selected what was our biggest and sharpest kitchen knife, which obviously had been placed next to the mobile phone. She'd put a lot of thought into this final encounter.

"So you can't shoot me, then. If you use that gun, your plan's gone."

"What? That gun? Do you mean the gun that's registered in your name, used by a woman being abused and ill-treated, a woman with a mental illness. It's a tough one, I admit, but I bet I can pull it off. Of course, Leoni here has seen everything. She's seen how you paw me, how you become aggressive at the drop of a hat. She was even in the house when you raped me and took advantage, so I think there are enough circumstances to make things a bit grey and doubtful."

I realized how hopeless the situation was. Then I had an impulse. It was no more than a subconscious instinct, and there was a distinct lack of evidence, but... "Laura's still alive, isn't she? You never killed her. That's why you're not telling me she's dead."

Caroline rolled her eyes, giving a false expression of sympathy. "Oh, hun. She's dead, very dead. It wasn't very nice, but she went to her maker all right. She'll bore him to tears."

"And George and Lillian? That was you."

"Not just me, but I did have a hand in it. Well somebody had to lure them out late at night." She gestured behind her. "Leoni's brother is quite a character, isn't he love? He quite likes heroin. In fact, he's very partial to it, so I bought him quite a lot. Oh, and thanks for the cash I withdrew using that new credit card you helped me get. I got him sorted."

"While I slept."

"Yes, that's the beauty of my old friend Temazepam. Guaranteed sleep. Never let me prepare you a drink in future." She laughed like a witch.

"Why kill them? They did nothing."

"Nothing." Her mouth become a massive sneer. "Those baby thieves gave your bitch the life I should have had. They did everything. Left me and my mother to die in that horrible house. I was born with nobody to help. Luckily, Judy was able to make a phone call or we wouldn't have this pleasure."

A look of finality came over Caroline's face and she turned to Leoni. "I need to kill this fucker now, so things are going to get messy. Might be best if you go to Costa, Starbucks or somewhere, after I've finished things here. In fact, go to Subway, and get me a sandwich."

"What sandwich?"

"BLT. Don't you know me?"

"There's no need for this to end like this." I felt like crying, but I had to stay strong.

"Shut up."

She stood in front of me and had the kitchen knife gripped with a real intensity, a twisted expression on her face.

I had to take a chance. I was probably going to die from a bullet but I had to do something. I found myself suddenly possessed by a combination of adrenaline, desperation and anger. I just had to find something deep inside me now. I twisted my body and sent my foot into the air, reaching out. It was freakish, and a throwback to the karate days of my early twenties but I managed to catch the bitch fully and with a decent impact in the side of the head with the heel of my shoe. She reeled from the blow but still had the knife in her hand.

I sprang up, knowing this was totally do or die. I sent a fierce punch that caught her in the temple. There were two of them, however, and, the next thing I knew, there was an explosion as Leoni fired, missing me.

With Caroline knocked down, I leapt across and grabbed hold of Leoni's arm causing her to drop the gun. I grabbed it and had it reassuringly in my hand. She backed away, realizing the tide was now turning. I quickly backed away too, so I had the two of them directly in front of me.

Caroline began to raise herself in front of me, so I pulled the trigger. Being unfamiliar with firearms of any description, the jolt of the weapon took me by surprise. A mark of red on the wall revealed that I had missed Caroline and caught Leoni.

At this point Leoni, squealing from her new pain, slipped out of the room, and I heard her move clumsily down the stairs.

Up here, I carried on the conflict, this time pushing Caroline to the ground with my free hand and considering my next move. Today was the first time I had ever hit a woman, but it felt so right.

"I'm going to phone the police."

"No you're not."

Suddenly, with surprising speed and a frightening degree of purpose, she was up against me and in my face, trying to wrestle the gun from my hand. She was showing strength as her nails dug into my wrist and her face was manically creased with determination as she tried, with bared teeth, to get close enough to my face to bite into it. I was struggling to hold on to the gun and attack her with my elbow simultaneously. This had become a wrestling match with the highest of stakes.

There was another gunshot. I wasn't feeling pain, although I wondered for a moment if this was a death where the victim doesn't feel pain.

Then I could see in Caroline's eyes that life was now seeping from her, that her strength was departing.

I snatched the gun away from her grip and she tumbled to the floor, the blood forming a large patch in the middle of her top. "Seems you're no longer in a position to dictate."

IN THE EYE OF THE HURRICANE

I woke up feeling hangover groggy and in the strangest of surroundings until my consciousness properly returned along with my memory of the previous night. I sat up on the half-hearted attempt at a bed, on a white tiled floor, like a half-completed chessboard on which I was the only piece. The cell was immaculately clean, surrounded by whitewashed walls. I hadn't slept well. The mattress had the same consistency as cardboard, with the room possessed by a devilish smell of bleach, that probably emanated from the seatless toilet in the corner of the room. Looking ahead of me, my eyes met a dark green door with a small rectangle at head height that I had seen on countless police shows on TV, for my jailers to peer through and check that I hadn't topped myself. And why would I do that?

Frustration had now taken full control of my existence. I was in a cleft stick for the killing and all my attempts to tell my story had met with total disbelief. I had kept asking myself through the night whether I would have believed it or not if I had been investigating and I kept returning to the same negative answer. It was pretty incriminating as far as the basic details I was giving were concerned, but surely they could see the truth in my face. After all, I had never been a convincing liar anyway.

I don't know when the interrogation had finished. I think I had become that shattered at the end that I was uttering gobbledygook. Two uniformed officers had brought me down here to this crappy little room on what I imagined was the ground floor, since there was a window with some light coming in, disturbing the dimness, and I could hear voices not so far away, the sounds of people not in my kind of predicament.

My only consolation was that the twisted Caroline was dead. My struggle went on, however.

* * *

They had listened to all of my story. Throughout most of it, they had made little response to my claims, other than Hawksworth persistently making notes and writing what looked like question marks after things I was saying. Taylor offered the full range of sarcastic and doubtful verbal responses, including "Do you expect us to believe that?" or "This is fantasy!" The tone was constantly one of irritation and impatience on their part, as if they were expecting a full and frank confession, with everything I said assisting them in their desire to consign me to the case closed section. Last night, however, I had had some fight in me and had tried to argue the truths and get them to consider the things I was telling them.

"You need to investigate the killing of George and Lillian Stewart. She was behind that."

"Who was behind that?"

"Caroline. Who else? She organized their murders."

"There is no Caroline. That's your fantasy. Who is this Caroline, anyway, a lost woman from your past, an old babysitter from your childhood?"

274

"As I've already told you, Caroline's the daughter of Judy Lawrence. She's in an old people's home in Chesterfield. You go there and check it out."

"No mate, not worth it. It doesn't really matter if she was visiting somebody in a home, or whether she was some long-lost daughter going under a different name, probably for reasons of secrecy. In fact, you were probably the cause of that secrecy, for all we know. You shot your wife."

"I killed a monster."

"So the woman you brutally murdered was a brutal murderer herself. Now what are the chances of that? That must be a hundred to one. Well worth a flutter."

"She was after the inheritance."

"And is that your motive then? To be rolling in it? I understand that couple were pretty well-off. Anybody benefitting from their deaths would be sitting pretty. Was that why you did it?"

"Once again, I didn't do it. I didn't do it." I felt my cheeks reddening and my fists were tightly clenched.

"Don't get angry, My Walker. That won't help. It's probably your temper that's got you into this mess."

The bespectacled Hawksworth came in at this point. "Why don't you drop the angry weird twin angle, Dominic? Just admit to us here and now that you killed her because you were angry. It happens. We all get angry sometimes, especially with our wives. I get angry with mine every day. Difficult thing, this marriage lark."

I stayed silent, so Taylor continued. "Did you have her followed because you suspected she was having an affair? Did James Clover discover something you aren't telling us? Was that why you killed her?"

"Ask him. Try to find him. He's vanished."

"How can he have vanished? People don't just vanish. Did you do something to him too? Bearer of bad news and all that?"

"No, I didn't. If you were able to find him, if Jamie's still alive, he would definitely confirm some of my story."

Taylor leaned back and opened his arms. "To be honest, he's not even been reported to us as missing, but we will get somebody to call on him in due course."

"I reported him missing."

"You did. And did you do that to cover your tracks?"

"No. I did it because he's my best friend and I was worried about him. Caroline killed him."

"How do you know that?"

"Because she told me. Just before I killed her."

"Well, that admission is good, Mr. Walker, because we're just waiting on a couple of bits and bobs then we're going to no doubt be charging you with murder. You need to prepare for that. Time to come clean, but in the meantime, we're remanding you downstairs for the night. Do you want to make a phone call? A solicitor, perhaps?"

"Not yet, but I would like a conversation with my sister."

* * *

I was just staring into space. This marked the end of something, but was it the end of everything? I had always scoffed at, scorned or failed to understand people who took their own lives, but here was I in a situation on this planet where nothing counted anymore. Everything I had cared about was now removed from my life: my wife, my parents, my job and even my best friend. There didn't seem to be anyway out of this. It appeared that, unless there was some miracle and Jamie turned up, with Caroline having lied to hurt me and he having had some kind of funny turn, I would be found guilty. I would face the intolerable prospect of too many years in prison. At the end of that, if I survived, which I didn't think was likely, as I knew

I was way too soft, I would emerge into a world that would be utterly strange and alienating. It would have no relevance to me and nothing and nobody in it to make my life worth living. Against this depressing backdrop, suicide wasn't that preposterous an idea. If done the right way, it would be a swift and hopefully painless conclusion.

While I was floating in this whirlpool of despair, there was the sound of a key in the lock and the door was opened. Kate was suddenly in front of me. I stood up and we hugged, without any words, and it seemed ironic now that she, my long-estranged sister, was the only remaining person of any importance in my life but I still had not even considered her as a reason to go on living.

"How are you, Dominic?" She was in her uniform, so I presumed she had used her role as an officer to gain access to me.

"I'm not good, Kate. I think I'm in a lot of trouble."

"What happened?"

"I killed a woman, Kate. The evil bitch was pretending to be my wife, but she killed Laura."

"How do you know she killed Laura?"

"She, Caroline, Laura's twin, showed me footage of her, in a chair, strapped down and dying." Something was starting to crystallize in my head, something not quite tangible, still in the form of a haze.

"Dom. I have to say this to you. Nobody outside this room believes your story."

"Don't you believe me?"

"I have no say in anything. You can't win in court with the story you're telling. Your solicitor will tell you that, when you eventually decide to employ one. Why don't you just tell the police what really happened? Let your brief argue for a reduced sentence on account of a confession. It sounds to me like you aren't a well man, and a judge might take that into consideration when you're sentenced. They often do."

I stood there staring at her, knowing then why she was here. It wasn't because I had asked for her at all, nothing to do with the devoted sister thing, but because they were using her to extract a confession from me. Bastards.

"Fucking Hell, Kate." I was angry now. "You've not been much of a sister to me over the years and here you are now, stabbing me in the back."

"I'm not stabbing you in the back, Dom. I just think it will save you unnecessary suffering and you'll get a worse sentence for not admitting it."

"But it's not the truth. But what could I expect from you, really?"

I could see regret suddenly lining her face, as if she placed more store on our desire to rekindle our relationship, however much it was threatened currently. Perhaps I was being harsh.

"It just makes me think…" I stopped. The haze had cleared somewhat inside my head. My mind had involuntarily gone back to the tracking of Caroline, then back further to documents, to undiscovered surprises. A thought now gripped me. "Kate, I will do what you say, but I want you to do one thing for me. One last thing."

"Just say it, Dom. I want to help you with this. I don't want us falling out. Not now."

"This is going to seem weird, and you need to take somebody with you because there's a psycho called Leoni still at large. I'll tell you about her. I want you to go to Wolstenholme Street, Chesterfield, check it out for me. I wasn't able to. Somewhere on that road is a house or flat or building, a number in the thirties, I think. I'm not saying there will be anything there, but I think you'll find out something if you investigate there. Documents for that house, number 34, I think, were in our papers and Caroline,

I mean Laura, if you like, was there on the day she died. Just do this one thing for me. You might not find anything, but it's a no-lose situation."

"But is there really a point to me doing that, Dom?"

"I hope so. Promise me you'll go there, Kate."

"I'll go there." I could see doubt in her face, where I needed certainty.

"On our Mother's grave."

Kate looked reluctant.

"On our Mother's grave, Kate, then I know you'll do it. I want you to check that house out like you're suspicious. No other attitude will do."

"OK, then," she replied, with irritation and doubt clear on her face. "I'll do it. I'll be back later today. But you must accept what is to be after I've done this. Follow legal advice in court."

"I will. Promise." For the first time in thirty years, I was going to say a prayer. This was such a long shot. The thing was, Laura had not been dead on that phone footage. I suddenly had the notion, that perhaps for some reason, one that could only be understood by someone with an equally twisted mind, she had wanted to keep Laura alive and suffering for a while, and perhaps had not actually got around to killing her. Of course, a visit by proxy to Wolstenholme Street was a bit of a long shot, but right now a long shot was all I had. Kate, even with her doubtful loyalty, was the only one who might possibly help me and I was praying that she would honour that promise and check out the house.

* * *

Hours passed. There was that prevailing sense of nothingness that dragged like a dull ache and was sending me crazy, as again I heard a key turn in the lock. Kate! Two uniformed officers came into the room and one of them placed a pair of handcuffs on me before I was escorted out.

"Have you heard from my sister?"

"I don't know what you're talking about. We're just escorting you upstairs."

I was led into a room identical to, if not the same, as the one I had been interrogated in.

Taylor and Hawksworth were already seated, awaiting my arrival. I sat down.

"Morning, Dominic. I'm formally charging you with the murder of Laura Walker. You don't have to say anything but anything you do say will be written down and may be used in evidence against you."

He said a few other things, but I was numb with dizziness. I had been a law-abiding citizen all of my life and here I was being formally charged with murder. They told me that I was now to be transferred to Leeds Prison, where I would be remanded until arraignment and my eventual trial. Everything had become a blur. It had been stupid pinning my hopes on Kate, with that utterly groundless idea, as if Laura wasn't dead and buried somewhere, probably with Jamie as a permanent companion. I allowed myself an ironic grin. Laying alongside Laura. He would have laughed wickedly at that idea.

I found myself again escorted out by the now grim-faced police officers and was taken along a long winding corridor and outside into what was some kind of courtyard, where a large white vehicle with small square windows, a 'meat wagon' was positioned, no doubt ready for that trip up the M1. Three other uniformed officers were outside the vehicle as I was led up to it. Was I actually considered dangerous at this point? Never a hard man at any point or in any way, emotional and sentimental to a fault, here I was being treated like Peter Sutcliff or Rose West. It was just so totally surreal, even if I had shot a woman dead.

I was pushed up into the vehicle and the two officers followed me in. They took seats on the opposite seats, making no eye contact. The doors were loudly and dramatically closed. I heard some shouting outside and presumed it was the instructions being given to the driver about the journey and the route he was going to take.

I was waiting for the sound of the truck's engines bursting into life but it didn't happen straight away. Was there a problem? Was there something wrong with the vehicle?

The back doors were, to the surprise of all three of us, opened again and a guy, whom I assumed to be a senior detective, told the officers to escort me back to the holding cell. What the fuck? I thought to myself. The detective looked at me. "There's a bit of a delay while we sort something out, Mr. Walker. We'll try not to keep you here any longer than we have to."

Back in the cell again, I spent what must have been another three hours in that wretched little hole.

For the third time that day, the cell door sprang open. This time the face that came through the door was a familiar one.

AFTER THE REVOLUTION

"What happened then?"

"Well, I had a cup of tea first, I have to be honest with you. And I did harbour the notion of not going. I was musing over it in the police canteen. I mean, it was a ridiculous idea of yours. But I had promised, and you were a shit playing that mother's grave trick on me."

"You went alone?"

"No. I heeded what you said. I don't know why. I was taking advice from a man who had clearly killed his wife. I took Sally, another constable, with me. She owed me a favour. Anyway, Wolstenholme Street is part of an industrial estate. The only house on there, and it is number 34, is a solitary house, an ugly block of a place that sits at the end of the road, pretty bleak, with an abandoned factory next to it."

"Was it Leoni's house?"

"No. It belonged to a woman called Caroline Lawrence. Ring any bells? Apparently, she's a known prostitute in the Chesterfield area, with something of a prison record. I could spend ten minutes just going through the details of that. Let's just say she's had a pretty prolific life. She's been chief suspect in a load of serious crimes."

"I could have predicted that."

"The curtains were shut and that was bit off-putting really, so I just sneaked up while Sally kept a look out for anything to be wary of, like the curtain opening. I knocked on the door first, but there was no answer. I tried again, but there was still nobody responding so I just opened the letter box. I looked in. There was nothing of note that I could see, just some dingy furniture, a dusty fireplace and some old wallpaper. It was the smell that did me."

"Through a letterbox?"

"Are you kidding? Do you remember when that freezer of ours broke down when we were away in Cornwall and the chicken had gone off?"

"Do I remember? It made me sick. Vilest smell ever. I can still smell it now."

"When somebody's been dead for a day or more that same smell happens and starts to spread, and what I could smell was definitely the smell of death. I'd smelled it before a few times, usually somebody old and lonely who died and decayed before anybody could care. To be honest, Dom, I had mixed stuff going through my head, because this is your wife we're talking about, and if you were somehow, against all expectations and reason, right and it was Laura dead in this house, I know how close you were. This was going to be more upset for you. It would hopefully cast serious doubt on your arrest, though."

The car pulled into a slip road to leave the M1. "How far is it now?"

"About three minutes. Anyway, I called for back-up from Derbyshire. That came in about fifteen minutes while Sally and I waited. To be honest, I fancied breaking the door down, but that's not how it works, not with forensics and that."

"Small potatoes, fifteen minutes, compared to the dreadful time I was in that cell. Very small, when placed alongside life imprisonment."

"Of course. When they came, they smashed the door and went straight in. The smell was coming from the cellar and it was overwhelming with the door open. I got kitted out in the whites and followed them down five minutes later. It was Jamie, Dom. He'd been stabbed and the lead forensics guy said he had slowly bled to death. Bit of a cruel bitch, the murderer, if you ask me."

"That's Caroline. Poor bloke. She killed him because he knew too much. He had already found stuff out about her. If he had carried on, he would have found out about her history and she couldn't have that. That was why she was going to kill me too."

"Laura was there too, lying in an adjacent room, like it was some kind of torture chamber. She had been through hell as well. Loads of bruising and stuff. Looks like whoever had held her there had put her through it."

"She had to cope with a load of hate and evil I suppose. Just like anybody else who crossed this bitch."

"You don't know the half of it. Stranger than fiction, her life. She'd killed before this."

"She do time for it?"

"No. They couldn't pin it on her. Looks like you gave her justice at last."

"Whatever comes next, Kate, I will always be grateful to you. I'm sure Laura will be too."

"What are your plans now, Dom?"

"Well I have to report to the police tomorrow for another interview. No doubt they're working out the questions to ask me as we speak."

"Well, it shouldn't be as harrowing this time. They know you didn't kill Laura. They know that Caroline killed Jamie.

The missing piece is Leoni Machin. Oh and her brother. They accept she and he hold the keys now to unlocking other stuff, including what happened to George and Lillian."

"To be honest I'm not sure what she knew. She always appeared pretty vacant and I felt she was very much the junior partner in what went on. Caroline's stooge."

"She was more than that. Leoni's police record, if that's who she was, is as long as Caroline's. She needs picking up, and pictures of her are already circulating. If she turns up at your house, get in touch straight away."

"I don't think she's that much of a threat. She lived in our house for a while and I would have sensed it."

"No, you wouldn't. Dom, Caroline was in the frame for a castration and assault. Leoni was her alibi. Do not underestimate Miss Machin."

"We're here. I'm going all goose pimply."

"That's understandable. We're dropping you right at the entrance. Remember, don't pressure her with questions. She's been through far too much."

"I won't."

* * *

I was sitting at the side of the bed looking across at my wife. This time, it wasn't an imposter, but the real thing, the unique individual who had been that good to me that she had made me soft and vulnerable and easy prey for somebody horrendous. There was one of those intravenous drip things going on and she looked very weak and out of it.

I took hold of her hand. It was meant to suggest that I would be there for her forever so I hoped it wasn't painful for her.

Laura was semi-conscious. At this point she knew none of the answers and would have plenty of questions, but I just wanted to help her enjoy her return to freedom. I was going to do my best to help her to forget the malicious bitch who had inflicted so much pain. Her eyes had suddenly half-opened.

"Hi, babe. I don't know what to say to you. I guess we've both been through some stuff."

She reached out for my hand. "What happened to her?"

"She did some horrible stuff but she's dead now. Her plan didn't work."

"Did you kill her?" Her voice was faint but her eyes were full of accusation.

"I had to. She was going to kill me and I thought she'd killed you. Horrible, especially with her being your twin."

She became puzzled. "She wasn't my twin. Looked nothing like me."

"Babe, I think you need to rest."

"OK. I do need to sleep now."

"Me too," I replied. "I'll see you later."

I put my arms around her. However ill she was, she would, I was sure, respond to a hug.

Laura was alive and we had a future.

I was looking out of the window. I was seeing everything like it was a new world, where the grass seemed a brighter green and even the buildings of Sheffield had been thoughtfully created. She had her eyes closed, hopefully recovering from the horror she had been forced to undergo.

Suddenly I noticed somebody. It was a woman wearing a familiar jacket. On the pavement across the road. She had that curly brown hair that I knew so well. She was looking up at this building we were in, glaring. I looked down. I was sure it was Leoni. I held Laura's hand tightly.

As I continued to look, I watched her turn and walk away with her back to me and I wasn't sure anymore.

The only thing that now mattered was getting this wonderful wife of mine healthy again and back home so that we could resume our lives. Nobody would get in the way of that, I was sure. We had come a long way, had been prised a long way apart for too long, and now was going to be a time of being together. Life was going to be good.

MALEVOLENCE

It's not over.

My beautiful friend died. That's not good, but that doesn't mean the end. Only the end means the end.

Things have to continue and I suppose that falls on me.

There is a couple who still need to learn lessons. Perhaps I can be the teacher.

Stranger things happen.

 **Matador**

For exclusive discounts on Matador titles,
sign up to our occasional newsletter at
troubador.co.uk/bookshop